THE SPARROWGRASS PAPERS.

MR. SPARROWGRASS DESCENDS TO THE INFERNAL REGIONS ON A DUMB WAITER.

"He came to the rescue with a bull-terrier, a Newfoundland pup, a lantern, and a revolver. The moment he saw me at the window he shot at me, but fortunately just missed me. I threw myself under the table, and ventured to expostulate."—PAGE 72.

"I managed to get the ring-leader of the swinish multitude into my parlor. He was a large, powerful-looking fellow with a great deal of comb, long legs, mottled complexion, and ears pretty well dogged. He stood for a moment at bay against the sofa, and then charged upon the dogs.."—PAGE 90

THE SPARROWGRASS PAPERS:

LIVING IN THE COUNTRY.

BY

FREDERIC S. COZZENS,

"To him who in the love of Nature holds
Communion with her visible forms, she speaks
A various language."

NEW YORK:
DERBY & JACKSON, 119 NASSAU ST.
CINCINNATI:—H. W. DERBY.
1856.

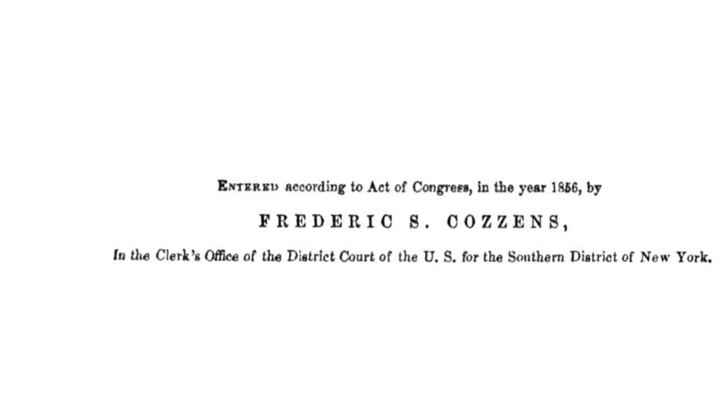

W. H. TINSON, Stereotyper. GEORGE RUSSELL & Co., Printers.

To

ONE OF THE GENTLEST OF HUMORISTS,

TO

THE REV. FREDERICK W. SHELTON,

AUTHOR OF

"LETTERS FROM UP THE RIVER,"

This Volume

IS AFFECTIONATELY INSCRIBED.

Gentle Reader!

Doubtless you have read, in the work of a quaint old commentator whose name has been quietly obscuring itself in the rust of nearly three centuries, these words—"It hath beene the custome of many men to make their introductions to their bookes, like to some Grecian Cities gates; so ample, that (as the Prouerbe ranne), their Citie was ready to steale thorow the same." You and I who appreciate wisdom—especially if it be a little mouldy, at once recognized the value of the hint conveyed by that piece of antiquated orthography. Therefore, to you, the brevity of this preface will, I trust, commend the book quite as much as though I had taken the matter in hand through the length and breadth of a score of pages. As there is nothing in it worth a smooth-faced prologue, nothing that would be the better for an apology, and nothing worth reviewing seriously, may I beg leave to present it without any introduction, except the very excellent designs of Mr. Darley?

Chestnut Cottage, *March 1st*, 1856.

CONTENTS.

CHAPTER XII.

CHAPTER XIII.

CHAPTER XIV.

CHAPTER XV.

CHAPTER XVI.

CHAPTER XVII.

THE

SPARROWGRASS PAPERS.

CHAPTER I.

Living in the Country—Rural Anticipations—Early Rising—Baked Hippopotami —Our New Chickens—A Discovery—The Advantages of having a Watch-Dog in the Country—A Finale to the First Garden, and Unpleasant Prospects for the Future.

It is a good thing to live in the country. To escape from the prison-walls of the metropolis—the great brickery we call "the city"—and to live amid blossoms and leaves, in shadow and sunshine, in moonlight and starlight, in rain, mist, dew, hoar-frost, and drouth, out in the open campaign, and under the blue dome that is bounded by the horizon only. It is a good thing to have a well with dripping buckets, a porch with honey-buds, and sweet-bells, a hive embroidered with nimble bees, a sun-dial mossed over, ivy up to the eaves, curtains of dimity, a tumbler of fresh flowers in your bedroom, a rooster on the roof, and a dog under the piazza.

When Mrs. Sparrowgrass and I moved into the country, with our heads full of fresh butter, and cool, crisp radishes for tea; with ideas entirely lucid respecting milk, and a looseness of calculation as to the number in family it would take a good laying hen to supply with fresh eggs every morning; when Mrs. Sparrowgrass and I moved into the country, we found some preconceived notions had to be abandoned, and some departures made from the plans we had laid down in the little back-parlor in Avenue G.

One of the first achievements in the country is early rising! with the lark—with the sun—while the dew is on the grass, "under the opening eyelids of the morn," and so forth. Early rising! What can be done with five or six o'clock in town? What may not be done at those hours in the country? With the hoe, the rake, the dibble, the spade, the watering-pot? To plant, prune, drill, transplant, graft, train, and sprinkle! Mrs. S. and I agreed to rise *early* in the country.

"Richard and Robin were two pretty men,
They laid in the bed till the clock struck ten:
Up jumped Richard and looked at the sky:
O Brother Robin! the sun 's *very* high!"

Early rising in the country is not an instinct; it is a sentiment, and must be cultivated.

A friend recommended me to send to the south side of Long Island for some very prolific potatoes—the real hippopotamus breed. Down went my man, and what, with expenses of horse-hire, tavern bills, toll-gates, and breaking a wagon, the hippopotami cost as much apiece as pine-apples. They were fine potatoes, though, with comely features, and large, languishing eyes, that promised increase of family without delay. As I worked my own garden (for which I hired a landscape gardener, at two dollars per day, to give me instructions), I concluded that the object of my first experiment in early rising should be the planting of the hippopotamusses. I accordingly rose next morning at five, and it rained! I rose next day at five, and it rained! The next, and it rained! It rained for two weeks! We had splendid potatoes every day for dinner. "My dear," said I to Mrs. Sparrowgrass, "where did you get these fine potatoes?'

"Why," said she, innocently, "out of that basket from Long Island!" The last of the hippopotamusses were before me, peeled, and boiled, and mashed and baked, with a nice thin brown crust on the top.

I was more successful afterwards. I did get some fine seed-potatoes in the ground. But something was the matter: at the end of the season, I did not get as many out as I had put in.

Mrs. Sparrowgrass, who is a notable house wife, said to me one day, "Now, my dear, we shall soon have plenty of eggs, for I have been buying a lot of young chickens." There they were, each one with as many feathers as a grasshopper, and a chirp not louder. Of course, we looked forward with pleasant hopes to the period when the first cackle should announce the milk-white egg, warmly deposited in the hay which we had provided bountifully. They grew finely, and one day I ventured to remark that our hens had remarkably large combs, to which Mrs. S. replied, "Yes indeed, she had observed that; but if I wanted to have a real treat, I ought to get up early in the morning and hear them crow." "Crow!" said I, faintly, "our hens crowing! Then, by 'the cock that crowed in the morn, to wake the priest all shaven and shorn,' we might as well give up all hopes of having any eggs," said I; "for, as sure as you live, Mrs. S., our hens are all roosters!" And so they were roosters! that grew up and fought with the neighbors' chickens, until there was not a whole pair of eyes on either side of the fence.

A *dog* is a good thing to have in the country. I have one which I raised from a pup. He is a good, stout fellow, and a hearty barker and feeder. The man of whom I bought him said he was thorough-bred, but he begins to have a mongrel look about him. He is a good watch-dog, though; for the moment he sees any suspicious-looking person about the premises, he comes right into the kitchen and gets behind the stove. First we kept him in the house, and he scratched all night to get out. Then we turned him out, and he scratched all night to get in. Then we tied him up at the back of the garden, and he howled so that our neighbor shot at him twice before day-break. Finally, we gave him away, and he came back; and now he is just recovering from a fit, in which he has torn up the patch that has been sown for our spring radishes.

A good, strong gate is a necessary article for your garden. A good, strong, heavy gate, with a a dislocated hinge, so that it will neither open nor shut. Such an one have I. The grounds before my fence are in common, and all the neighbors' cows pasture there. I remarked to Mrs. S., as we stood at the window in a June sunset, how placid and picturesque the cattle looked, as they strolled about, cropping the green herbage. Next morning, I found the innocent creatures in my garden. They had not left a green thing in it. The corn in the milk, the beans on the poles, the young cabbages, the tender lettuce, even the thriving shoots on my young fruit-trees had vanished. And there they were, looking quietly on the ruin they had made. Our watch-dog, too, was foregathering with them. It was too much, so I got a large stick and drove them all out, except a young heifer, whom I chased all over the flower-beds, breaking down my trellises, my woodbines and sweet-briers, my roses and petunias, until I cornered her in the hot-bed. I had to call for assistance to extricate her from the sashes, and her owner has sued me for damages. I believe I shall move in town.

CHAPTER II.

We conclude to give the Country another Year's Trial—Spring Birds—Mr. Sparrowgrass becomes the Owner of a Boat—A Visit from a Friend—First Experience with a Fish-net—An Irishman in a Fyke—Exchange of Civilities and Cucumbers—Bate's Cow, and a Hint to Horticulturists—Local Designations.

MRS. SPARROWGRASS and I have concluded to try it once more: we are going to give the country another chance. After all, birds in the spring are lovely. First, come little snow birds, *avant-courriers* of the feathered army; then, blue-birds, in national uniforms, just graduated, perhaps, from the ornithological corps of cadets, with high honors in the topographical class; then follows a detachment of flying artillery—swallows; sand-martens, sappers, and miners, begin their mines and countermines under the sandy parapets; then cedar birds, in trim jackets faced with yellow—aha, dragoons! And then the great rank and file of infantry, robins, wrens, sparrows, chipping-birds; and lastly—the band!

"From nature's old cathedral sweetly ring
The wild bird choirs—burst of the woodland band,
—who mid the blossoms sing;
Their leafy temple, gloomy, tall, and grand,
Pillared with oaks, and roofed with Heaven's own hand."

There, there, that is Mario. Hear that magnificent chest note from the chesnuts! then a crescendo, falling in silence—*à-plomb!*

Hush! he begins again with a low, liquid monotone, mounting by degrees and swelling into an infinitude of melody—the whole grove dilating, as it were, with the exquisite epithalamium.

Silence now—and how still!

Hush! the musical monologue begins anew; up, up, into the tree-tops it mounts, fairly lifting the leaves with its passionate effluence, it trills through the upper branches—and then dripping down the listening foliage, in a cadenza of matchless beauty, subsides into silence again.

"That's a he cat-bird," says my carpenter.

A cat-bird? Then Shakespeare and Shelly have wasted powder upon the sky-lark; for never such "profuse strains of unpremeditated art" issued from living bird before. Sky-lark! pooh! who would rise at dawn to hear the sky-lark, if a cat-bird were about, after breakfast?

I have bought me a boat. A boat is a good thing to have in the country, especially if there be any water near. There is a fine beach in front of my house. When visitors come, I usually propose to give them a row. I go down—and find the boat full of water; then I send to the house for a dipper; and prepare to bail; and, what with bailing and swabbing her with a mop, and plugging up the cracks in her sides, and struggling to get the rudder in its place, and unlocking the rusty padlock, my strength is so much exhausted that it is almost impossible for me to handle the oars. Meanwhile, the poor guests sit on stones around the beach, with woe-begone faces. "My dear," said Mrs. Sparrowgrass, "why don't you sell that boat?"

"Sell it? ha! ha!"

One day, a Quaker lady from Philadelphia paid us a visit. She was uncommonly dignified, and walked down to the water in the most stately manner, as is customary with Friends. It was just twilight, deepening into darkness, when I set about preparing the boat. Meanwhile our Friend seated herself upon *something* on the beach. While

I was engaged in bailing, the wind shifted, and I became sensible of an unpleasant odor; afraid that our Friend would perceive it too, I whispered Mrs. Sparrowgrass to coax her off, and get her further up the beach.

"Thank thee, no, Susan, I feel a smell hereabout, and I am better where I am."

Mrs. S. came back, and whispered mysteriously, 'that our Friend was sitting on a dead dog, at which I redoubled the bailing, and got her out in deep water as soon as possible.

Dogs have a remarkable scent. A dead setter one morning found his way to our beach, and I towed him out in the middle of the river; but the faithful creature came back in less than an hour—that dog's smell was remarkable, indeed.

I have bought me a fyke! A fyke is a good thing to have in the country. A fyke is a fish-net, with long wings on each side; in shape like a night-cap with ear-lappets; in mechanism like a rat-trap. You put a stake at the tip end of the night-cap, a stake at each end of the outspread lappets; there are large hoops to keep the night-cap distended, sinkers to keep the lower sides of the lappets under water, and floats, as large as musk-melons, to keep the upper sides above the water. The stupid fish come down stream, and rubbing their noses against the wings, follow the curve towards the fyke, and swim into the trap. When they get in they cannot get out. That is the philosophy of a fyke. I bought one of Conroy. "Now," said I to Mrs. Sparrowgrass, "we shall have fresh fish, to-morrow, for breakfast;" and went out to set it. I drove the stakes in the mud, spread the fyke in the boat, tied the end of one wing to the stake, and cast the whole into the water. The tide carried it out in a straight line. I got the loose end fastened to the boat, and found it impossible to row back against the tide with the fyke. I then untied it, and it went down stream, stake and all. I got it into the boat, rowed up, and set the stake again. Then I tied one end, to the stake, and got out of the boat myself, in shoal water. Then the boat got away in deep water; then I had to swim for the boat. Then I rowed back and untied the fyke. Then the fyke got away. Then I jumped out of the boat to save the fyke, and the boat got away. Then I had to swim again after the boat, and row after the fyke, and finally was glad to get my net on dry land, where I left it for a week in the sun. Then I hired a man to set it, and he did; but he said it was "rotted." Nevertheless, in it I caught two small flounders and an eel. At last, a brace of Irishmen came down to my beach for a swim, at high tide. One of them, a stout, athletic fellow, after performing sundry aquatic gymnastics, dived under and disappeared for a fearful length of time. The truth is, he had dived into my net. After much turmoil in the water, he rose to the surface with the filaments hanging over his head, and cried out, as if he had found a bird's nest: "I say, Jimmy! be gorra here's a foike?" That unfeeling exclamation to Jimmy, who was not the owner of the net, made me almost wish that it had not been "rotted."

We are worried about our cucumbers. Mrs. S. is fond of cucumbers, so I planted enough for ten families. The more they are picked, the faster they grow; and if you do not pick them, they turn yellow, and look ugly. Our neighbor has plenty, too. He sent us some one morning, by way of a present. What to do with them we did not know, with so many of our own. To give them away was not polite; to throw them away was sinful; to eat them was impossible. Mrs. S. said, "Save them

them for seed." So we did. Next day, our neighbor sent us a dozen more. We thanked the messenger grimly, and took them in. Next morning, another dozen came. It was getting to be a serious matter; so I rose betimes the following morning, and when my neighbor's cucumbers came, I filled his man's basket with some of my own, by way of exchange. This bit of pleasantry was resented by my neighbor, who told his man to throw them to the hogs. His man told our girl, and our girl told Mrs. S., and, in consequence, all intimacy between the two families has ceased; the ladies do not speak even, at church.

We have another neighbor, whose name is Bates; he keeps cows. This year our gate has been fixed; but my young peach-trees, near the fences, are accessible from the road; and Bates's cows walk along that road, morning and evening. The sound of a cow bell is pleasant in the twilight. Sometimes, after dark, we hear the mysterious curfew tolling along the road, and then, with a louder peal, it stops before our fence, and again tolls itself off in the distance. The result is, my peach-trees are as bare as bean-poles. One day, I saw Mr. Bates walking along, and I hailed him: "Bates, those are your cows there, I believe." "Yes, sir—nice ones, ain't they?" "Yes," I replied, "they are *nice* ones. Do you see that tree there?"—and I pointed to a thrifty peach, with about as many leaves as an exploded sky-rocket. "Yes, sir." "Well, Bates, that red-and-white cow of yours, yonder, ate the top off that tree: I saw her do it." Then I thought I had made Bates ashamed of himself, and had wounded his feelings, perhaps too much. I was afraid he would offer me money for the tree, which I made up my mind to decline, at once. "Sparrowgrass," said he, "it don't hurt a tree a single mossel to chaw it, ef it's a young tree. For my part, I'd rather have my young trees chawed than not. I think it makes 'em grow a leetle better. I can't do it with mine, but you can, because you can wait to have good trees, and the only way to have good trees is to have 'em chawed."

I think Mrs. Sparrowgrass is much improved by living in the country. The air has done her good. The roses again bloom in her cheeks, as well as freckles, big as butter-cups. When I come home in the evening from town, and see her with a dress of white dimity, set off by a dark silk apron, with tasteful pockets, and a little fly-away cap, on the back of her head, she does look bewitching. "My dear," said Mrs. Sparrowgrass, one evening, at tea, "what am I?"

The question took me at an unguarded moment, and I almost answered, "A beauty;" but we had company, so I said, with a blush, "A female, I believe."

"Nonsense," she replied, with a toss of the "know-nothing" cap; "nonsense; I mean this:—when I was in Philadelphia, I was a Philadelphian; when in New York, a New-Yorker; now we live in Yonkers, and what am I?"

"That," said I, "is a question more easily asked than answered. Now, '*Yonker*,' in its primary significance, means the eldest son, the heir of the estate, and 'Yonker's' is used in the possessive sense, meaning 'the Yonker's,' or the *heir's* estate. If, for instance, you were the owner of the town, you might, with propriety, be called the Yonkeress."

Mrs. Sparrowgrass said she would as soon be called a tigress!

"Take," said I, "the names of the places on the Hudson, and your sex makes no difference in regard to the designation you would derive from a locality. If, for instance, you lived at Spuyten Devil, you would be called a Spuyten-Deviller!"

Mrs. Sparrowgrass said nothing would tempt her to live at Spuyten Devil.

"Then," I continued, "there is Tillietudlem—you'd be a Tillietudlemer."

Mrs. Sparrowgrass said, that, in her present frame of mind, she didn't think she would submit to it.

"At Sing Sing, you would be a Sing-Singer; at Sleepy Hollow, a Sleepy Hollower."——

Mrs. Sparrowgrass said this was worse than any of the others.

"At Nyack, a Nyackian; at Dobb's Ferry, a Dobb's Ferryer."——

Mrs. Sparrowgrass said that any person who would call her a "Dobb's Ferryer," was destitute of a proper sense of respect.

"You might be a Weehawkite, a Carmansvillan, a Tubby Hooker."——

Mrs. Sparrowgrass, quite warm and indignant, denied it.

"A Tarrytownian—a Riverdalean."

Mrs. Sparrowgrass said she thought a village on

the tip-top of a hill could not be called River-*dale* with any show of reason.

"A Simpson's Pointer—a Fordhammer."

"A what?"

"A Fordhammer."

Mrs. Sparrowgrass said she thought, at first, I was getting profane. "But," she added, "you do not answer my question. I live at Yonkers, and what am I?"

"That," said I, "Mrs. Sparrowgrass, is a question I *cannot* answer, but I will make it a public matter through these pages."

"What is the proper, local, or geographical appellation by which an inhabitant of Yonkers should be known?"

CHAPTER III.

The Clouds in the Country—A Thunder-Shower—Mr. Sparrowgrass buys a Bugle—Ineffectual Music—A Serenade and an Interruption—First Fruits—A Surprise, and the Entire Loss of our Cherry Crop.

Mrs. Sparrowgrass says that summer sketches should not come out in the winter. She thinks what was written in June is not fit to be read in December, and a paper made in July is out of season in January. "The one you are putting in your overcoat pocket, now," she says, "was written last August, and I know it." At first, I was as much confused as if I had been caught in some flagrant act of impropriety, but I rallied a little, for a lucky thought struck me. "Mrs. Sparrowgrass," said I, "I will put the August paper in print, now; but, at the same time, request them not to read it until warm weather." This admirable and original piece of finesse pleased my wife highly. "That will do," she said, "but do not forget to tell them not to read it until then." So now, good reader, when you have reached this point, fold up the leaf, and do not open it until Sirius is in the noon-day sky.

We begin to enjoy the clouds since we have moved out of town. The city sky is all strips and patches; but the sky of the country forms a very comfortable whole. Then, you have the horizon, of which you get but an imperfect idea if you live in a crooked street; and besides, you can see distant rain storms passing over far-off landscapes, and as the light-winged breeze comes sweeping up and you feel the approaching dampness, there is a freshness and fragrance in it which is not at all like the miasmatic exhalations of a great city. Then, when the rain does come it is not simply an inconvenience, as it always is in town, but a real blessing, which even the stupid old cabbages know enough to enjoy. I think our musk-melons feel better now, as they lie there in sandy beds sucking the delicious fluid through their long vinous tubes. I think our Shaker corn, as he gives himself a rousing shake, and flings the big drops around him, does so with a species of boisterous joy, as if he could not have too much of it; and Monsiour Tomate, who is capering like Humpty Dumpty on the wall, is evidently in high feather, which is not the case with our forlorn rooster, who is but poorly protected under the old basket, yonder. The rain came from the southwest. We saw the clouds rolling up over the Palisades in round masses, with a movement like puffs of smoke rolling up from the guns of a frigate. It was a dead calm; not a pensile leaf twinkled; the flat expanse of the river was without a ripple. We saw the conglomerated volumes of snow-white vapor ascending to the zenith, and below lay the Hudson, roughening in the now audibly approaching breeze. Meanwhile the sky grew ashy pale in the southwest, and the big clouds overhead were sometimes veined with lightning, which was reflected momently by the darkening water. Just below us we heard the quick rattle of the rings, as the wood sloops dropped and reefed their broad sails in anticipation of the squall. Everything around us reposed in a sort of supernatural twilight, the grass turned grey and old, the tree trunks changed to iron, the air seemed denser, sullener, sultrier. Then a little breeze prattled through the chestnuts, and whitened the poplars. Then it subsided. Then the white cloud above appeared a tangle of dazzling light, and a sharp fusilade followed on the instant. Then Mrs. Sparrowgrass got frightened, and said she must go in, and as she said so, the wind pounced upon her and carried up her sunbonnet at least three hundred feet above tide water. Then it slammed to every door in the house, prostrated my Lima beans, howled down the chimney, roared and whistled through the trees, tore the dust from the roads, and poured it through our open windows, hurried off the big gate, laid it on my pie-plants, blew down my beehive, liberated all my bees, who instantly settled upon our watch dog and stung him so that he ran away and did not return until the following Sunday.

Nevertheless, the scenery around was marvellously beautiful. South of us a grey rain-curtain was drawn across the river, shutting out everything beyond, except the spectral masts and spars of a schooner riding at anchor. The Palisades started up in the gloom, as their precipitous masses were revealed by the flashes of unearthly light that played through the rolling clouds. The river before us, flecked with snow, stretched away to the north, where it lay partly in sunshine, under a blue sky, dappled with fleecy vapors. Inland, the trees were twisted in attitudes strikingly picturesque and novel; the scud flew before the blast like spray, and below it the swells and slopes of livid green had an aspect so unusual that it seemed as if I had been transported into a strange place—a far countrie. Our cottage, too, which I had planned and built, changed its tinted walls to stark, staring white, with window-panes black as ink. From room to room Mrs. Sparrowgrass flitted like a phantom, closing the sashes, and making all secure. Then the electric prattled overhead for a moment, and wound up with a roar like the explosion of a stone quarry. Then a big drop fell and rolled itself up in a globule of dust in the path; then another—another—another. Then I bethought me of my new straw hat, and retreated into the house, and then—it rained!

Reader, did you ever see rain in the country? I hope you have; my pen is impotent; I cannot describe it. The storm hushed by degrees, and went off amid saffron flushes, and a glitter of hail. The western sky parted its ashy curtains, and the rugged Palisades lay warm and beautiful under the evening sun. Now the sun sinks amid melted topaz and rubies; and above it, on one side, stretching aloft from the rocky precipices high up in the azure, is a crescent of crimson and golden fragments of clouds! Once more in the sunlight, and so we will throw open all the windows and let in the cool air.

The splendor falls on castle walls,
  And snowy summits old in story;
The long light shakes across the lakes,
  And the wild cataract breaks in glory.
Blow, bugle, blow! set the wild echoes flying!
Blow, bugle! answer echoes, dying, dying, dying!

I have bought me a bugle. A bugle is a good thing to have in the country. The man of whom I bought it said it had an easy draught, so that a child could fill it. He asked me if I would try it. I told him I would prefer not, as my wind was not in order; but that when I got out in my boat, the instrument should be critically tested. When I reached home, I could scarcely finish my tea on account of my bugle. The bugle was a secret. I meant to surprise Mrs. Sparrowgrass. Play, I could not, but I would row off in the river, and blow a prolonged note softly; increasing it until it thrilled across the night like the dolorous trumpet of Roland, at the rout of Roncevalles. I slipped away, took the hidden instrument from the bushes, handled the sculls, and soon put five hundred feet of brine between me and the cottage. Then I unwrapped the brown paper, and lifted the copper clarion to my lips. I blew until I thought my head would burst, and could not raise a toot. I drew a long breath, expanded my lungs to the utmost, and blew my eyes almost out of their sockets, but nothing came of it, saving a harsh, brassy note, within the metallic labyrinth. Then I attempted the persuasive, and finally cajoled a faint rhythmic sound from it that would have been inaudible at pistol-shot distance. But this was encouraging—*I had gotten the hang of it.* Little by little I succeeded, and at last articulated a melancholy B flat, whereupon I looked over at the cottage. It was not there—the boat had drifted down stream, two miles at least; so I had to tug up against the tide until I nearly reached home, when I took the precaution of dropping an anchor to windward, and once more exalted my horn. Obstinacy is a Sparrowgrassic virtue. My upper-lip, under the tuition of the mouth-piece, had puffed out into the worst kind of a blister, yet still I persevered. I mastered three notes of the gamut, and then pulled for the front of the cottage. Now, said I, Mrs. Sparrowgrass, look out for an unexpected serenade.

"Gnar-ty, Gnar-rra-raa-poo-poo-poop-en-arr-ty! Poo-poo-ta! Poo-poo-ta! Poo-poo-ta-rra-noop-en taa-ty! Poopen te noopan ta ta! 'np! 'np! Graa-too-pen-tar-poopen-en-arrty!"

"Who is making that infernal noise?" said a voice on the shore.

"Rrra-ty! 'traa-tar-poopen-tarty!"

"Get out with you!" and a big stone fell splash in the water. This was too much to bear on my own premises, so I rowed up to the beach to punish the offender, whom I found to be my neighbor.

"Oh, ho," said he, "was that you, Sparrow-grass?"

I said it was me, and added, "You don't seem to be fond of music?"

He said, not as a general thing, but he thought a tune on the fiddle, now and then, wasn't bad to take.

I answered, that the relative merit of stringed and wind instruments had never been exactly settled, but if he preferred the former, he might stay at home and enjoy it, which would be better than intruding on my beach, and interrupting me when

I was practising. With this I locked up my boat, tucked the bugle under my arm, and marched off. Our neighbor merely laughed, and said nothing.

> The man who hath no music in himself,
> Nor is not moved with concord of sweet sounds,
> Is fit for treasons, stratagems, and spoils :
> The motions of his spirit are dull as night,
> And his affections dark as Erebus :
> Let no such man be trusted."

When I reached my domicile, Mrs. Sparrowgrass asked me who that was, "blowing a fish-horn?" I have in consequence given up music as a source of enjoyment since that evening.

Our fruit did not turn out well this season on account of the drought. Our apple trees blossomed fairly, but the apples were stung by the curculio, and finished their growth by the time they got to look like dried prunes. I had the satisfaction, however, of producing a curious hybrid in my melon patch, by planting squashes in the next bed. I do not know which to admire most—the influence of the melon on the squash, or the influence of the squash on the melon. Planted side by side, you can scarcely tell one from the other, except from appearance; but if you ever do eat a musk melon boiled, or a squash raw, you will have some idea of this singular and beautiful phenomenon.

On the Fourth of July we had company from town. "Dear," said Mrs. S., "have you seen our cherry?" I answered, that I had set out many trees of that kind, and did not know which one she alluded to (at the same time a hopeful vision of "cherry pie on the Fourth of July" flitted across my pericranics). As we all walked out to see the glorious spectacle, I told our guests aside, the young trees were so luxuriant in foliage that I had not observed what masses of fruit might be concealed underneath the leaves, but that Mrs. S. had a penetrating eye, and no doubt would surprise me as well as them. When we came to the tree, my wife turned around, after a slight examination, and coolly observed, she thought it was there, but some boy must have picked it off.

"Picked *it* off," said I, as the truth flashed in my mind. "Yes," she replied, with a mournful accent, "picked off the only cherry we ever had."

This was a surprise, indeed, but not what I had expected. Mrs. Sparrowgrass, how could you expose me in such a way? How could you, after all my bragging to these city people about our fine garden, make a revelation that carried away the foundations of my pride in one fell swoop? How could you, Mrs. Sparrowgrass?

CHAPTER IV.

Mrs. Sparrowgrass discourses of Social Life in the Rural Districts—Town and Country—A Rural Party—The Advantages of dressing in a Plain Way—Our New Dog—Autumnal Scenery—A Family Acqueduct.

"WE have an invitation to a party," said Mrs. Sparrowgrass, "on Friday next, and I think a party is a very pleasant thing in the country. There is more sociability, more hospitality, warmer welcomes, less dress, and less style than there is in the city." Here Mrs. Sparrowgrass handed me an engraved card of rather formidable dimensions, which I must confess looked anything but *rural*. I took the missive with some misgivings, for I have a natural horror of parties. "I wonder," said I, in the most playful kind of bitter irony, "whether we will meet out here that young lady that never sings herself, but is always so passionately fond of music?" Mrs. Sparrowgrass said she thought not; she said she heard she was married.

"And that gentleman," I continued, "who was

a stranger to me, that always wanted to be presented to some young lady that I didn't know?"

Mrs. Sparrowgrass said she believed he had gone to California.

"And that lady who prized confectionery above good-breeding, and went home with her pockets well stuffed with mottoes, in defiance of the eighth commandment, and the laws of propriety?"

Mrs. Sparrowgrass said she knew the lady to whom I alluded, but she assured me she was yet in New York, and had not been seen about our village.

"Then," said I, "Mrs. Sparrowgrass, we will go to the party. Put my best shirt, and the white waistcoat in Monday's wash. Never mind expense. Get me a crumb of bread, and bring me my old white gloves. I am going to be gay."

"I think," said Mrs. Sparrowgrass, "that a party in town is nothing but an embarrassment." "True," said I. "Don't you remember," said she, "what a fuss I used to make about getting my hair fixed, and how put out I was that night when you forgot the japonica?" "Certainly." "And then, when we were all dressed and ready, how we used to wait for fear of getting there too early, and after we did reach the house, how we always got in a corner, and made happy wall-flowers of ourselves, and some old friends." "Of course I do." "Where nobody took any notice of us." "Exactly." "Then what difference did it make how I was dressed—whether I wore Honiton lace or cotton edging?" "I am afraid," said I, "Mrs. Sparrowgrass, if you had made a point of wearing cotton lace, you would not have been invited." At this palpable *double entendre* I felt that secret satisfaction which every man must feel when he has said a good thing. It was lost upon Mrs. Sparrowgrass. "Here," she continued, "we expect a simple, old-fashioned entertainment." Then I chimed in—"No gas-lights to make your eyes ache—no patent-leather to make your feet ache—no fashionable follies to make your heart ache—and no overheated, ill-ventilated rooms, boned-turkies, game, ice-cream, Charlotte Russe, pâtés, champagne, and chicken-salad, to make your head ache next morning." "There will be oysters and ice-cream," said Mrs. Sparrowgrass, dubiously. "I wish," said I, "there was a prospect of apples and cider instead. The moment I get inside the doors, and breathe the mingled odors of oysters and geraniums, it will carry me back to town, and for one evening, at least, I shall forget that we are living in the country.

——'I could be content
To see no other *verdure* than its own;
To feel no other breezes than are blown
Through its tall woods;'

but we must succumb; we will go like plain, sensible people, won't we?"

"If you were me, what would you wear?" said Mrs. Sparrowgrass.

"Something very plain, my dear."

"Then," said Mrs. Sparrowgrass, "I have nothing very plain, suitable for a party, and to-morrow I must go to town and do a little shopping."

"I am afraid," said I (after the second day's hard shopping in town) "your dress is going to be too plain, my dear. Every hour brings a fresh boy, with a fresh bundle, and a fresh bill, to my office." Mrs. Sparrowgrass said, "that if I thought so, perhaps she had better get something expensive when she went to buy the trimmings." I told her I thought her dress would do without trimming. She said, "it would be ridiculous without gimp or galloon; but perhaps I would prefer velvet ribbon, on account of the flounces?" I told her she had better get the velvet ribbon, and omit the gimp and galloon. Mrs. Sparrowgrass said, "very well," and the next day another boy brought another bundle, and another bill, which convinced me that extras form an important item in rural architecture. Then we had a dressmaker for several days, and the stitching went on by sun-light and lamp-light, and on the last day Mrs. S. discovered that she had nothing for her head, and the new bonnet was taken to pieces to get at the feathers for a coiffure. Then when the night fell, there fell, too, a soaking rain; and I had forgotten the carriage, so I was obliged to go a mile in the mud to order one from the village livery stable. Then I had to walk back, as the man said "it was out;" but he promised to send it for us right straight off. Then I had to get dressed over again. Then Mrs. Sparrowgrass could not find her best handkerchief, and I dropped five spermacetti blotches on the new silk dress looking for it. Then she found the handkerchief. Then our girl said that the new dog had run off with one of my boots. Then I had to go out in the mud in my slippers after the dog. Then I got the boot and put it on so as to make that sure. Then we waited for the carriage. We were all dressed and ready, but no carriage. We exercised all the patience we could muster, on account of the carriage, and listened at the windows to see if we could hear it. Two months have elapsed, and it hasn't come yet. Next day we heard that the party had been an elegant affair. That everybody was there, so we concluded the carriage had not been able to come for us on account of business.

I have bought me another dog. I bought him on account of his fine, long ears, and beautiful silky tail. He is a pup, and much caressed by the young ones. One day he went off to the butcher's, and came back with no more tail than a toad. The whole bunch of young Sparrowgrasses began to bawl when he reached the cottage, on account of his tail. I did not know him when I came home, and he could not recognize me—he had lost his organ of recognition. He reminded me of a dog I once heard of, that looked as if he had been where they wanted a tail merely, and had taken his, and thrown the dog away. Of course I took my stick, and went to see the butcher. Butcher said "he supposed I was something of a dog fancier, and would like to see my dog look stylish." I said on the contrary, that I had bought him on account of his handsome silky tail, and that I would give ten dollars to have it replaced. Then the idea of having it replaced seemed so ludicrous that I could not restrain a smile, and then the butcher caught the joke, and said there was no way to do it except with fresh putty. I do love a man who can enjoy a joke, so I took a fancy to that butcher. When I got home and saw the dog, I thought less of the butcher, but put a piece of black court-plaster on the dog, and it improved his appearance at once. So I forgave the butcher, and went to bed at peace with all mankind.

I love to lie a-bed in these autumnal mornings, and see the early sunlight on those grim old Palisades. A vast stretch of rock, gaunt and grey, is not a cheerful view from the south window. Shut your eyes for a minute, and now look. That faint red cornice, reaching rough-cast along the rugged tops, ten miles or more, from Closter to Tillietudlum, is not unpicturesque. And although we have not the odor of spring lilacs and summer roses, breathing through the windows, yet there is something not less delightful to the senses in this clear frosty atmosphere. Below, the many-colored woods that burgeon on the sides seem to retain the verdure of early spring in those cool depths of shadow. As the sunlight broadens on the crags, the illusion disappears, and we behold once more the brilliant vagaries of vegetation, the hectic hints of yesterday. I wish Kensett could see that pure blue sky and yonder melancholy sloop on the river, working her passage down, with bricks from Haverstraw, and a sail like an expanded rose leaf. It is a pleasant thing to watch the river craft in these autumnal mornings. Sometimes we see a white breasted covey coming up in the distance—from shore to shore a spread of dimity. Here and there are troops of shining ones with warm illuminated wings, and others creeping along in shadow with spectral pinions, like evil spirits. Yonder schooner is not an unfair image of humanity; beating up against adverse winds with one black and one white sail. That dogged old craft, just emerging from obscurity into sunlight, is but a type of some curmudgeon passing from poverty to affluence, and there is another, evidently on the wrong track, stretching away from the light of prosperity into the gloom of misfortune. I do not love the country less because of her teachings by these simple symbols.

There are many things to be learned from watching the old wood-sloops on the river.

Our neighbor has been making an improvement in his house. He has had a drain made in the kitchen, with a long earthen pipe ending in a cess-pool at the end of his garden. The object of it is to carry off the superfluous water from the house. It was a great convenience, he said, "on wash days." One objection might be urged, and that was, after every heavy rain he found a gully in his garden path, and several cart loads of gravel in his cess-pool. Besides, the pipe was of an equal width, and one obstruction led to another; sometimes it was a silver spoon and a child's frock; sometimes it was a scrubbing-brush, a piece of soap, and a handkerchief. I said that if he had made a square wooden trough, gradually widening from end to end, it would have cleared itself, and then I thought it would be a good thing for me to have such a one myself. Then I had a cess-pool built at the bottom of the wall, under the bank, which is about one hundred and fifty feet from the kitchen, and told my carpenter to make a trough of that length. Carpenter asked me "how big I wanted it?" I told him about eight inches in diameter at the end nearest to the house, and then gradually widening all the way for the whole length. As I said this, my carpenter smiled, and said he never heard of such a thing. I told him no, that the idea was an original one of my own. He asked me how much I would like to have it widened. I thought for a moment, and said, "about half an inch to the foot." He said very well, and the next week he came with two horses, and an edifice in his cart that looked like a truncated shot-tower. I asked him what that was? He said it was the big end of my pipe. When he laid it on the ground on its side I walked through it, and could not touch the upper side with my hand. Then I asked the carpenter what he meant by it, and he said it was made according to directions. I said not at all, that I told him to increase the diameter at the rate of half an inch to the foot, and he had made it about a foot to the foot, as near as I could judge. "Sparrowgrass," said he, a little nettled, "jest take your pencil and put down eight inches." "Well, that's the diameter of the small end, I believe?" I told the carpenter he was right so far. "Now, for every foot there is an increase of half an inch in the width; that's according to directions, too, ain't it?" Yes.

"Well, then, put down one hundred and fifty half inches, how much does that make, altogether, in feet?" Six feet eleven inches. "Now," said he, "jest you take my rule, and measure the big end of that 're pipe." "Carpenter," said I, "I see it all; but the next time I build an aqueduct I will be a little more careful in the figures." "Sparrowgrass," said he, pointing to the pipe, "didn't you tell me that that was an original idea of your own?" I answered that I believed I did make a remark of that kind. "Well," said he, with a sort of muffled laugh, "that is the first time that I see an original idea come out at the big end."

CHAPTER V.

Children in Town and Country—A Mistake about a Lady—The Menagerie—Amusement for Children—Winter Scenery—Another Amusement for Children—Sucker Fishing—General Washington.

IT is a good thing to have children in the country. Children in the country are regular old-fashioned boys and girls, not pocket editions of men and women as they are in town. In the metropolis there is no representation of our species in the tadpole state. The word "lad" has become obsolete. Fast young men and fast young women repudiate the existence of that respectable, antique institution, childhood. It is different in the country. My eldest does not call me "Governor," but simply "Father;" and although in his ninth year, still treats his mother with some show of respect.

Our next boy (turned seven) has prematurely given up smoking ratan; and our four-year-old girl is destitute both of affectation and dyspepsia. As for the present baby, his character is not yet fully developed, but having observed no symptoms of incipient depravity in him up to this time, we begin to believe the country is a good place for children. One thing about it is certain, children in the country get an immense deal of open-air-training that is utterly impracticable in town. A boy or girl, brought up "under glass" (to use a horticultural phrase) is apt to "blow" prematurely; but, although it is rather rough culture, still I think the influence of rocks, rivers, leaves, trees, buds, blossoms, birds, fresh air, and blue sky, better, for the undeveloped mind of a child, than that of a French nurse, no matter how experienced she may be. *I* think so, and so does Mrs. Sparrowgrass.

There is one thing, however, that is mortifying about it. When our friends come up from town with their young ones, our boys and girl look so fat and gross beside them, that we have to blush at the visible contrast. Mrs. Peppergrass, our respected relative, brought up her little girl the other day, a perfect French rainbow so far as dress went, and there they sat—the *petite*, pale Parisienne of four years, and the broad chested, chubby, red-cheeked rustic of the same age, with a frock only diversified by the holes scratched in it, and a clean dimity apron just put on, with a gorget of fruit marks on the breast that spoke plainly of last summer—there they sat, side by side, cousins both, and who would have known it. "My dear," said I, to Mrs. Sparrowgrass, after our respected relative had departed, "did you observe the difference between those children? one was a perfect little lady, and the other"— "Yes," interrupted Mrs. Sparrowgrass, "I did; and if I had had a child behave in that way, I would be ashamed to go anywhere. That child did nothing but fret, and tease her mother for cake, from the time she came into the house till she went out of it. Yes, indeed, our Louise was, as you say, a real little lady beside her."

Finding I had been misunderstood, I kept silent. I do not know anything so sure to prevent controversy as silence—especially in the country.

"Speech is silver, silence is golden."

There is one institution, which, in a child's-eye point of view, possesses a majesty and beauty in the country altogether unappreciable in a large city. I allude to the *Menagerie!* For weeks, juvenile curiosity has been stimulated by pictorial representations at the Dépôt and Post-office. There is the likeness of the man who goes into the cage with the wild beasts, holding out two immense lions at arms' length. There is the giraffe with his neck reaching above a lofty palm tree, and the boa constrictor with a yawning tiger in his convoluted embrace. If you observe the countenances of the small fry collected in front of a bill of this description in the rural districts, you will see in each and all, a remarkable enlargement of the eye, expressive of wonder.

"Conjecture, expectation, and surmise,"

are children's bedfellows, and the infantile pulse reaches fever heat long before the arrival of the elephant. At last he comes, the "Aleph"* of the procession! swinging his long cartilaginous shillalah in solemn concord with the music. Then follow wagons bearing the savage animals in boxes with red panels; then a pair of cloven-footed

* *Aleph*, the first letter of the Hebrew alphabet. *Probably* the elephant was the first thing Adam saw, and hence, the name *Aleph-ant.*

camels; then other wagons all mystery and red panels; then pie-bald horses and ponies, and then the rear-guard of the caravan drags its slow length along. "My dear," said Mrs. Sparrowgrass, "we must take the children and go to the menagerie." This seemed a reasonable request, and of course we went. When we approached the big tent we heard the music of wind instruments, the sound of a gong, and the roaring of lions. This divided our juvenile party at once, one half wanted to go in, and the other half wanted to keep out; Mrs. Sparrowgrass joined the seceders, and in consequence, we separated at the entrance of the canvas edifice. When we got in we heard that the lion-tamer had finished his performance, and that the elephant had been around, but there was a great deal of sport going on in the ring—the monkey was riding on his pony. At this announcement the young ones were immensely excited, and tried to get a peep at it, but, although I held them up at arms' length, they could see neither monkey nor pony. Then I tried to work a passage for them to the front, but the ring being invested with a border of country people thirteen deep, this was out of the question. So I concluded to wait until the crowd dispersed, and to keep the young Sparrowgrasses in good humor, I held them up and let them read the signs on the tops of the cages. "ROYAL BENGAL TIGER"—"BLACK LION FROM NUBIA"—"YELLOW ASIATIC LION"—"THE GNU"—"WHITE POLAR BEAR," &c., &c. By and by the clapping of hands announced the close of the performance in the ring, and the dense mass of people became detached, so we made our way through the crowd towards the elephant. All of a sudden we saw a general rush of the crowd in our direction, and we heard somebody say that "something had broke loose!" Not being of an inquisitive turn of mind, I did not ask what it was, but at once retired under a wagon load of pelicans, and put the young Sparrowgrasses though a door which I made in the side of the tent with my pruning-knife. The people poured out of the big door and from under the edges of the tent, but they had not run far before they stopped, and proceeded to make inquiries. Some said it was the polar bear, whereupon several respectable looking men suddenly climbed over a fence; others said it was a monkey, at which all the boys set up a shout. The intrepid conduct of the cash-taker had much to do with restoring confidence. He stood there, at the entrance of the tent, smoking a cigar with imperturbable firmness. So we all concluded to go back again and see the rest of the show. When we got to the door we found the entrance fee was twenty-five cents. We represented that we had been in before. "That may be," replied the cash-taker, "but we don't sell season tickets at this establishment."

Finding the discussion was likely to be violent upon this point, I retired, with some suspicions of having been slightly swindled. When I got home, Mrs. S. asked me "if we had seen the elephant?" I told her the whole story. "Well," said she, "that's just the way I thought it would be. I'm glad I did not go in."

It seems to me the country is marvellously beautiful in winter time. The number of bright days and moonlight nights is surprising. The sky is not less blue in January than in June, nor is a winter landscape without its charms. The lost verdure of the woods is compensated by the fine frost-work woven in the delicate tracery of the trees. To see a noble forest wreathed in icy gems, is one of the transcendental glories of creation. You look through long arcades of iridescent light, and the vision has an awful majesty, compared with which the most brilliant cathedral windows pale their ineffectual fires. It is the crystal palace of Jehovah! Within its sounding aisles a thought even of the city seems irreverent. We begin to love the country more and more.

> " Its dewy morn, and odorous noon, and even,
> With sunset; and its gorgeous ministers,
> And solemn midnight's tingling silentness;
> And autumn's hollow sighs in the sere wood,
> And winter, robing with pure snow and crowns
> Of starry ice the grey grass and bare boughs;
> And spring's voluptuous pantings when she breathes
> Her first sweet kisses."

Here you begin to apprehend the wonderful order of creation, the lengthening days after the winter solstice; all the phenomena of meteoric machinery, every change in the wind, every change in the temperature; in the leafless trees you see a surprising variety of forms. The maple, the oak, the chestnut, the hickory, the beech, have each an architecture as distinct as those of the five orders. Then the spring is tardy in town, but if you have a hot-bed in the country, you see its young green firstlings bursting from the rich mould long before the city has shaken off the thraldom of winter.

One day in the month of March, I heard there was to be some sport on the Nepperhan in the way of fishing, so I took my young ones to see it. The Nepperhan is an historical river—the Tiber of Yonkers. It runs in a straight line for about forty yards from the Hudson, then proudly turns to the right, then curves to the left, and in fact exhibits all the peculiarities of the Mississippi without its turbulence and monotony. It was a cold day in spring, the air was chill, the sky grey, the Palisades still ribbed with snow. As we approached the stream we saw that a crowd had collected on the deck of a wrecked coal-barge moored close to the bank, and on the side of the bank opposite to the barge, a man was standing, with one foot in the water, holding up the end of a net stretched across the tide. The other end of the net was fastened to the barge, and the bight, as the sailors say, was in the water. In the middle of the crowd there stood upright a fair, portly-looking man of good presence. His face looked like a weather-beaten, sign-board portrait of General Washington with white whiskers. He was looking up the stream, which from this point made a rush for the south for about one hundred feet, then gave it up, and turned off due east, around a clump of bushes. What particular animosity General Washington had to this part of the stream I could not imagine, but he was damning that clump of bushes with a zeal worthy of a better cause. I never heard such imprecations. The oaths flew from his lips, up stream, as the sparks fly from an express locomotive at midnight. Dr. Slop's remarks concerning the knots in the string of the green bag of surgical instruments, beside them, was like tender pity. Such ill-natured, uncharitable, unamiable, mordacious, malignant, pitiless, ruthless, fell, cruel, ferocious, proscriptive, sanguinary, unkind execrations were never fulminated against a clump of bushes before. By-and-by a flat-boat, filled with men, turned the corner and came broadside down stream. The men were splashing the water on every side of the flat-boat to drive the fish towards the net! They had oars, sticks, boards, boughs, and branches. Then I understood General Washington. He had been offended because the flat-boat was behind time.

Now it was all right: I saw a placid expression spreading over his weather-beaten countenance, as a drop of oil will spread over rough water, and mollify its turbulent features. The flat-boat, or scow, was long enough to stretch almost from shore to shore. The shouts and splashes were frightening the fish, and below us, in the water, we could occasionally see a spectral sucker darting hither and thither. I looked again at General Washington. He had untied the end of the net, and was holding it in his hand. His face expressed intense inward satisfaction—deep—not vain-glorious. Near and nearer swept the broadside of the boat, down stream was the net, between both were the accumulating fish. General Washington's hand trembled—he was getting excited. Here it comes, close upon us, and then—by the whiskers of the Great Mogul! one end of the scow grounded on the opposite bank, the bow rounded to, and cat-fish, perch, bull-head, and sucker, darted through the gap, and made tracks for the most secluded parts of the Nepperhan! But he who held the net was equal to the emergency—he cursed the boat out at right angles in an instant—a small minority of the fish still remained, and these were driven into the net. General Washington, with an impulse like that of a Titan rooting up an oak, pulled up his end of the net—the fish were fairly above the water—a smile gleamed out of his weather-beaten face like a flash from a cannon—and then—then it was—just then—the treacherous mesh *split!* and like a thread of silver fire, the finny prey disappeared through the rent, and made a bee-line for the Hudson.

"Nary fish!" said an innocent bystander. General Washington turned an eye upon him that was like a Drummond light, dropped the net, took off his hat, and then proceeded to give that individual such an account of his birth, parentage and family connections, from the earliest settlement of Westchester county to the present time, that a parental regard for the ears of the young Sparrowgrassii, induced me to hurry them off the coal-barge in the quickest kind of time. But long after the scene was out of sight, I could hear, rolling along the face of the rocky Palisades, the reverberations of the big oaths, the resonant shadows of the huge anathemas, that had been the running accompaniments to the sucker fishing on the Nepperhan!

CHAPTER VI.

An Event—Wolfert's Roost—The Nepperhan and its Legends—Mr. Sparrowgrass descends to the Infernal Regions on a Dumb Waiter—Carrier Pigeons and Roosters—The great Polish Exile—Poetry—Altogether a Chapter of Birds.

WE have had an event in our family. The children are half crazy about it; Mrs. Sparrowgrass says she cannot lay it down for a moment; when she does, Miss Lobelia, our niece, takes it up, and there she will sit over it, in her lap, for hours together. It is called "WOLFERT'S ROOST," a new book, by Washington Irving. When I brought it home in my carpet-bag, and opened it at our winter tea-table, and read all about the Nepperhan (our river) to the boys, their eyes dilated so, that I seemed to be surrounded with the various mill-ponds of that celebrated stream. Here we are within the enchanted ground, and the shadow of the great "Katrina Van Courtland, with one foot resting on Spiting Devil Creek, and the other on the Croton River," is over us. It is pleasant to know that, in case of invasion, we are in the same county with the lusty goose-gun of the lion-hearted Jacob Van Tassel; and, even in this biting winter-weather, there is a sort of local pride in the reflection that the north wind cannot approach us, without making all the weathercocks on the "Roost" point towards Yonkers.

As for our eldest, the reading to him of "The Adalantado of the Seven Cities," and "The Three Kings of Bermuda" has filled his head with ships, sails, anchors, salt-water, and ambergris,

> "Nothing of him——
> But doth suffer a sea-change
> Into something rich and strange."

And while perusing "Mountjoy," I observed our niece, Miss Lobelia, glancing contemplatively more than once at her slipper. "Uncle Sparrowgrass," said she, "you have been to Wolfert's Roost, I believe?" I answered, with all the humility I could muster, that I had, and proceeded to give a full and minute account of the particulars; how L. G. C. and I walked from "Dobb his ferry," upon the rigid back-bone of the aqueduct, to Dearman's one memorable summer day; how the Roost looked, and everything about it—the rough-cast walls, overclung with Abbotsford ivy, and trumpet creeper—the crow-step gables—the Sunny-side pond, with its navy of white, topsail ducks—the Spanish chestnut that stood on the bank—the splendid tulip-trees in the ravine back of the Roost—Gentleman Dick in the stable—the well-worn tiles in the hall, the Stadt-House weathercock on the peak of the roof. Miss Lobelia interrupted me—"Is Mr. a—a—I mean, what became of the heroine of the footsteps?" "Oh, ho!" thought I, "I see where the shoe pinches," and then gravely answered, "Mountjoy is still a bachelor;" at which our niece glanced furtively again at her little slipper, and a fleeting dimple faded from her cheek, as I have seen a farewell ship gleam for a moment in the sun, then vanish in shadow.

There's magic in the book, it has bewitched everybody!

What I most admire in it is, the juvenile air it has; there is a freshness about Wolfert's Roost, a sort of spring-like freshness, which makes it more attractive than anything else Irving ever wrote. It is a younger brother of the Sketch Book, not so scholarly, perhaps, but sprightlier; fuller of fine impulses—genius—fire—spirit! And then it has mentioned our village once or twice; and the beloved Nepperhan river rolls along, no longer a dumb feeder of mill-ponds, but a legended stream, that "winds, for many miles, through a lovely valley, shrouded by groves, and dotted by Dutch farm-houses, and empties itself into the Hudson, at the ancient Dorp of Yonkers!"

> "The intelligible forms of ancient poets,
> The fair humanities of old religion,
> The power, the beauty, and the majesty,
> That had her haunts in dale, and piny mountains,
> Or forest by slow stream, or pebbly spring,
> Or chasms and watery depths,"

may now visit the sacred shores of the Saw-Mill river—the Nepperhan. A touch of Irving's quill, and lo, it is immortal! As Arno to the Tuscan, or Guadalquivir to the Andalusian; as the Ganges to the Hindoo, or the Nile to the Egyptian, henceforth and for ever the Nepperhan to the Yonk—to the future citizens of the ancient Dorp of Yonkers.

"Bottom, thou art translated."

We, too, have our traditions, and some remain

untold. One is that of the horse-ghost, who may be seen every Evacuation night, after twelve, on a spectral trot towards the City of New York; and the other is the legend of the Lop-horned Buck, who sometimes, in a still summer evening, comes through the glen, to drink from Baldwin's phantom-haunted pond. When these are recorded, in a future Wolfert's Roost, then will the passenger, by loitering steamboat, or flying train, draw a long breath as he passes our village, and say, "there! look! behold! the ancient Dorp of Yonkers!"

We have put a dumb waiter in our house. A dumb waiter is a good thing to have in the country, on account of its convenience. If you have company, everything can be sent up from the kitchen without any trouble, and, if the baby gets to be unbearable, on account of his teeth, you can dismiss the complainant by stuffing him in one of the shelves, and letting him down upon the help. To provide for contingencies, we had all our floors deafened. In consequence, you cannot hear anything that is going on in the story below; and, when you are in an upper room of the house, there might be a democratic ratification meeting in the cellar, and you would not know it. Therefore, if any one should break into the basement, it would not disturb us; but to please Mrs. Sparrowgrass, I put stout iron bars in all the lower windows. Besides, Mrs. Sparrowgrass had bought a rattle when she was in Philadelphia; such a rattle as watchmen carry there. This is to alarm our neighbor, who, upon the signal, is to come to the rescue with his revolver. He is a rash man, prone to pull trigger first, and make inquiries afterwards.

One evening, Mrs. S. had retired, and I was busy writing, when it struck me a glass of ice-water would be palatable. So I took the candle and a pitcher, and went down to the pump. Our pump is in the kitchen. A country pump, in the kitchen, is more convenient; but a well with buckets is certainly most picturesque. Unfortunately, our well water has not been sweet since it was cleaned out. First I had to open a bolted door that lets you into the basement-hall, and then I went to the kitchen-door, which proved to be locked. Then I remembered that our girl always carried the key to bed with her, and slept with it under her pillow. Then I retraced my steps; bolted the basement-door, and went up in the dining-room. As is always the case, I found, when I could not get any water, I was thirstier than I supposed I was. Then I thought I would wake our girl up. Then I concluded not to do it. Then I thought of the well, but I gave that up on account of its flavor. Then I opened the closet doors, there was no water there; and then I thought of the dumb waiter! The novelty of the idea made me smile; I took out two of the movable shelves, stood the pitcher on the bottom of the dumb waiter, got in myself with the lamp; let myself down, until I supposed I was within a foot of the floor below, and then let go!

We came down so suddenly, that I was shot out of the apparatus as if it had been a catapult; it broke the pitcher, extinguished the lamp, and landed me in the middle of the kitchen at midnight, with no fire, and the air not much above the zero point. The truth is, I had miscalculated the distance of the descent—instead of falling one foot, I had fallen five. My first impulse was, to ascend by the way I came down, but I found that impracticable. Then I tried the kitchen door, it was locked; I tried to force it open; it was made of two-inch stuff, and held its own. Then I hoisted a window, and there were the rigid iron bars. If I ever I felt angry at anybody it was at myself, for putting up those bars to please Mrs. Sparrowgrass. I put them up, not to keep people in, but to keep people out.

I laid my cheek against the ice-cold barriers and looked out at the sky; not a star was visible; it was as black as ink overhead. Then I thought of Baron Trenck, and the prisoner of Chillon. Then I made a noise! I shouted until I was hoarse, and ruined our preserving-kettle with the poker. That brought our dogs out in full bark, and between us we made night hideous. Then I thought I heard a voice, and listened—it was Mrs. Sparrowgrass calling to me from the top of the stair-case. I tried to make her hear me, but the infernal dogs united with howl, and growl, and bark, so as to drown my voice, which is naturally plaintive and tender. Besides, there were two bolted doors and double deafened floors between us; how could she recognize my voice, even if she did hear it? Mrs. Sparrowgrass called once or twice, and then got frightened; the next thing I heard was a sound as if the roof had fallen in, by which I understood that Mrs. Sparrowgrass was springing the rattle! That called out our neighbor, already wide awake; he came to the rescue with a bull-terrier, a Newfoundland pup, a lantern, and a revolver. The moment he saw me at the window, he shot at me, but fortunately just missed me. I threw myself under the kitchen table and ventured to expostulate with him, but he would not listen to reason. In the excitement I had forgotten his name, and that made matters worse. It was not until he had roused up everybody around, broken in the basement door with an axe, gotten into the kitchen with his cursed savage dogs and shooting-iron, and seized me by the collar, that he recognized me—and then, he wanted me to explain it! But what kind of an explanation could I make to him? I told him he would have to wait until my mind was composed, and then I would let him understand the whole matter fully. But he never would have had the particulars from me, for I do not approve of neighbors that shoot at you, break in your door, and treat you, in your own house, as if you were a jail-bird. He knows all about it, however—somebody has told him—*somebody* tells everybody everything in our village.

That *somebody* reminds me of a queer fowl that roosts in the village, and in all villages, to hatch disturbances among weak-minded people. I allude to the Carrier Pigeon. The Carrier Pigeon tells you all your friends say of you, and tells your friends all you say of them. The mode of tactics is somewhat in this wise. She goes to Mrs. Kornkobbe's, takes tea with that lady, pets the children, takes out her needle and thread, opens her little basket, pulls out a bit of linen, with a collar pattern pencilled upon it, puts on her thimble, then stitches away, and innocently asks Mrs. K. if she has heard that ridiculous story about her husband.

Mrs. Kornkobbe has not heard of it, but bridles up, and would like to know *who* has had the impudence to say anything about her husband! The Carrier Pigeon does not like to mention names, but vaguely hints that something is in the wind. Mrs. K., of course, is anxious to know the particulars. Carrier Pigeon would not for the world hurt Mrs. K.'s feelings, but, just for her own satisfaction, she would like to ask "where Mr. Kornkobbe's father was born?" Mrs. K. is completely nonplused by this question, for, to use a mercantile phrase, she had never been posted up in regard to the incubation of her father-in-law, deceased some twenty years before she was married and two years before she was born. Carrier Pigeon, seeing Mrs.

K.'s trepidation, adds, carelessly, as it were, "Your husband is an American, I believe?" Mrs. K. catches at that, and answers "Yes." "German name?" Mrs. K. replies in the affirmative. "That is all I want to know," sighs the Carrier Pigeon. Whereupon Mrs. K., who is wrought up to fever point, answers, "But that is not all *I* want to know;" and, by dint of a deal of persuasion, finally draws out the important secret; the Carrier Pigeon has heard it reported all over the village, that Mr. Kornkobbe's father was nothing but a low German shoemaker. Now, if there is any information that Mrs. K. desires next in the world, it is to have the name of the person who said so; and Carrier Pigeon, after a temporary struggle between duty and propriety, finally, but reluctantly, gives up Mrs. Marshmallow as the author, at which Mrs. Kornkobbe lets loose all the pent-up fury in her soul upon the whole Marshmallow tribe, from the old grandfather, who hands around the plate in church, down to the youngest member of the family, just recovering from the united attacks of sprue, measles, hooping cough, and chicken pox.

The next day Mrs. Marshmallow, who really loves Mrs. K. like a sister, and who possibly might have repeated by way of a mere joke, and not as a reflection, that Kornkobbe, senior, had been a Teutonic cordwainer—the next day, Mrs. Marshmallow is visited by the Carrier Pigeon. Now, Mrs. M. is a lady of much stronger mind than Mrs. K.; not so easily excited by any means; but Carrier Pigeon, by dint of hints, innuendoes, and all the artillery of shrugs and smiles, finally manages to excite *her* curiosity; and then, when pressed to divulge, after binding up Mrs. Marshmallow not to tell a living soul, and taking other precautions of like nature, reluctantly, after struggling again through duty and propriety, allows Mrs. Marshmallow to draw from her all and everything Mrs. Kornkobbe had said about *her* the previous evening; but, of course, does not say a word of the use she had made of Mrs. Marshmallow's name, by which the fire had been kindled so as to bring Mrs. K. up to the scalding point. And, as the tone of the Carrier Pigeon would lead Mrs. M. to believe that all her friend, Mrs. Kornkobbe, had said, was gratuitous, she at once makes up her mind that Mrs. Kornkobbe is a base, cold-blooded, double-faced, malicious slanderer. How pleased she is that she has found her out. Explanation is out of the question; neither Mrs. K. nor Mrs. M. will condescend to notice each other, and Mr. Marshmallow and Mr. Kornkobbe go down to town in separate cars from that time and for ever.

I love to see the Carrier Pigeon; to admire its pretty glossy neck, its mild eyes, its chaste and elegant plumage; but Mrs. Sparrowgrass and I have determined never to listen to its dulcet voice, whether it bring accounts of how our neighbors look, or how we look ourselves when others see us.

We have gotten another rooster. Our Bantam disappeared one day; but we do not think it a serious loss, as he was of very little use. While he remained with us he kept up a sort of rakish air, and swaggered among the young pullets, just as you sometimes see an old bachelor with a bevy of buxom damsels; but the dame Partlets did not have much respect for him, and I am afraid he was terribly hen-pecked by Leah and Rachel. He left us one day. Probably he made away with himself—there is a great deal of vanity in a rooster, and wounded vanity is often the cause of suicide. One evening, on my return from the city, Mrs. Sparrowgrass said she had a surprise for me—a present from a friend. It was a Rooster; a magnificent black Poland cock, with a tuft of white feathers on his crown, and the most brilliant plumage in Westchester county. There he stood, one foot advanced, head erect, eye like a diamond, tail as high as his top-knot. There, too, was his mate, a matron-like, respectable looking female, who would probably conduct herself according to circumstances, and preserve her dignity amid the trying difficulties of her new position. "A present from Judge Waldbin," said Mrs. Sparrowgrass. "So I thought," said I; "generous friend! Do you know what I intend to do with his rooster?" Mrs. Sparrowgrass was frightened, and said she did not know. "Put him in verse," said I. Mrs. Sparrowgrass said she never heard of such a thing. But I will, Mrs. S., though I cannot write verse except upon great occasions. So, after a hearty supper and two cigars, I composed the following:—

TO MY POLAND ROOSTER.

"O thou, whatever title please thine ear,"
He-chicken, Rooster, Cock, or Chanticleer;
Whether on France's flag you flap and flare,
Or roost and drowse in Shelton's elbow-chair;
Or wake the drones, or please the female kind,
And cluck and strut with all your hens behind;

As symbol, teacher, time-piece, spouse, to you
Our praise is doubtless, Cock-a-doodle, due.

Oviparous Sultan, Pharaoh, Cæsar, Czar,
Sleep-shattering songster, feathered morning-star;
Many-wived Mormon, cock-pit Spartacus,
Winner alike of coin and hearty curse;
Sir Harem Scarum, knight by crest and spur,
Great, glorious, gallinaceous Aaron Burr,
How proud am I—how proud yon corn-fed flock
Of cackling houris are—of thee, Old Cock!

Illustrious Exile! far thy kindred crow
Where Warsaw's towers with morning glories glow;
Shanghai and Chittagong may have their day,
And even BRAHMA-POOTRA fade away;
But thou shalt live, immortal Polack, thou,
Though Russia's eagle clips thy pinions now,
To flap thy wings and crow with all thy soul,
When Freedom spreads her light from Pole to Pole.

"I think," said Mrs. Sparrowgrass, "I have heard something like that before."

"No doubt you have," said I; "part is from Pope, part from Halleck, especially the pun in the first stanza; but how can you make decent poetry in the country without borrowing a little here and there, unless you have the genius of a Homer, or of an Alexander Smith, Mrs. Sparrowgrass?"

CHAPTER VII.

A Country Fire-place—Lares and Penates—Sentiment—Spring Vegetables in the Germ—A Garden on Paper—Warm Weather—A Festa—An Irruption of Noseologists—Constitutional Law, and so forth.

IT is a good thing to have an old-fashioned fire-place in the country; a broad-breasted, deep-chested chimney-piece, with its old-fashioned fender, its old-fashioned andirons, its old-fashioned shovel and tongs, and a goodly show of cherry-red hickory, in a glow, with its volume of blue smoke curling up the thoracic duct. "Ah! Mrs. Sparrowgrass, what would the country be without a chimney corner and a hearth? Do you know," said I, "the little fairies dance upon the hearth-stone when an heir is born in a house?" Mrs. Sparrowgrass said she did not know it, but, she said, she wanted me to stop talking about such things. "And the cricket," said I, "how cheerful its carol on the approach of winter." Mrs. S. said the sound of a cricket made her feel melancholy. "And the altar and the hearth-stone: symbols of religion and of home! Before one the bride—beside the other the wife! No wonder, Mrs. Sparrowgrass, they are sacred things; that mankind have ever held them inviolable, and preserved them from sacrilege, in all times, and in all countries. Do you know," said I, "how dear this hearth is to me?" Mrs. Sparrowgrass said, with hickory wood at eight dollars a cord, it did not surprise her to hear me grumble. "If wood were twenty dollars a cord I would not complain. Here we have everything—

> '——content,
> Retirement, rural quiet, friendship, books,
> Ease and alternate labor, useful life;'

and as I sit before our household altar," said I, placing my hand upon the mantel, "with you beside me, Mrs. S., I feel that all the beautiful fables of poets are only truths in parables when they relate to the hearth-stone—the heart-stone, I may say, of home!"

This fine sentiment did not move Mrs. Sparrowgrass a whit. She said she was sleepy. After all, I begin to believe sentiment is a poor thing in the country. It does very well in books, and on the stage, but it will not answer for the rural districts. The country is too genuine and honest for it. It is a pretty affectation, only fit for artificial life. Mrs. Peppergrass may wear it, with her rouge and diamonds, in a drawing-room, but it will not pass current here; any more than the simulated flush of her cheeks can compare with that painted in the skin of a rustic beauty by the sun and air.

"Mrs. Sparrowgrass," said I, "let us have some nuts and apples, and a pitcher of Binghamton cider; we have a good cheerful fire to-night, and why should we not enjoy it?"

When Mrs. Sparrowgrass returned from giving directions about the fruit and cider, she brought with her a square, paper box full of garden seeds. To get good garden seeds is an important thing in the country. If you depend upon an agricultural warehouse you may be disappointed. The way to do is, to select the best specimens from your own raising: then you are sure they are fresh, at least. Mrs. Sparrowgrass opened the box. First she took out a package of seeds, wrapped up in a newspaper —then she took out another package tied up in brown paper then she drew forth a bundle that was pinned up—then another that was taped up—

then another twisted up—then out came a bursted package of watermelon seeds—then a withered ear of corn—then another package of watermelon seeds from another melon—then a handful of split okra pods—then handsful of beans, peas, squash seeds, melon seeds, cucumber seeds, sweet corn, evergreen corn, and other germs. Then another bursted paper of watermelon seeds. There were watermelon seeds enough to keep half the county supplied with this refreshing article of luxury. As the treasures were spread out on the table, there came over me a feeling that reminded me of Christmas times, when the young ones used to pant down stairs, before dawn, lamp in hand, to see the kindly toy-gifts of Santa Claus. Then the Mental Gardener, taking Anticipation by the hand, went forth into the future garden; peas sprouted out in round leaves, tomato put forth his aromatic spread; sweet corn thrust his green blades out of many a hillock; lettuce threw up his slender spoons; beans shouldered their way into the world, like Æneases, with the old beans on their backs; and watermelon and cucumber, in voluptuous play, sported over the beds like truant school-boys.

> "Here are sweet peas, on tiptoe for a flight:
> With wings of gentle flush o'er delicate white,
> And taper fingers catching at all things,
> To bind them all about with tiny rings."

"Now," said I, "Mrs. Sparrowgrass, let us arrange these in proper order; I will make a chart of the garden on a piece of paper, and put everything down with a date, to be planted in its proper time." Mrs. Sparrowgrass said she thought that an excellent plan. "Yes," I replied, tasting the cider, "we will make a garden to-night on paper, a ground plan, as it were, and plant from that; now, Mrs. S., read off the different packages." Mrs. Sparrowgrass took up a paper and laid it aside, then another, and laid it aside. "I think," said she, as the third paper was placed upon the table, "I did not write any names on the seeds, but I believe I can tell them apart; these," said she, "are water-melon." "Very well, what next?" "The next," said Mrs. S., "is either muskmelon or cucumber seed." "My dear," said I, "we want plenty of melons, for the summer, but I do not wish to plant half an acre of pickles by mistake; can't you be sure about the matter?" Mrs. Sparrowgrass said she could not. "Well, then, lay the paper down and call off the next." "The next are not radishes, I know," said Mrs. S., "they must be summer cabbages." "Are you sure now, Mrs. Sparrowgrass?" said I, getting a little out of temper. Mrs. Sparrowgrass said she was sure of it, because cabbage seed looked exactly like turnip seed. "Did you save turnip seed also?" said I. Mrs. Sparrowgrass replied, that she had provided some, but they must be in another paper. "Then call off the next; we will plant them for cabbages, whether or no." "Here *is* a name," said Mrs. Sparrowgrass, brightening up. "Read it," said I, pen in hand. "Watermelons—not so good," said Mrs. S. "Lay that paper with the rest and proceed." "Corn," said Mrs. Sparrowgrass, with a smile. "Variety?" "Pop, I am sure." "Good, now we begin to see daylight." "Squash," said Mrs. Sparrowgrass. "Winter or Summer?" "Both." "Lay that paper aside, my dear." "Tomato." "Red or yellow?" Mrs. Sparrowgrass said she had pinned up the one and tied up the other, to distinguish them, but it was so long ago, she had forgot which was which. "Never mind," said I, "there is one comfort, they cannot bear without showing their colors. Now for the next." Mrs. Sparrowgrass said, upon tasting the tomato seed, she was sure they were bell peppers. "Very well, so much is gained, we are sure of the capsicum. The next." "Beans," said Mrs. Sparrowgrass.

There is one kind of bean, in regard to which I have a prejudice. I allude to the asparagus bean, a sort of long-winded esculent, inclined to be prolific in strings. It does not climb very high on the pole, but crops out in an abundance of pods, usually not shorter than a bill of extras, after a contract; and although interesting as a curious vegetable, still not exactly the bean likely to be highly commended by your city guests, when served up to them at table. When Mrs. Sparrowgrass, in answer to my question, as to the particular species of bean referred to, answered, "Limas," I felt relief at once. "Put the Limas to the right with the sheep, Mrs. S., and as for the rest of the seeds sweep them into the refuse basket. I will add another stick to the fire, pare an apple for you, and an apple for me, light a cigar, and be comfortable. What is the use of fretting about a few seeds more or less? But, next year, we will mark all the packages with *names*, to prevent mistakes, won't we, Mrs. Sparrowgrass?"

There has been a great change in the atmosphere within a few days. The maple twigs are all scarlet and yellow fringes, the sod is verdurous and moist; in the morning a shower of melody falls from the trees around us, where blue birds and "pewees" are keeping an academy of music. Off on the river there is a long perspective of shad-poles, apparently stretching from shore to shore, and, here and there, a boat, with picturesque fishermen, at work over the gill-nets. Now and then a shad is held up; in the distance it has a star-like glitter, against the early morning sun. The fruit trees are bronzed with buds. Occasionally a feeble fly creeps along, like a valetudinarian too early in the season at a watering-place. The marshes are all a-whistle with dissipated bull-frogs, who keep up their revelry at unseemly hours. Our great Polander is in high cluck, and we find eggs in the hens' nests. IT IS SPRING! It is a good thing to have spring in the country. People grow young again in the spring in the country. The world, the old globe itself, grows young in the spring, and why not Mr. and Mrs. Sparrowgrass? The city, in the spring, is like the apples of Sodom, "fair and pleasant to behold, but dust and ashes within." But who shall sing or say what spring is in the country?

> "——To what shall I compare it?
> It has a glory, and naught else can share it:
> The thought thereof is awful, sweet, and holy,
> Chasing away all worldliness and folly."

"Mrs. Sparrowgrass," said I, "the weather is beginning to be very warm and spring-like; how would you like to have a little *festa?*" Mrs. Sparrowgrass said that, in her present frame of mind, a fester was not necessary for her happiness. I replied, "I meant a *festa*, not a fester; a little fête, a few friends, a few flowers, a mild sort of spring dinner, if you please; some music, claret, fresh lettuce, lamb and spinach, and a breakfast of eggs fresh laid in the morning, with rice cakes and coffee." Mrs. Sparrowgrass said she was willing. "Then," said I, "Mrs. S., I will invite a few old friends, and we will have an elegant time." So, from that day we watched the sky very cleverly for a week, to ascertain the probable course of the clouds, and consulted the thermometer to know what chance there was of having open windows for the occasion. The only drawback that stood in the way of perfect enjoyment was, our lawn had been half rooted out of existence by an irruption of predatory pigs. It was vexatious enough to see our lawn bottom-side up on a festive occasion. But I determined to have redress for it. Upon consulting with the best legal authority in the village, I was told that I could obtain damages by identifying the animals, and commencing suit against the owner. As I had not seen the animals, I asked Mrs. Sparrowgrass if she could identify them. She said she could not. "Then," said I to my legal friend, "what can I do?" He replied that he did not know. "Then," said I, "if they come again, and I catch them in the act, can I fire a gun among them?" He said I could; but that I would be liable for whatever damage was done them. "That," said I, "would not answer; my object is to make the owner suffer, not the poor quadrupeds." He replied that the only sufferers would probably be the pigs and myself. Then I asked him, if the owner recovered against me, whether I could bring a replevin suit against him. He said that, under the Constitution of the United States, such a suit could be brought. I asked him if I could recover. He said I could not. Then I asked him what remedy I could have. He answered that if I found the pigs on my grounds, I could drive them to the pound, then call upon the fence-viewers, get them to assess the damages done, and by this means mulct the owner for the trespass. This advice pleased me highly; it was practical and humane. I determined to act upon it, and slept soundly upon the resolution. The next day our guests came up from town. I explained the lawn to them, and having been fortified on legal points, instructed them as to the remedy for trespass. The day was warm and beautiful; our doors and windows were thrown wide open. By way of offset to the appearance of the lawn, I had contrived, by purchasing an expensive little bijou of a vase, and filling it with sweet breathing flowers, to spread a rural air of fragrance thoughout the parlor. The doors ot the bay-window open on the piazza; in one doorway stood a tray of delicate confections, upon two slender quartette tables. These were put in the shade to keep cool. I had suborned an Italian to bring them up by hand, in pristine sharpness and beauty of outline. I was taking a glass of sherry with our old friend, Capt. Bacon, of the U.S. Navy, when suddenly our dogs commenced barking. We keep our dogs chained up by daylight. Looking over my glass of sherry, I observed a detachment of the most villainous looking pigs rooting up my early pea-patch. "Now," said I, "Captain," putting down my glass deliberately, "I will show you some fun; excuse me for a few minutes;" and with that I bowed significantly to our festal guests. They understood at once that etiquette must give way when pea-patch was about being annihilated. I then went out, unchained the dogs, and commenced driving the pigs out of the garden. After considerable trampling of all my early vegetables, under the eyes of my guests, I managed to get the ringleader of the swinish multitude into my parlor. He was a large, powerful looking fellow, with a great deal of comb, long legs, mottled complexion, and ears pretty well dogged. He stood for a moment at bay against the sofa, then charged upon the dogs, ran against the centre table, which he accidentally upset, got headed off by Captain Bacon, who came to the rescue, darted under our quartette tables—making a general distribution of confectionery, and finally got cornered in the piazza.

By this time I was so much exasperated that I was capable of taking the life of the intruder, and probably should have done so had my gun not been at the gunsmith's. In striking at him with a stick, I accidentally hit one of the dogs such a blow as to disable him. But I was determined to capture the destroyer and put him in the pound. After some difficulty in getting him out of the piazza, I drove him into the library and finally out in the ground. The rest of his confederates were there, quietly feeding on the remains of the garden. Finally I found myself on the hot, high road, with all my captives and one dog, in search of the pound. Not knowing where the pound was, after driving them for a quarter of a mile, I made inquiry of a respectable looking man, whom I met, in corduroy breeches, on the road. He informed me that he did not know. I then fell in with a colored boy who told me the only pound was at Dobb's Ferry. Dobb's Ferry is a thriving village about seven miles north of the Nepperhan. I made a bargain with the colored boy for three dollars, and by his assistance the animals were safely lodged in the pound. By this means I was enabled to return to my guests. Next day I found out the owner. I got the fence-viewers to estimate the damages.

The fence-viewers looked at the broken mahogany and estimated. I spoke of the vase, the flowers, [green-house flowers] and the confectionery. These did not appear to strike them as damageable. I think the fence-viewers are not liberal enough in their views. The damages done to a man's temper and constitution shall be included, if ever I get to be fence-viewer; to say nothing of exotics trampled under foot, and a beautiful dessert ruthlessly destroyed by unclean animals. Besides that, we shall not have a pea until everybody else in the village has done with peas. We shall be late in the season with our early peas. At last an advertisement appeared in the county paper, which contained the decision of the fence-viewers, to wit:

WESTCHESTER COUNTY, } *ss.*
Town of Yonkers. }

WE, THE SUBSCRIBERS, FENCE-VIEWERS of said town, having been applied to by Samson Sparrowgrass of said town to appraise the damages done by nine hogs, five wintered, [four spotted and one white,] and four spring pigs, [two white] distrained by him doing damage on his lands, and having been to the place, and viewed and ascertained the damages, do hereby certify the amount thereof to be three dollars, and that the fees for our services are two dollars. Given under our hands, this —— day of ——, 185-.

DANIEL MALMSEY, } Fence-viewers.
PETER ASSMANSHAUSER, }

The above hogs are in the Pound at Dobb's Ferry.

CORNELIUS CORKWOOD, Pound Master.

"Under the circumstances," said I, "Mrs. Sparrowgrass, what do you think of the pound as a legal remedy?" Mrs. S. said it was shameful. "So I think, too; but why should we repine? The birds sing, the sky is blue, the grass is green side up, the trees are full of leaves, the air is balmy, and the children, God bless them! are happy. Why should we repine about trifles? If we want early peas we can buy them, and as for the vase, flowers, and confectionery, they would have been all over with, by this time, if the pigs had not been here. There is no use to cry, like Alexander, for another world; let us enjoy the one we have, Mrs. Sparrowgrass."

CHAPTER VIII.

Mr. Sparrowgrass concludes to buy a Horse—Reminiscences of Bloomingdale—The difference between now and then—A Horse as can go—An Artist Story—Godiva—Homeward and Outward bound—The Curtained Dais of the Life School—A new "Lady of Coventry."

I HAVE bought me a horse! A horse is a good thing to have in the country. In the city, the persevering streets have pushed the Bloomingdale road out of reach. Riding-habits and rosy cheeks, bright eyes, round hats and feathers, are banished from the metropolis. There are no more shady by-paths a little way out of town to tempt equestrians. There are no visions of Die Vernon and Frank Osbaldiston at "Burnam's" now. Romance no longer holds the bridle-rein while the delicate slipper is withdrawn from the old red morocco stirrup. A whirl of dust, a glitter of wheels, a stretch of tag-rag and bobtail horses, and the young Potiphars are contesting time with Dusty Bob and the exquisite Mr. Farobank. That is the picture of the

Bloomingdale road now. It is the everyday picture too. Go when you will, you see the tag-rag and bobtail horses, the cloud of dust, the whirl of wheels, the young Potiphars, Dusty Bob, and the elegant Mr. Farobank.

There was a time when I could steal away from the dusky counting-room to inhale the fragrant hartshorn of the stable, while the hostler was putting the saddle on "Fanny." Fanny was a blooded filly, a descendant of the great Sir Henry. Her education had been neglected. She had been broken by a couple of wild Irishmen, who used to "*hurrup*" her, barebacked, morning and evening, through the lonely little street in the lower part of the city, where the stable was situated. As a consequence, the contest between her high blood and low breeding made her slightly vicious. The first time I backed her, she stood still for half an hour, no more moved by the whip than a brass filly would have been; then deliberately walked up the street, turned the corner with a jump that almost threw me on the curb-stone, then ran away, got on the sidewalk, and stopped suddenly, with her fore feet planted firmly in front of a steep flight of area steps, which happened to be filled with children.

I dismounted, and, in no time, was the centre of an angry swarm of fathers and mothers, who were going to immolate me on the spot for trying to ride down their ragged offspring. There is much difficulty in making an *explanation* under such circumstances. As the most abusive person in the crowd happened to be a disinterested stranger who was passing by, it soon became a personal matter between two of us. Accordingly, I asked him to step aside, which he did, when I at once hired him to lead the filly to the ferry. Once on a country road, I was at home in the saddle, and a few days' training made Fanny tractable. She would even follow me with great gentleness, like a trained dog, and really behaved in a very exemplary way, after throwing me twice or so. Then Fanny and I were frequently on the Bloomingdale road, in summer evenings and mornings, and so were ladies and gentlemen. I do not think the fine buildings that usurp those haunted paths an improvement. Those leafy fringes on the way-side had a charm that freestone cannot give. That stretch of vision over meadows, boulders, wild shrubbery and uplifted trees, down to the blue river, is not compensated by ornate façades, cornices, and vestibules. Where are the birds? In my eyes, the glimmer of sultry fire-flies is pleasanter in a summer night than the perspective gas-lights in streets.

> "There's not a charm improvement gives like those it takes away,
> When the shadowing trees are stricken down because they do not pay;
> 'Tis not from youth's smooth cheek the blush of health alone is past,
> But the tender bloom of heart departs, by driving horses fast."

Poor Fanny! my Bloomingdale bride! I believe I was her only patron; and when the stable burnt down, she happened to be insured, and her mercenary owner pocketed her value with a grin.

I have bought me a horse. As I had obtained some skill in the *manége* during my younger days, it was a matter of consideration to have a saddle-horse. It surprised me to find good saddle-horses very abundant soon after my consultation with the stage-proprietor upon this topic. There were strange saddle-horses to sell almost every day. One man was very candid about his horse: he told me, if his horse had a blemish, he wouldn't wait to be asked about it; he would tell it right out; and, if a man didn't want him then, he needn't take him.

He also proposed to put him on trial for sixty days, giving his note for the amount paid him for the horse, to be taken up in case the animal were returned. I asked him what were the principal defects of the horse. He said he'd been fired once, because they thought he was spavined; but there was no more spavin to him than there was to a fresh-laid egg—he was as sound as a dollar. I asked him if he would just state what were the defects of the horse. He answered, that he once had the pink-eye, and added, "now that's honest." I thought so, but proceeded to question him closely. I asked him if he had the bots. He said, not a bot. I asked him if he would go. He said he would go till he dropped down dead; just touch him with a whip, and he'll jump out of his hide. I inquired how old he was. He answered, just eight years, exactly—some men, he said, wanted to make their horses younger than they be; he was willing to speak right out, and own up he was eight years. I asked him if there were any other objections. He said no, except that he was inclined to be a little gay; "but," he added, "he is so kind, a child can drive him with a thread." I asked him if he was a good family horse. He replied that no lady that ever drew rein over him would be willing to part with him. Then I asked him his price. He answered that no man could have bought him for one hundred dollars a month ago, but now he was willing to sell him for seventy-five, on account of having a note to pay. This seemed such a very low price, I was about saying I would take him, when Mrs. Sparrowgrass whispered, that I had better *see the horse first.* I confess I was a little afraid of losing my bargain by it, but, out of deference to Mrs. S., I did ask to see the horse before I bought him. He said he would fetch him down. "No man," he added, "ought to buy a horse unless he's saw him." When the horse came down, it struck me that, whatever his qualities might be, his personal appearance was against him. One of his fore legs was shaped like the handle of our punch-ladle, and the remaining three legs, about the fetlock, were slightly bunchy. Besides, he had no tail to brag of; and his back had a very hollow sweep, from his high haunches to his low shoulder-blades. I was much pleased, however, with the fondness and pride manifested by his owner, as he held up, by both sides of the bridle, the rather longish head of his horse, surmounting a neck shaped like a peapod, and said, in a sort of triumphant voice, "three-quarters blood!" Mrs. Sparrowgrass flushed up a little, when she asked me if I intended to purchase *that* horse, and added, that, if I did, she would never want to ride. So I told the man he would not suit me. He answered by suddenly throwing himself upon his stomach across the back-bone of his horse, and then, by turning round as on a pivot, got up a-straddle of him; then he gave his horse a kick in the ribs that caused him to jump out with all his legs, like a frog, and then off went the spoon-legged animal with a gait that was not a trot, nor yet precisely pacing. He rode around our grass plot twice, and then pulled his horse's head up like the cock of a musket. "That," said he, "is *time*." I replied that he did seem to go pretty fast. "Pretty fast!" said his owner. "Well, do you know Mr. ——?" mentioning one of the richest men in our village. I replied that I was acquainted with him. "Well," said he, "you know his horse?" I replied that I had no personal acquaintance with him. "Well," said he, "he's the fastest horse in the county—jist so—I'm willin' to admit it. But do you know I offered to put my horse agin' his to trot? I had no money to put up, or, rayther, to spare; but I offered to trot him, horse agin' horse, and the winner to take both horses, and I tell you —*he wouldn't do it!*"

Mrs. Sparrowgrass got a little nervous, and twitched me by the skirt of the coat. "Dear," said she, "let him go." I assured her I would not buy the horse, and told the man firmly I would not buy him. He said very well—if he didn't suit 'twas no use to keep a-talkin': but he added, he'd be down agin' with another horse, next morning, that belonged to his brother; and if he didn't suit me, then I didn't want a horse. With this remark he rode off.

When I reached our rural dwelling in the evening, I brought with me the pleasant memory of a story I had heard amid the crash and roar of the great city. To preserve it, I wrote it down on paper. Then I brought it in to Mrs. Sparrowgrass, and, with a sort of premonitory smile, asked her if she remembered "Godiva." Mrs. S. seemed puzzled at the question. I believe she was enumerating the names of our former servant girls in her mind—girls that had been discharged or gone off of themselves, from a disinclination to cleanliness, coupled with a certain amount of work. "Godiva," said I, " or Godina, was the wife of Lord Leofrick, of Coventry, in Warwickshire, England. He oppressed the citizens with heavy taxes, and destroyed their privileges. His wife interceded with him, begged him to remit the weighty burden for her sake. In jest, he promised to do so upon one consideration." " I remember it," said Mrs. Sparrowgrass. "The condition was, that she should ride through the streets of Coventry stark naked." Mrs. Sparrowgrass blushed up to her eyes. "But, like a noble woman, she undertook the task, and redeemed their liberties, by fulfilling his jest in earnest." " Poor thing," said Mrs. S. " You remember," I continued, " how splendidly Tennyson has painted the legend :

'Then fled she to her inmost bower, and there
Unclasp'd the wedded eagles of her belt,
The grim Earl's gift ; but ever at a breath
She lingered, looking like a summer moon,
Half dipt in cloud : anon she shook her head,
And shower'd the rippled ringlets to her knee ;
Unclad herself in haste ; adown the stair
Stole on ; and, like a creeping sumbeam, slid
From pillar unto pillar, until she reached
The gateway ; there she found her palfry trapt

> In purple blazoned with armorial gold.
> Then she rode forth, clothed on in chastity.' "

" How noble !" said Mrs. S. " Yes," I replied, " and now, after this, I want to read you my story. I call it

THE NEW GODIVA.

Sometime after the year eighteen hundred and fifty, a young Englishman landed at one of the quays that afford accommodation to packet ships, around the city of New York He had come to the New World full of hope and enthusiasm, and he stepped upon the quay without a penny in his pocket. Seldom does an American find himself in this condition, in a foreign port. Here it is so familiar, so much of an every-day occurrence, that sympathy has grown callous to the repetition of the old story ;—so this emigrant found, by bitter experience. His fine, intelligent face, under a check-cloth cap, presented itself at various counting-rooms of the city. Check-cloth caps, in search of employment, are common enough; and few merchants can spare time to analyze the lineaments of a fine, intelligent countenance.

So the young emigrant found no employment in

the busy, active city; the fine, intelligent countenance suffered by unwholesome resting-places, among funeral mahogany at night, and by pride struggling with hunger in the day, until at last the check-cloth cap bent over a stone mallet to beat down the city cobble stones, for a corporation contractor. Oh, the dreary, desolate city, crowded with strangers! Oh, the bright alien sunshine, that never lighted up a sympathetic face! Oh, the green shores of Merrie England, that he had seen sinking in the distant sea, with misty eyes! There they all were; mother and brothers, and she, the dear one—all! and every blow of the stone-rammer went down like a sob. In no period of life is disappointment so poignant as in youth. The dreams of maturity are limited by experience, and the awakening is almost anticipated. But youth believes its gorgeous visions, and looks upon the real, work-day world as a monstrous fable. But, oh, the touch of the Ithuriel spear!

The stone-rammer, for months, steadily beat down the cobble-stones. The check-cloth cap had lost its pristine freshness; the fine, intelligent countenance became dead, dull, apathetic. There was a trifling sum deposited weekly in the Emigrants'

Saving Bank. It was all withdrawn one day. It was the day the "Devonshire" Liverpool packet sailed. From that day the check-cloth cap, and the fine, intelligent countenance were seen no more by the corporation contractor.

The "Devonshire" packet ship had a fine passage out, and was beating up towards the Mersey in little more than a fortnight after she bade farewell to the American city. There she met another packet ship, outward bound. The ships came so near each other that passengers could recognize faces on either deck. Amid the multitude of emigrants, thronging the side of the outward-bound packet, one face had particularly attracted the attention of the passengers on the "Devonshire." It was that of an emigrant girl, a right English face, in a Dunstable bonnet, but still strikingly lovely. It was a face not simply beautiful only, it was ideally so; one of those faces to inspire love in a woman, adoration in a man, and respect in coarser natures. It was not surprising, then, when one of the younger passengers on the "Devonshire" proposed at dinner, "*the health of that English girl*," that everybody understood it—that ladies and all joined in the toast with enthusiasm.

One person alone, a steerage passenger on the "Devonshire," had been insensible to the excitement occasioned by the passing ships. From the time the blue land hove in sight, the inevitable check-cloth cap, and fine intelligent countenance had been turned shorewards, from the bowsprit. Never once had that eager gaze been diverted from the land; never once had it turned towards the packet, outward bound!

A fragment of his history must be inserted in the mosaic of the story. When he left home to seek his fortune in the Western republic, he did so with a feeling, a faith that seemed prophetic of success. His talents, for he had talents; his perseverance, for he had perseverance; his indefatigable industry, for he had that also, assured him there could be no failure. Nor would there have been, in time. Industry, perseverance, and talent, may fearlessly *begin* with the stone rammer, or even with a lower calling. Begin, begin, somewhere—anywhere—only begin. There is no position, no dignity, without the inevitable steps. If need be, take the lowest and surmount them. Here, then, might have been laid the foundation of his fortunes, had pride permitted; but that young, ardent spirit, crushed by drudgery, saw the future only as a continuation of the present; the busy world had rudely thrust him aside; it is true, pride had succumbed to hunger, and beat down the cobble stones, but this, to him, was not the dawn of hope, but the sequel. Henceforth, one thought controlled his mind. "Home, home! return, return!" rang out from the flinty pavements. There was the face of mother, there were the faces of brothers, there was *her face*, the face of his beloved one—his betrothed, to whom, in his anguish, he had not written since he first stepped upon the shores of the busy, heartless New World. "Home, home!" was the constant burthen, until the "Devonshire" packet carried him, with his slender fortunes, once more across the Atlantic. What was that outward-bound ship to him, when his eyes were fixed again on Merrie England, where they all were?

Not very long after this period, Mr. Ultramarine, the famous artist, was arranging the drapery on his lay-figure. A lay-figure is a huge doll, usually about five feet three in height, kept in artists' studios. Its joints are flexible, back, arms, neck, et cetera, movable at will; it can be made to stand up, to sit down or lie down, in fact, may be put in any posture; its limbs, bust, body, are stuffed out so as to cleverly represent womanity, in perfect and divine proportions; its ordinary use is to be dressed up as a lady, and to act as such in the studio. For example, Mrs. Honiton is sitting for her portrait, the lovely face, the rounded arms, the taper fingers, are transferred to the canvas; but Mrs. Honiton's elaborate dress must also be painted, and a two hours' sitting, day after day, is tiresome and tedious. The lay-figure then becomes useful, and plays a brief part in society. For a period, it represents Mrs. Honiton. While Mr. Ultramarine is finishing the picture, it wears her brocades, velvets, shawl, bertha, bracelets, lace-sleeves, with becoming dignity. There is one peculiarity in lay figures, sometimes objectionable. They are apt to transfer an air of stiffness to the likeness; this, however, may be also in the original, and then the effect is wonderful.

Mr. Ultramarine could not arrange the drapery on the lay-figure to suit his fancy. The delicate, careless curve of Mrs. Honiton's arm, holding the thrown-off shawl, was beyond the lay-figure's ability. So Mr. Ultramarine gave it up, and went on setting his pallet, with now and then a fiendish look at his lay-figure. There was that rigid arm, stiffly holding out the shawl, with the precision of porcelain; completely excluding the idea Mr. U. wished to portray, of carelessness.

There is always, in every studio, of every artist in the city of New York, in the morning, before visitors arrive, a respectable, elderly female. Her duties are sweeping and dusting. By constantly breathing its magic atmosphere, she often gains an intuitive conception of art, beyond even the skill of the newspaper critic. The respectable elderly female who was putting Mr. Ultramarine to rights, understood the difficulty at once. She glanced at the artist and at the shawled manikin. Then she hushed the music of the broom, and said, timidly, "Please, sir, there is a poor creature, a young English girl, sir, at my room, a living with me, that would be glad to earn a shilling or two; and she would hold yon shawl just as you want it." Mr. Ultramarine squeezed a little vermilion out of the capsule upon his pallet, and looked up. "Hum," he replied, "a coarse creature, I presume." This was said in a kind voice, with a lingering accent on "coarse creature," that did not convey harshness by any means. "No, sir," she answered, "I would call her an English beauty. The finest face and figure, sir." "Dear me," said the artist, "why did you not speak of it before? Can you bring her now, Mrs. Hill?" "I can, sir," she replied, "immegently." So Mrs. Hill left the studio for the model, and Mr. U. went on preparing Mrs. Honiton's toilet on his pallet. He squeezed a tiny pod of blue in one place, then mixed it with white, in a variety of tints; then he smeared another place over with Vandyke brown; then he dropped a curious little worm of yellow ochre, out of another capsule; then the pallet-knife dipped into a patch of white, and then the ochre was graduated into various tints; then he dug a mass of magilp out of a bottle, and put that on the board; then glanced on the lovely Honiton, and again took up another capsule, from which he pressed a cogent blush of carmine. Then the door opened, after a short knock, and in walked Mrs. Hill and the model. Under a plain English bonnet was the same face the passengers on the "Devonshire" had seen looking over the side of the packet, outward-bound.

Mr. Ultramarine was a painter, and felt the divine inspiration of his professicn realized in that face. But when the model had been arrayed by

Mrs. Hill in the ante-room in the splendid dress of Mrs. Honiton, and stood upon the dais, the effect was bewildering. "Such," said the artist to himself, "was the face Raphael knew and painted, and men turned from Divinity to worship art in the ideal Virgin. It is not surprising the church has made so many proselytes."

Mr. Ultramarine was an artist; he set to work manfully and painted the shawl. There was an ease and grace in the careless curve of the living arm holding it, that made lay-figure absolutely repulsive. He put lay-figure in one corner of his studio, and covered her all over with old coats, pantaloons, a rug, and bit of curtain, besides piling on his fishing-rod, and laying a cracked pallet on top, by way of cap-stone. In a few days Mrs. Honiton was done. Alas, Mr. Ultramarine had not another lady sitter just then; there were a score of gentlemen whose portraits had to be painted. They must be painted; he had a family to support, and not much to do it with. He must pay the model and send her away. So he told her simply and kindly, and then——

The model turned deadly pale, essayed to speak, failed, and fainted outright.

Mr. Ultramarine took it into his head that the model had fallen in love with him. Never was he more mistaken, nor more relieved when he found he was mistaken. He carried the helpless form to a chair, bathed the Madonna face with water, and brought the model to.

Then came the story. She was betrothed; her lover had left England for America months ago; she had waited patiently to hear from him by letter; steamer after steamer arrived, but no letter. In the seclusion of her native village suspense had become intolerable. She determined to follow him. Not for an instant doubting his faith, but fearing all that woman can fear save that. Never did she think she could not find him; no, not if he were in the world. She had traced him even in the wilderness of New York, until at last she found he had taken passage to England again by the "Devonshire." For her there was but one thought, one hope, one overpowering desire. That was also to return, speedily, instantly, if possible, but——she was almost penniless.

When she had concluded, a bright idea suggested itself to Mr. Ultramarine, and played with a lambent light over his features. "My child," said he, "it would be impossible for me to assist you with means sufficient for your purpose, but I can tell you of a way by which you can make enough to enable you to return, and make it speedily too. We are in want of a nude model for the National Academy of Design. Our present models have been so long on the carpet that they have grown too stringy even for high art. You understand me, we are in want of a nude model for the life school. If you will consent to sit, you can speedily earn enough to enable you to return, say in a few weeks."

What was passing in that young mind while the artist was saying this, in a plain matter-of-fact way? What terrible thoughts were being balanced there? What years of blinding toil, to earn even a pittance for daily support, with no hope of regaining far-off England, were being weighed against this startling alternative? With all there was a little flush of hope;—in a month she could be on the broad ocean; once more she would see him for whom she had suffered so much; and in that pure, maiden heart arose the determination to make the sacrifice. So, when the burning blush left her features, and she had heard all, it was a face as calm as marble that bowed assent, meekly but firmly, and then she went forth from the studio.

In the National Academy of Design there are two schools of art—the Antique and the Life. The first comprises casts of the famous statues, the Farnese Hercules, the Venus de Medici, the Apollo Belvidere, Thorwaldsen's Mercury with the pipe, and Venus with the apple, the Nymph of the bath, Venus Victrix, the Greek Suppliant, and other immortal achievements. Here the neophytes of the Academy assemble in winter to draw from the casts. In the adjoining room maturer students copy from life. In no place is the ennobling influence of art more apparent than in the Life-school. The sacred stillness of the place, the calm, earnest faces of the sketchers, the statue-like repose of the living model; the analytical experience constantly suggested by the nude figure—the muscles, first round and firm, then flattened, then lax and shrunken by the hour's duty, teaching the physical aspects of nature in various conditions, from which the true painter draws the splendid corollary, "*that art represents nature best, when art comprehends nature in all its developments.*"

Was there no shrinking in that young creature's

heart when they had left her alone in the unrobing room? Was there no touch of unconscious pride as she stood at last, in her abundant beauty, before the mirror? Did she not hesitate as she opened the door, and stepped forth upon the curtained dais? Or, was that pure, innocent breast so unsullied, that even to shame it was alien? The truly good alone can answer this question.

To the most discreet, the wisest, and the gravest counsellors of the Academy is confided the delicate task of arranging the *pose* of the nude model on the dais. Then the curtains are drawn, and the figure is revealed to the students. There are usually three of these counsellors; for, "in a multitude of counsellors is wisdom." This time no artistic interference was needed. The natural posture of the nude figure upon the dais-sofa was one of such exquisite grace that it rivalled even the Greek marble. So the wise greybeards of the Academy besought the model to sit perfectly still, and with this slight premonition, the curtains were swept away, and a flood of light fell upon the dais and Godiva.

Thou white chastity! Amid that blaze of eager eyes now fastened upon thy beauties, there is not a soul so base as to harbor one evil thought of thee!

Here, where "art's pure dwellers are," thou art secure as in a shrine!

The hour's probation is over: the curtains close. And now the touching history of her love is told by Mr. Ultramarine to the listening students, and ere the Madonna face is hidden again in the Dunstable bonnet, the artists before the curtain have a little gift for the model. It is a purse, not heavy, but sufficient. Young artists cannot give much. But there was an unanimous determination that she should be protected by them until such time as she could be safely placed on a steamer "outward bound." And before a week had elapsed she stood again upon a deck; and never were farewells, waved to the departing passengers of the "Atlantic," fuller of generous sympathy, than those that bade adieu to Godiva!

"Is that all?" said Mrs. Sparrowgrass, as I rolled up the manuscript. "That is all, my dear." "Did she find her lover?" said Mrs. Sparrowgrass. "I do not know," I replied; "but I suppose she did." "I hope she did," said Mrs. S., "from the bottom of my heart I do."—(A pause.)—"Come," said I, "it is late. To-morrow we must rise early, for you know the man is to bring the other horse here;—the one that belongs to his brother, Mrs. Sparrowgrass."

CHAPTER IX.

A Horse of another color—Ancient and Modern Points of a Horse—A suspected Organ and Retrograde Movement—Mr. Sparrowgrass buys the Horse that belongs to the Man's Brother—A valuable Hint as to Stable-building—A Morning Ride, and a Discovery—Old Dockweed—An Evening Ride, and a Catastrophe.

"IT rains very hard," said Mrs. Sparrowgrass, looking out of the window next morning. Sure enough, the rain was sweeping broadcast over the country, and the four Sparrowgrassii were flattening a quartette of noses against the window-panes, believing most faithfully the man would bring the horse that belonged to his brother, in spite of the elements. It was hoping against hope: no man having a horse to sell will trot him out in a rain-storm, unless he intend to sell him at a bargain—but childhood is so credulous! The succeeding morning was bright, however, and down came the horse. He had been very cleverly groomed, and looked pleasant under the saddle. The man led him back and forth before the door. "There, squire, 's as good a hos as ever stood on iron." Mrs. Sparrowgrass asked me what he meant by that. I replied, it was a figurative way of expressing, in horse-talk, that he was as good a horse as ever stood in shoe-leather. "He's a handsome hos, squire," said the man. I replied that he did seem to be a good-looking animal, but, said I, "he does not quite come up to the description of a horse I have read." "Whose hos was it?" said he. I replied it was the horse of Adonis. He said he didn't know him, but, he added, "there is so many hosses stolen, that the descriptions are stuck up now pretty common." To put him at his ease (for he seemed to think I suspected him of having stolen the horse), I told him the description I meant had been written some hundreds of years ago by Shakspeare, and repeated it—

"Round-hooft, short-joynted, fetlocks shag and long,
Broad brest, full eyes, small head, and nostril wide,
High crest, short ears, strait legs, and passing strong,
Thin mane, thick tail, broad buttock, tender hide."

"Squire," said he, "that will do for a song, but it ain't no p'ints of a good hos. Trotters now-a-days go in all shapes, big heads and little heads, big eyes and little eyes, short ears or long ones, thick tail and no tail; so as they have sound legs, good l'in, good barrel, and good stifle, and wind, squire, and speed well, they'll fetch a price. Now, this animal is what I call a hos, squire; he's got the p'ints, he's stylish, he's close-ribbed, a free goer, kind in harness—single or double—a good feeder." I asked him if being a good feeder was a desirable quality. He replied it was; "of course," said he, "if your hos is off his feed, he ain't good for nothin'. But what's the use," he added, "of me tellin' you the p'ints of a good hos? You're a hos man, squire: you know"— "It seems to me," said I, "there is something the matter with that left eye." "No, *sir*," said he, and with that he pulled down the horse's head, and, rapidly crooking his fore-finger at the suspected organ, said, "see thar—don't wink a bit." "But he should wink," I replied. "Not onless his eye are weak," he said. To satisfy myself, I asked the man to let me take the bridle. He did so, and, so soon as I took hold of it, the horse started off in a remarkable retrograde movement, dragging me with him into my best bed of hybrid roses. Finding we were trampling down all the best plants, that had cost at auction from three-and-sixpence to seven shillings apiece, and that the more I pulled, the more he backed, I finally let him have his own way, and jammed him stern-foremost into our largest climbing rose that had been all summer prickling itself, in order to look as much like a vegetable porcupine as possible. This unexpected bit of satire in his rear changed his retrograde movement to a sidelong bound, by which he flirted off half the pots on the balusters, upsetting my gladioluses and tuberoses in the pod, and leaving great splashes of mould, geraniums, and red pottery in the gravel walk. By this time his owner had managed to give him two pretty severe cuts with the whip, which made him unmanageable, so I let him go. We had a pleasant time catching him again, when he got among the Lima bean-poles; but his owner led him back with a very self-satisfied expression. "Playful, ain't he, squire?" I replied that I thought he was, and asked him if it was usual for his horse to play such pranks. He said it was not. "You see, squire, he feels his oats, and hain't been out of the stable for a month. Use him, and he's as kind as a kitten." With that he put his foot in the stirrup, and mounted. The animal really looked very well as he moved around the grass plot, and, as Mrs. Sparrowgrass seemed to fancy him, I took a written guarantee that he was sound, and bought him. What I gave for him is a secret; I have not even told Mrs. Sparrowgrass.

It is a mooted point whether it is best to buy your horse before you build your stable, or build your stable before you buy your horse. A horse without a stable is like a bishop without a church. Our neighbor, who is very ingenious, built his stable to fit his horse. He took the length of his horse and a little over, as the measure of the depth of his stable; then he built it. He had a place beside the stall for his Rockaway carriage. When he came to put the Rockaway in, he found he had not allowed for the shafts! The ceiling was too low to allow them to be erected, so he cut two square port-holes in the back of his stable and run his shafts, through them, into the chicken-house behind. Of course, whenever he wanted to take out his carriage, he had to unroost all his fowls, who would sit on his shafts, night and day. But that was better than building a new stable. For my part, I determined to avoid mistakes, by getting the horse and carriage both first, and then to build the stable. This plan, being acceptable to Mrs. Sparrowgrass, was adopted, as judicious and expedient. In consequence, I found myself with a horse on my hands with no place to put him. Fortunately, I was acquainted with a very honest man who kept a livery stable, where I put him to board by the month, and in order that he might have plenty of good oats, I bought some, which I gave to the ostler for that purpose. The man of whom I bought the horse did not deceive me, when he represented him as a great feeder. He ate more oats than all the rest of the horses put together in that stable.

It is a good thing to have a saddle-horse in the country. The early morning ride, when dawn and dew freshen and flush the landscape, is comparable to no earthly, innocent pleasure. Look at yonder avenue of road-skirting trees. Those marvellous trunks, yet moist, are ruddy as obelisks of jasper! And above—see the leaves blushing at the east! Hark to the music! interminable chains of melody linking earth and sky with its delicious magic. The little, countless wood-birds are singing! and now rolls up from the mown meadow the fragrance of cut grass and clover.

"No print of sheep-track yet hath crushed a flower ;
The spider's woof with silvery dew is hung
As it was beaded ere the daylight hour :
The hookéd bramble just as it was strung,
When on each leaf the night her crystals flung,
Then hurried off, the dawning to elude."

* * * * *

"The rutted road did never seem so clean,
There is no dust upon the way-side thorn,
For every bud looks out as if but newly born."

Look at the river with its veil of blue mist! and the grim, gaunt old Palisades, as amiable in their orient crowns as old princes, out of the direct line of succession, over the royal cradle of the heir apparent!

There is one thing about early riding in the country; you find out a great many things which, perhaps, you would not have found out under ordinary circumstances. The first thing I found out was, that my horse had the heaves. I had been so wrapt up in the beauties of the morning, that I had not observed, what perhaps everybody in that vicinity had observed, namely, that the new horse had been waking up all the sleepers on both sides of the road with an asthmatic whistle, of half-a-mile power. My attention was called to the fact by the village teamster, old Dockweed, who came banging after me in his empty cart, shouting out my name as he came. I must say, I have always disliked old Dockweed's familiarity; he presumes too much upon my good nature, when he calls me Sparrygrass before ladies at the dépôt, and by my Christian name always on the Sabbath, when he is dressed up. On this occasion, what with the horse's vocal powers and old Dockweed's, the affair was pretty well blown over the village before breakfast. "Sparrygrass," he said, as he came up, "that your hos?" I replied, that the horse was my property. "Got the heaves, ain't he? got 'em bad." Just then a window was pushed open, and the white head of the old gentleman, who sits in the third pew in front of our pew in church, was thrust out. "What's the matter with your horse?" said he. "Got the heaves," replied old Dockweed, "got 'em bad." Then, I heard symptoms of opening a blind on the other side of the road, and as I did not wish to run the gauntlet of such inquiries, I rode off on a cross road; but not before I heard, above the sound of pulmonary complaint, the voice of old Dockweed explaining to the other cottage, "Sparrygrass—got a hos—got the heaves—got 'em bad." I was so much ashamed, that I took a round-about road to the stable, and instead of coming home like a fresh and gallant cavalier, on a hand gallop, I walked my purchase to the stable, and dismounted with a chastened spirit.

"Well, dear," said Mrs. Sparrowgrass, with a face beaming all over with smiles, "how did you like your horse?" I replied that he was not quite so fine a saddle-horse as I had anticipated, but I added, brightening up, for good humor is sympathetic, "he will make a good horse, I think, after all, for you and the children to jog around with in a wagon." "Oh, won't that be pleasant!" said Mrs. Sparrowgrass.

Farewell, then, rural rides, and rural roads o' mornings! Farewell, song birds, and jasper colonnades; farewell misty river, and rocky Palisades; farewell mown honey-breath, farewell stirrup and bridle, dawn and dew, we must jog on at a foot pace. After all, it is better for your horse to have a pulmonary complaint than have it yourself.

I had determined not to build a stable, nor to buy a carriage, until I had thoroughly tested my horse in harness. For this purpose, I hired a

Rockaway of the stable-keeper. Then I put Mrs. Sparrowgrass and the young ones in the double seats, and took the ribbons for a little drive by the Nepperhan river road. The Nepperhan is a quiet stream that for centuries has wound its way through the antient dorp of Yonkers. Geologists may trace the movements of time upon the rocky dial of the Palisades, and estimate the age of the more modern Hudson by the foot-prints of sauriæ in the strata that fringe its banks, but it is impossible to escape the conviction, as you ride beside the Nepperhan, that it is a very old stream—that it is entirely independent of earthquakes—that its birth was of primeval antiquity—and, no doubt, that it meandered through Westchester valleys when the Hudson was only a fresh water lake, land-locked somewhere above Poughkeepsie. It was a lovely afternoon. The sun was sloping westward, the meadows

> ———————" were all a-flame
> In sunken light, and the mailed grasshopper
> Shrilled in the maize with ceaseless iteration."

We had passed Chicken Island, and the famous house with the stone gable and the one stone chimney, in which General Washington slept, as he made it a point to sleep in every old stone house in Westchester county, and had gone pretty far on the road, past the cemetery, when Mrs. Sparrowgrass said suddenly, "Dear, what is the matter with your horse?" As I had been telling the children all the stories about the river on the way, I had managed to get my head pretty well inside of the carriage, and, at the time she spoke, was keeping a look-out in front with my back. The remark of Mrs. Sparrowgrass induced me to turn about, and I found the new horse behaving in a most unaccountable manner. He was going down hill with his nose almost to the ground, running the wagon first on this side and then on the other. I thought of the remark made by the man, and turning again to Mrs. Sparrowgrass, said, "Playful, isn't he?" The next moment I heard something breaking away in front, and then the Rockaway gave a lurch and stood still. Upon examination I found the new horse had tumbled down, broken one shaft, gotten the other through the check-rein so as to bring his head up with a round-turn, and besides had managed to put one of the traces in a single hitch around his off hind leg. So soon as I had taken all the young ones and Mrs. Sparrowgrass out of the Rockaway, I set to work to liberate the horse, who was choking very fast with the check-rein. It is unpleasant to get your fishing-line in a tangle when you are in a hurry for bites, but I never saw fishing-line in such a tangle as that harness. However, I set to work with a penknife, and cut him out in such a way as to make getting home by our conveyance impossible. When he got up, he was the sleepiest looking horse I ever saw. "Mrs. Sparrowgrass," said I, "won't you stay here with the children until I go to the nearest farm-house?" Mrs. Sparrowgrass replied that she would. Then I took the horse with me to get him out of the way of the children, and went in search of assistance. The first thing the new horse did when he got about a quarter of a mile from the scene of the accident, was to tumble down a bank. Fortunately the bank was not over four feet high, but as I went with him, my trowsers were rent in a grievous place. While I was getting the new horse on his feet again, I saw a colored person approaching, who came to my assistance. The first thing he did was to pull out a large jack-knife, and the next thing he did was to open the new horse's mouth and run the blade two or three times inside of the new horse's gums. Then the new horse commenced bleeding. "Dah, sah," said the man, shutting up his jack-knife, "ef 't hadn't been for dat yer, your hos would a' bin a goner." "What was the matter with him?" said I. "Oh, he's ony jis got de blind-staggers, das all. Say," said he, before I was half indignant enough at the man who had sold me such an animal, "say, ain't your name Sparrowgrass?" I replied that my name was Sparrowgrass. "Oh," said he, "I knows you, I brung some fowls once down to you place. I heerd about you, and you hos. Dats de hos dats got de heaves so bad, heh! heh! You better sell dat hos." I determined to take his advice, and employed him to lead my purchase to the nearest place where he would be cared for. Then I went back to the Rockaway, but met Mrs. Sparrowgrass and the children on the road coming to meet me. She had left a man in charge of the Rockaway. When we got to the Rockaway we found the man missing, also the whip and one cushion. We got another person to take charge of the Rockaway, and had a pleasant walk home by moonlight. I think a moonlight night delicious, upon the Hud-

Does any person want a horse at a low price? A good, stylish-looking animal, close-ribbed, good loin, and good stifle, sound legs, with only the heaves and blind-staggers, and a slight defect in one of his eyes? If at any time he slips his bridle and gets away, you can always approach him by getting on his left side. I will also engage to give a written guarantee that he is sound and kind, signed by the brother of his former owner.

CHAPTER X.

Children—An Interrupted Discourse—Mrs. Sparrowgrass makes a Brilliant Remark—Philadelphia Phrases—Another Interruption—Quakers—A few Quakeristics—A Quaker Baby—The Early Quakers—John Woolman—Thomas Lurting—Broadbrims in a Cathedral—And a Friendly Suggestion.

CHILDREN, God bless them! Who can help loving them! Children, God bless them! are the only beings for whom we have no "imperfect sympathies." We love them through and through. There is nothing conventional in the hearty laugh of a child. The smile of a child is unsuspectable of artifice. I once corrected one of my little ones, and put him to bed, for having been stubborn at his letters. Then I waited until he fell asleep, and then I watched beside him until he slumbered out his sorrows. When he opened his eyes, he stretched out his little arms, smiled up in my face, and forgave me. The Lord forgive me for the whaling I gave him! I owe him an apology, which I intend to make so soon as he is old enough to understand it. There is nothing so odious to the mind of a child as injustice, and young married people are prone to expect too much, and exact too much of their eldest born. If then we are unjustly severe from our want of experience, it seem to me there is something due, some reparation on our part, due to the individual whose feelings we have injured. If we lose temper with a gentleman six feet high, and call him hard names, we often find it convenient to apologize. It seems to me that three feet of wounded sensibility is, at least, entitled to respectful consideration. What do you think of that, Mrs. Sparrowgrass? Mrs. Sparrowgrass said she thought it was true. "How much," I continued, reflectively, "children occupy the father's mind." "Yes," said Mrs. Sparrowgrass, "and the mother's." "Children," said I, "are to the father as weights are to the clock—they keep him steady and they keep him busy."

Mrs. Sparrowgrass looked up from the plaid patch of new gingham she was needling into the breast of a faded gingham apron, and nodded significantly: "True," said she, "you are the hour hand, but I am the minute hand."

As this was the most brilliant remark Mrs. S. had made for months, I was silent for some time.

"My dear," said I, after a pause, "speaking of children, I wish you would not teach the young ones so many of your Philadelphia phrases." Mrs. Sparrowgrass looked surprised. "You know, my dear," I continued, "how proud I am this year, and justly proud, too, of our musk-melons?" "Well?" "And when Uncle Sourgrass was here the other day, what should Ivanhoe do but ask him to go out to look at the cantelopes." "Well, what of that?" said Mrs. S. "Cantelope," said I, "in this part of the world, is the name of a very inferior species of melon, and I would not have had Uncle Sourgrass think we had nothing but cantelopes in the garden, upon any account." "You wouldn't?" "No! You call *all* kinds of melons 'cantelopes' in Philadelphia, but permit me to say that it is a local error, which should not be transplanted and trained in juvenile minds on the banks of the Hudson." Mrs. Sparrowgrass was much impressed by this horticultural figure. "Then, when visitors come, you always will take them to see that patch of 'Queen Margarets,' and everybody gets disappointed to find they are only China-asters." "Well?" "And there is another thing too Mrs. Sparrowgrass; next Christmas Santa Claus, if you please—no Kriss Kringle. Santa Claus is the patron saint, Mrs. Sparrowgrass, of the New Netherlands, and the ancient Dorp of Yonkers; he it is who fills the fireside stockings; he only can come down Westchester chimneys, and I would much prefer not to have the children's minds, and the flue, occupied with his Pennsylvania prototype. And, since I must speak of it, why will you always call a quail a partridge? All you Philadelphians will call a quail a partridge. Did you ever read Audubon?" Mrs. Sparrowgrass said she never had. "Wilson?" "Never." "Charles Bonaparte?" (A dead silence.) "Nor any other work on ornithology?" Mrs. Sparrowgrass said there was a little bundle of remnants and patches in the upper part of the closet, which she wished I would reach down. "A quail," I continued, as I reached down the bundle, "is not a partridge, my dear." Mrs. Sparrowgrass said the next time we had partridges she would call them all quails, as she supposed I knew which was correct better than she did. With that she unrolled the bundle and drew therefrom a long, triangular piece of faded, mouse-colored silk.

There are moments when I feel as if I would like to launch into a little sea of language, and spread a nautilus sail in delicate air. The great, three-deckers of thought, the noble orators and splendid statesmen, require the broader and more turbulent ocean for their ponderous movements. But for me, who have seen something of the eloquent world, from the magnates of the senate, in palmy days, down to the present windy representatives of the great metropolis in Common Council assembled, there seems to be a more captivating charm in those lighter crafts that float in safety over the shallows of polite conversation, and venture securely amid the rocks and whirlpools of social argument. Who has not felt as if he would like to preach for half an hour or so upon some favorite text or topic? Who has not, in some auspicious instant, been so fortified in argument as to absolutely suffer for the stimulant of opposition, to enable him to unload his mind and be comfortable? Mrs. Sparrowgrass, by an ill-timed, brilliant remark, had broken the thread of my discourse upon children, and she had put an end to my argument against local phrases, by requesting me to reach down a piebald bundle of patches. But from that roll of remnants she had drawn forth a long, triangular piece of mouse-colored silk. The tint was suggestive. It was a text, a thesis, that would bear amplifying. So I at once started off. "My dear, do you know I have long felt as if I would like to be one of the society called 'Friends?'" Mrs. Sparrowgrass replied, she did not know I had contemplated so serious a departure from the rules of propriety. "My dear," I said, "no person has a greater feeling of respect and regard than I have for the sect that so unjustly bears the name of

QUAKERS.

"There is something, in the very aspect of a 'Friend,' suggestive of peace and good will. Verily, if it were not for the broad-brimmed hat, and the straight coat, which the world's people call 'shad,' I would be a Quaker. But for the life of me I cannot resist the effect of the grotesque and the odd. I must smile, oftenest at myself. I could not keep within drab garments and the bounds of propriety. Incongruity would read me out of meeting. To be reined in under a plain hat would be impossible. Besides, I doubt whether any one accustomed to the world's pleasures could be a Quaker. Who, once familiar with Shakspeare and the opera, could resist a favorite air on a hand organ, or pass, undisturbed, 'Hamlet!' in capital letters on a play bill? To be a Quaker, one must be a Quaker born. In spite of Sydney Smith, there is such a thing as a Quaker baby. In fact, I have seen it—a diminutive demurity, a stiff-plait in the bud. It had round blue eyes, and a face that expressed resignation in spite of the stomach-ache. It had no lace on its baby-cap, no embroidered nonsense on its petticoat. It had no beads, no ribbons, no rattle, no bells, no coral. Its plain garments were innocent of inserting and edging; its socks were not of the color of the world's people's baby. It was as punctiliously silent as a silent meeting, and sat up rigidly in its mother's lap, twirling its thumbs and cutting its teeth without a gum-ring. It never cried, nor clapped its hands, and would not have said 'papa' if it had been tied to the stake. When it went to sleep it was hushed without a song, and they laid it in a drab-colored cradle without a rocker. Don't interrupt me, I have seen it, Mrs. Sparrowgrass!

"Something I have observed too, remarkably, strikingly Quakeristic. The young maidens and the young men never seem inclined to be fat. Such a thing as a maiden lady, nineteen years of age, with a pound of superfluous flesh, is not known among Friends. The young men sometimes grow outside the limits of a straight coat, and when they do, they quietly change into the habits of ordinary men. Either they are read out of meeting, or else they lose their hold when they get too round and too ripe, and just drop off. Remarkably Quakeristic, too, is an exemption the Friends appear to enjoy from diseases and complaints peculiar to other people. Who ever saw a Quaker marked with the small-pox, or a Quaker with the face-ache? Who ever saw a cross-eyed Quaker, or a decided case of mumps under a broad-brimmed hat? Nobody. Mrs. Sparrowgrass, don't interrupt me. Doubtless much of this is owing to their cleanliness, duplex cleanliness, purity of body and soul. I saw a face in the cars, not long since—a face that had calmly endured the storms of seventy yearly meetings. It was a hot, dry day, the windows were all open;

dust was pouring into the cars; eye-brows, eye-lashes, ends of hair, mustachios, wigs, coat-collars, sleeves, waistcoats, and trowsers of the world's people, were touched with a fine tawny color. Their faces had a general appearance of humidity in streaks, now and then tatooed with a black cinder; but there, within a satin bonnet (Turk's satin), a bonnet made after the fashion of Professor Espy's patent ventilator, was a face of seventy years, calm as a summer morning, smooth as an infant's, without one speck or stain of dust, without one touch of perspiration, or exasperation, Mrs. S. No, nor was there, on the cross-pinned 'kerchief, nor on the elaborately plain dress, one atom of earthy contact; the very air did seem to respect that aged Quakeress.

"Mrs. Sparrowgrass, don't interrupt me. Did you ever, my dear, 'get the writings of John Woolman by heart, and love the early Quakers,' as beloved Charles Lamb recommends? No? Then let me advise you to read the book, and learn something of one who had felt the efficacy of that power, which, as he says, 'prepares the creature to stand like a trumpet, through which the Lord speaks to his people.' Here is a little story of his early childhood, which I want you to read to the children now and then.

"'Once going to a neighbor's house, I saw, on the way, a *Robin* sitting on her nest, and, as I came near, she went off; but, having young ones, flew about, and, with many cries, expressed her concern for them. I stood and threw stones at her, till, one striking her, she fell down dead. At first, I was pleased with the exploit; but, after a few minutes, was seized with horror, as having, in a sportive way, killed an innocent creature while she was careful of her young. I beheld her lying dead, and thought those young ones, for which she was so careful, must now perish for the want of their dam to nourish them; and, after some painful considerations on the subject, I climbed up the tree, took all the young birds, and killed them, supposing that better than to leave them to pine away and die miserably; and believed, in this case, that Scripture proverb was fulfilled, "The tender mercies of the wicked are cruel." I then went on my errand; but, for some hours, could think of nothing else but the cruelties I had committed, and was much troubled. Thus He, whose tender mercies are above all his works, hath placed a principle in the human mind, which incites to exercise goodness toward every living creature; and this being singly attended to, people become tender-hearted and sympathizing; but being frequently and totally rejected, the mind becomes shut up in a contrary disposition.'

"Don't interrupt me, my dear. And Thomas Lurting, too; his adventures are well worth reading to the children. A Quaker sailor, the mate of a Quaker ship, manned with a Quaker crew, every one of which had a straight collar to his pea-jacket, and a tarpaulin, with at least three feet diameter of brim. Thomas Lurting, whose ship was captured by Algerine pirates after a hard chase, and who welcomed them on board as if they had been brothers. Then, when the Quaker vessel and the Algerine were separated by a storm, how friendly those salt-water non-resistants were to their captors on board their own vessel; with what alacrity did they go aloft to take in sail, or to shake out a reef, until those heathen pirates left the handling of the ship entirely to their broad-brimmed brethren, and went to sleep in the cabin; and then, what did the Quakers do but first shut the cabin doors, and fasten them, so that the Turks could not get out again?

And then, fearless of danger, they steered for the Barbary coast, and made those fierce, mustached pirates get into a small boat (they had been for ever locked up else), and rowed them to the shore; and when the Turks found themselves in a small boat with but a small crew of broad-brims, and gave signs of mutiny, what did the brave Thomas Lurting? Lay violent hands on them? Draw a cutlass, or cock a pistol? No, he merely struck the leader 'a pretty heavy blow with a boat-hook, telling him to sit still and be quiet,' as he says himself, 'thinking it was better to stun a man than to kill him.' And so he got the pirates on shore, and in their own country. Brave Thomas Lurting! True? Of course, it is true.

"The most singular spectacle I ever witnessed was the burial-service over a Quaker, in a Catholic cathedral. He had formerly been the rigidest of his sect—a man who had believed the mitre and crozier to be little better than the horns and tail of the evil one—a man who had looked upon church music and polygamy with equal abhorrence, and who would rather have been burnt himself than burn a Roman candle on the anniversary of the national jubilee. Yet, by one of those inexplicable inconsistencies, peculiar to mere men, but rare among Quakers, he had seceded from the faith of his fathers, and become one of the most zealous of papists.

"The grand altar was radiant with wax tapers; the priests on either side, in glittering dresses, were chanting responses; the censer boys, in red and white garments, swung the smoke of myrrh and frankincense into the air, and as the fragant mist rolled up and hung in rosy clouds under the lofty, stained-glass windows, the great organ panted forth the requiem. Marvellously contrasted with this pomp and display appeared the crowd of broad-brims and stiff-plaits, the friends and relatives of the deceased. Never, perhaps, had such an audience been grathered in such a place in the world before. The scene, to the priests themselves, must have been novel and striking. Instead of the usual display of reverence, instead of the customary show of bare heads and bended knees, every Quaker stood stoutly on his legs, with his broad-brimmed hat clinging to his head as strongly as his faith to his heart. Disciplined as they had been in many a silent meeting, during the entire mass not one of the broad-brims moved an inch until the service was over. Then the coffin was opened and solemnly, silently, decorously, the brethren and sisters moved towards it to look, for the last time, upon the face of the seceder. Then silently, solemnly, decorously, they moved from the Popish temple. 'I saw,' said one of the sisters, 'that he (meaning the departed ex-Quaker) had on worked slippers with silver soles, what does thee think that was for?' The person spoken to wore a hat with a goodly brim. Without moving his head, he rolled around, sideways, two Quakeristic eyes, large blue eyes, with little inky dots of pupils, like small black islands in oceans of buttermilk, and said, awfully—'I suppose they was to walk through Purgatory with.'"

"I do not believe it," said Mrs. Sparrowgrass. "Nevertheless, my dear, it is true," I replied; "true, every word of it. You have not seen all the world yet, my dear; it is a very large place—a very large place, indeed, Mrs. Sparrowgrass."

CHAPTER XI.

Our new Horse improves—He is loaned to to a Neighbor, and disgraces himself —Autumnal Vegetation—The Palisades and *Rock Cataract*—An agreeable Surprise—Mr. Sparrowgrass takes a short trip to the County of Broome— —Meets with a Disappointment on his Return, but indulges in a flowing vein of "Adversity's sweet milk."

OUR new horse waxes fat. He takes kindly to his feed, and has already eaten himself into the shape of a bell-pear. As he was suffering from want of exercise, I loaned him, for a few days, to a neighbor, who was moving his chattels into a new house. He was quite serviceable for a time, and really would have done very well, but for a sudden return of his epilepsy as he was carrying a load of crockery. I think our neighbor has acquitted me of any malicious intention in letting him have the animal, but his wife always meets me with a smile as fine as a wire. In fact, she told Mrs. Sparrowgrass it was of no consequence, that it was all right, and she never would have thought of it at all, if it had not been for an old family teapot that had belonged to her grandmother, that could not be replaced—"a thing, my dear, the family has always set a great deal of store by." Confound the family teapot! If it were really so choice a piece of porcelain, what did they put it in the wagon for? Why didn't they carry it by hand? I suppose we will have that broken teapot alluded to, every now and then, at village tea-parties, for years to come.

Our horse waxes fat. I had serious thoughts of parting with him once, but the person who was negotiating for him wanted me to take another horse in exchange, and pay him a sum of money to boot, which seemed to be, at least, as much as, if not more than, both horses were worth. Upon consultation with Mrs. S., I declined the trade.

Notwithstanding the continued warm weather, the leaves already manifest the visible approaches of autumn. Earliest of all, the velvet-podded sumach hangs its fringe of fire, here and there, in the heart of the deep old wood. Then the sugar-maples, golden at the top, and the deeper green leaves of the swamp-maple, are bound with a florid border. The pointed foliage of the gum-tree comes out with a chromatic spread of tints, and, around the trunks, and up in the heavy verdure of cedar and oak, the five-fingered creeper winds its threads of gleaming crimson. Countless little purple flowers scatter between the trees, and margin the roads; white asters, large and small, put forth their tufts of stars; and above them the golden rod waves in the wind its brilliant sceptre. Down by the plashy spring, the wild-rose thickets are densely spotted with round, red berries, beautiful to behold, and, if you look in the grass, you will often find a yellow jewel, a sort of wild lady's-slipper.

But, oh, the glory of those grand old Palisades! Those bald, storm-splintered crags, that overlook the river! Far as the vision stretches, reach their grim, grey precipices, gorgeous, in autumnal tartan, to the waist, but bare, disrobed, and regal to the summit. Brave old thunder-mockers, they. I once suggested, to some of my neighbors, the propriety of having them white-washed, for appearance sake, but I do most heartily repent me of the irreverent jest. Truth to say, I had no intention in it, although the project was taken seriously, and as seriously objected to, partly on the ground that there were *other things* about the village, to be done, of more pressing importance, and partly on account of the expense.

There is another hint of the coming of autumn; the evening music of the insect world hath ceased; the iterated chirp of the cricket, the love-lorn cry of Katy-did, and the long, swelling monotone of the locust, have departed. But we have brought forth the antique andirons, and the winter-wood lies piled up in the shed, and, with the first crackle of the hickory, we shall hear, at least, one summer-voice, on the earth. We shall miss our beetles, though; we shall see no more of those window-visitors who used to bump against the centre-lamp and then go crawling, in a very improper way, over the table, with a segment of white shirt sticking forth from their nether garments behind. We shall miss our beetles. The swamps and ponds, too, are silent. The frogs no longer serenade us with their one-pronged jews-harps, and, oh, saddest of all, the birds! the summer birds! now pipe in other lands, and under alien skies.

> "The melancholy days are come,
> The saddest of the year."

Take it all in all, our garden, this season, has

redeemed itself. To be sure, our fruit-trees blossomed away their energies, attempting to make too much of a show in the spring. But we do not care a great deal for pears, and as one cherry-tree put out quite a respectable show of ox-hearts, we were content. As for musk and water-melons, we had much to brag of; and our potatoes have yielded an abundant crop of all sizes. When we get in our tomatoes, we shall feel pretty comfortable for the winter; at present, they are green, but thrifty.

It is a good thing to have an agreeable surprise, now and then, in the country. I have been tempted lately, by the fine moonlight evenings, to take short rides in the saddle by the haunted shores of the Nepperhan. I love to note the striking contrasts of massive foliage in deep shadow, silvery water in breaks and bends, a pond here, a mill-dam there, with its mimic cascade, and at times the red glare of a belated cottage window. I enjoy these rides, even at the risk of a tumble. And this custom was the cause of a pleasant surprise. One evening, I returned rather early from the river, on account of the fog, and tied our new horse under the shed, intending to ride him over to the stable at the usual hour. But finding some visitors at home, the pleasure of conversation, in regard to the fall crops, beguiled me, and I went to bed, leaving the new horse tied under the shed. When I woke up next morning he was gone. Some person had stolen him in the night. I do not believe he got very far with him before he found out it was easier to get him away than to bring him back. At all events, he was off, and I paid his bill at the stable, to date, with great pleasure. At first I thought I would tell my wife, and then I concluded to keep the good news for a while, and break it to her gradually. There is a great deal in keeping a good thing to yourself for a while. You can turn it over and over in your mind, and enjoy, in anticipation, the effect it will produce when you come to relate it to another. This was too good, though, to keep very long. Here was a snub-nosed, blear-eyed, bandy, legged horse-thief, with a pocketful of oats, and a straw in his mouth, covertly sneaking off at midnight with an animal he did not know anything about—a horse that was an ostrich, in appetite only—a horse that would keep him, by night and by day, constantly busy, in doing nothing else but stealing his food. A horse that was a *weaver!* And of all hard feeders, a weaver is the worst. A weaver, that would stand weaving his head from side to side, like a shuttle, over the manger, eating away with a sinister look in his one eye expressive of—

> "You, nor I, nor nobody knows,
> Where oats, peas, beans, and barley grows."

It was too good to keep. Once or twice I came very near letting it out; but by great presence of mind I succeeded in keeping it in.

By and by it will be a great joke for *somebody!*

We have had a slight frost. The first tender touch of winter's jewelled finger. A premonition, no more. How kindly the old dame moves in the country—how orderly. How cleverly she lays everything to sleep, and then folds over all her delicate drapery! It is a grand sight to see the snow driving across the rocky face of the Palisades. We shall welcome in the winter with pleasure. Sleep, little flowers, for a time; the kind old nurse will be beside your tiny cradles, and wrap you up softly in light blankets! Sleep, little hard-shell beetles, rest Katy-did, and you—nocturnal bugler, mosquito, rest!

We have had again warmer weather and fogs. We love to see a fog in the country. Look over the wide expanse of the river, smooth as looking-glass—two miles across; see the morning sunlight on the eternal precipices. Look at the variegated foliage fused to lava under the thin screen of mist. It seems as if nature had poured down in floods of melted sulphur, vermilion, and orpiment. And now the slight veil sweeps away, and the round masses of vegetation jut forth in light and shadow. Once more we recognize the bare strip that indicates the course of the ROCK CATARACT! If you watch the summit now, you will see something. The blasters are at work with gunpowder. There! Puff number one! Up rolls the blue smoke, and hark at the echoes! You do not see the blown out mass, as it falls sheer down the barren cliff; but now watch the yellow cloud of dust that whirls along, as the huge fragment bounds, hundreds of feet below, over the steep sloping earth, until it buries itself, amid the uproar, at the very brink of the river. Follow its course to the city, and you will behold it, and its brethren, rising in massive piles of architecture; but look at the grand old rocks again, and tell if there be a scar or spot left, to indicate whence it fell. Strange that you cannot, for it is a great quarry that—over there.

Not a person knows anything concerning the horse's hegira, yet. Old Dockweed, the inquisitive old sand-piper, asked me, "how that horse was getting along with his heaves?" I replied, he was getting on pretty well. I mean to ask Mrs. S., some day, how much she thinks my stable bill has been for the past week or two. How she will open her eyes, when I tell her that expense is at an end. And horse-shoes too; what a costly luxury a blacksmith is, in the country.

I shall leave home to-morrow, for a short sojourn in Broome county with a friend. When I return, it will be time enough to tell Mrs. S. about our good luck. How surprised she will be.

It is a good thing to travel in the country—to go from one country place to another country place—to meet old friends with fresh welcomes, old hearths, and old wood, old side-boards, old wine, and, above all--old stories. I love an old story. There is no place where you will find so many old stories as in the country. Our village is full of old stories. They have a flavor of antiquity, too, that commends them always to the connoisseur. The old stories of Broome county have a rarer merit—some of them are good. How pleasant it was to sit with my old friend by his hospitable hearth-stone, and enjoy the warmth of his fire, his wine, and his welcome! How pleasant it was to listen to *his* old stories, like the chime of some old bell, or the echo of some old song, bringing up again days, men, scenes, and scores of happy memories! How we went into the deep green cover to shoot woodcock; how I bagged my first bird; how we stopped at the spring, and could not find the flask, but we did not mean the powder-flask; how we got Mr. Peapod to fire at the mark, but forgot to put the shot in his gun; and all about our old friends on the Susquehanna, the rides, the drives, the junketings—up above, where the broad river sweeps on behind the garden, or where the brook ramps over the rocks, and rambles musically down through the glen. Those, indeed, were fine old stories.

I love, too, to sleep in an old-fashioned house—to hear the dew drip from the eaves at night, and the rustle of autumnal leaves around the porch—to wake with the cheery crow of the rooster, and the chirrup of the coffee-mill—to look forth from the low-browed window upon the early morning, and to see clouds, and hills, and ever so many rural pictures. It is a good thing to travel sometimes in the country.

When I returned home, I determined to break the whole matter to Mrs. Sparrowgrass about the horse. There is such a thing as keeping a secret too long from the partner of one's bosom. This thought oppressed me. So, after I had deposited my over-coat and carpet-bag in the hall, I could scarcely keep the secret quiet until the proper moment. The children never seemed to be so pertinaciously curious as they did on the evening of my return. I think we should never refuse answering the questions children put to us, unless they ask questions it would be improper to answer. To tell the truth, I was not sorry when they were cased in their Canton-flannel long-drawers, and ready for bed. Then I had to tell Mrs. Sparrowgrass all about the journey; but first she had to tell me all about everything that had occurred during my absence. Then I commenced: "My dear," said I, "do you know notwithstanding the extraordinary large crops this fall, that feed still remains very high?" Mrs. S. replied that she had neglected to speak of the horse; but as I had reminded her of it—"My dear," said

I, interrupting her, "I know what you want to say. You want me to part with him, even if I give him away." Mrs. Sparrowgrass replied that she did. "What," I continued, "do you suppose he has cost me within the two past weeks?" Mrs. Sparrowgrass answered that I would find he had cost more than he was worth, twice over. "You think so, do you?" said I. "Then, my dear, I want to tell you something that will gratify and surprise you." Then I followed it up: "In the first place, do you remember, about two weeks ago, that I returned home from a moonlight ride beside the romantic shores of the Nepperhan?" Mrs. Sparrowgrass replied that she remembered it. "Well, then, that night I tied our horse under the shed, and I forgot him. The next morning he was missing." Mrs. Sparrowgrass requested me to go on.

There is a great deal, sometimes, in the manner of saying those two words, "go on." It sometimes implies that you have arrived at the end of what you have to say, and that the other party has something yet to add. There was a pause.

"Go on," said Mrs. Sparrograss, "tell your story, and then let me tell mine!" "Wasn't he stolen?" said I, beginning to fear that some news of an unpleasant nature was in store for me. "I do not know whether he was stolen or whether he strayed away; but at all events he has been found, my dear," replied Mrs. S. "Where did they find him, Mrs. S.?" said I, feeling a little nervous. "*In the Pound!*" replied Mrs. Sparrowgrass, with a quiet, but impressive accent on the last word. "In the pound!" I echoed, "then, Mrs. S., we will leave him in the hands of the village authorities." "Bless me!" replied Mrs. S., "I had him taken out immediately, so soon as I heard of it. Why you would not have your horse kept in the pound, my dear, for everybody to make remarks upon? He is in the stable, my dear, and as fat as ever; the man that keeps him said it would do you good to see him eat the first day he got back. You will have to pay a pretty nice bill, though. There are the fees of the pound-master, and the damages to the Rev. Mr. Buttonball, for breaking into his carrot patch, where he was found, and then you will have to get a new saddle and bridle, and "———

"Mrs. Sparrowgrass," said I, interrupting the catalogue of evils, by putting up my hand with the palm turned toward her like a monitor, "Mrs. S., there are times when trifles occupy too conspicuous a position in the human mind. Few people lose their night's rest from a superabundance of joy, but many suffer from a species of moral nightmare. Do not let this matter, then, give you any more uneasiness." Mrs. Sparrowgrass said it did not give her any uneasiness at all. "If this wretched animal is again upon our hands, we must make the best of him. While I was away, I heard in the country there was a prospect of oats not being able to keep up this winter. Next year we can put him out to pasture. I also learn that a new and fatal disease has broken out among horses lately. We must hope, then, for the best. Let us keep him cheerfully, but do not let us be *haunted* with him. He is, at least, a very nice looking animal, my dear. Excuse me a moment——

> 'Let Fate do her worst, there are relics of joy,
> Bright dreams of the past, which we cannot destroy.'

You had, at least, the pleasure of riding after him once; and I had the pleasure of hearing that he was stolen—once. Perhaps somebody may take a fancy to him yet, Mrs. Sparrowgrass."

CHAPTER XII.

Our New Barber—Reminiscences of our Old Barber—A Dog of another Color—October Woods—A Party on the Water—Home, Sweet Home, with Variations (flute obligato)—A row to the Palisades—Iroquois Legend—Return to the Cottage.

WE have gotten a new barber in the village. It is a good thing to have a barber in the country. You hear all the news, all the weddings, the engagements, the lawsuits, and other festive matters, in his aromatic shop. Our former Master Nicholas has left us suddenly. "*Maese Nicolas, quando barbero, del mismo pueblo.*" We miss him very much. I used to admire his long and learned essay upon the 'uman 'air. The 'uman 'air, for want of capillary attraction, could not maintain its place upon the 'uman 'ead, without the united juices of one hundred and fifty-five vegetables. So long as he devoted himself to procuring the necessary vegetables, and hung his argument upon a hair, he did very well. It was pleasant to doze under his glib fingers and his vegetative philosophy. But unfortunately he got into politics. Barbers usually have excitable temperaments. The barber of our village became the softest of the softs. He was ready to argue with anybody, and everybody, in his "garden of spices."

One day while I was under his tuition, at the end of a prolonged debate with one of his sitters, by way of clinching his point, he did me the honor of tapping me twice upon the cranium with the back of his hair-brush. "Sir," said he (tap), "I tell you *that* is *so*" (heavy tap). In consequence, I predicted his speedy downfall. Sure enough, he laid a wager that his candidate would have a majority in our village over all the rest of the candidates, and the next election only gave his candidate *two votes*. Next day our barber was missing. Public vandalism had crushed him.

We have procured a new barber. He is in the dyeing line of business. It is the color, not the quantity of hair, that engages all his lubricating efforts. To convert the frost of age into a black or brown scalp is the highest ambition of his genius. Not only that: he anticipates time, and suggests preventive treatment to younger men. To me he is excessively tiresome.

I have bought me a new dog. A snow-white terrier, with rose-colored ears and paws. She is as white as new-plucked cotton, or February clouds. All our other dogs, Jack, Zack, and Flora, are black; Juno, by contrast, looks strikingly white. One day, I found *four* black dogs under the porch. Of the four, I should say Juno was the blackest. She had been to the barber's on a visit, and he had given her a coat of his confounded Praxitiles balsam. Now she is growing out of it, but her present appearance is so repulsive the other dogs will not associate with her. Some day I mean to give that barber a talking to about the matter.

Who that loves nature can forsake the country in October? Before the leaves fall, before "the flying gold of the woodlands drive through the air," we must visit our old friends opposite—the Palisades. We must bring forth our boat once more, and "white-ash it" over the blue river to the "*Chimneys.*" "What do you think of it, Mrs. Sparrowgrass?" Mrs. S. replied, she was willing. So, then, on Saturday, if the weather be fair, we will make our final call upon them. The weather was fair, the air warm, the sky clear, the river smooth, the boat in order, and over we went. I had invited a German gentleman, Mr. Sumach, to accompany us, on account of his flute. He is a very good performer on that instrument, and music always sounds to great advantage upon the water. When we approached the great cliffs, Mr. Sumach opened his case and took therefrom the joints of an extraordinarily large flute. Then he moistened the joints and put it together. Then he held it up and arranged the embouchure to his satisfaction, and then he wiped it off with his handkerchief. Then he held it up again at right angles, and an impudent boy in another boat, fishing, told him he'd better take in his boom if he did not want to jibe. Then Mr. Sumach ran rapidly through a double octave, executed a staccato passage with wonderful precision, and wound up with a prolonged bray of great brilliancy and power. Then the boy, by way of jibing himself, imitated the bleating of a sheep. Then I bent the white ash oars to get out of the reach of the boy, and the blisters on my hands became painfully bloated. Then Mr. Sumach, who had been trilling enough to make anybody nervous, proposed that we should sing something. Then Mrs. Sparrowgrass suggested "Home, Sweet Home." Then we commenced (flute obligato.)

HOME, SWEET HOME!

WITH VARIATIONS.

"Mid (taw-tawtle) pala—(tawtle)
Though–oh! (tawtle-taw!)
Be it (taw-tawtle) hum—(tawtle)
Taw, tawtle-taw! (*rapid and difficult passage, ending with an inimitable shake*).
A cha—(tawtle) skies! (tawtle) halo (taw, taw)
Which (taw-tawtle) world (taw) not (taw-tawtle) where.
Home! (*trill B flat*) Hoem! (*rapid and difficult passage*)
Sweet! (toodle) sweet! (toodle) home! (toodle)
Be it (tawtle-de-doodle-diddle-doodle—taw) 'ble,
There's no–oh! (toodle!) home!"

By this time we had reached the base of the Palisades.

Now then—here we are! A segment of sand you might cover with a blanket, and all the rest of the beach a vast wreck of basaltic splinters! Rocks, rocks, rocks! From bits not larger than a watermelon, up to fragments the size of the family tea-table. All these have fallen off those upper cliffs you see rising from the gold, brown, and crimson of autumnal leaves. Look up! No wonder it makes you dizzy to look up. What is that bird? Mrs. Sparrowgrass, that is an eagle!

It was a pleasant thing, after we had secured the boat by an iron grapnel, to pick our way over the sharp rocks; now holding by a lithe cedar, now swinging around a jutting crag by a pendulous, wild grape-vine, anon stepping from block to block, with a fine river view in front and below; and then coming suddenly upon the little nook where lay the flat stone we were in quest of; and then came the great cloth-spreading, and opening of the basket! And we took from the basket, first a box of matches, and a bundle of choice segars of delicate flavor. Next two side bottles of claret. Then we lifted out carefully a white napkin, containing only one fowl, and that not fat. Then two pies, much the worse for the voyage. Then two more bottles of claret. Then another centre-piece—ham sandwiches. Then a bundle of knives and forks, a couple of cork-screws, a tier of plates, six apples, and a half bottle of olives. Then twenty-seven hickory nuts, and a half dozen nut-crackers. And then came the cheese, and the manuscript.

Oh, golden November sky, and tawny river! bland distance and rugged foreground! wild, crimson vines, green cedars, many-colored, deciduous foliage, grey precipices, and delicious claret! What an afternoon that was, *under the Palisades!*

"Mr. Sumach," said I, after the pippins and cheese, "if you will cast your eyes up beyond the trees, above those *upper* trees, and follow the face of the precipice in a direct line for some four hundred feet perpendicularly, you will see a slight jutting out of rock, perhaps twenty feet below the top of the crags." Mr. Sumach replied, the sun was shining so brilliantly, just then, upon that identical spot, that he could see nothing at all. As, upon careful inspection, I could not see the spot myself, I was obliged to console myself with another sip of claret. Yet there it was! Just above us!

"Mr. Sumach," said I, "I wish you could see it, for it is one of the curiosities of our country. You know we have five wonders of the world in America—the Falls of Niagara, the Natural Bridge in Virginia, the Mammoth Cave of Kentucky, Trenton Falls, and the Palisades. Now, sir, just above us, almost at the brink of that dizzy height, there is a singular testimony of the freaks of nature.

That tough old rock, sir, has had a piece taken out of it—squarely out, by lightning probably, and the remnants of the vast mass now lie around us, covered with lichens, nutshells, dead leaves, tablecloth, and some claret bottles. If you will go with me, some two miles north, there is a path up the mountains, and we can then walk along the top of the vast precipice to the spot directly over us." Mr. Sumach declined, on the ground of not being accustomed to such rough walking. "Then, sir, let me describe it to you. From that jutting buttress of rock in front, to the opening there, just back of you, there is a flat platform above us, wide enough for a man to lie down with his head close to the inner wall and his feet a few inches over the precipice. That platform is probably one hundred and fifty feet long; the wall behind it is some twenty feet high; there is a little ravine, indicated by the gap up there, by which you can reach the platform. Once on it, you will see the wall back of you is very flat and even, as well as the stone floor you tread upon." Mr. Sumach answered, "Very well?" in a tone of inquiry. "Now," said I, "here in this paper is the Legend of the Palisades, and as we are upon legendary ground, I will read it to you." Mr. Sumach, with a despairing look at his giant flute-case, said he would like much to hear it. So, after another sip of claret, I unrolled the manuscript and read

A LEGEND OF THE PALISADES

Long before the white sails of Europe cast their baleful shadows over the sunny waters of the western continent, a vast portion of this territory, bounded by perpetual snows and perpetual summer, was occupied by two mighty nations of red men. The Iroquois, by far the most warlike nation, dominated, with its united tribes, the inland from Canada to North Carolina, and east and west from Central Pennsylvania to Michigan; while the great Algonquin race peopled the sea-board, from Labrador almost to the Floridas, and extending itself westward, even to the borders of Oregon, again stretched away beyond the waters of the Mississippi, unto the hunting-grounds of the swarthy Appalachians. This bright river, in those days, flowed downward to the sea under some dark, Indian name; and where yonder village glitters with its score of spires and myriad windows, the smoke of numerous camp-fires curled amidst pointed wigwams, of poles, and skins, and birch-bark wrought with barbaric characters.

Of the Algonquin tribes, that formerly inhabited the banks of this mighty stream, tradition has scarcely preserved a name. A handful of colored, earthen beads, a few flint arrow-heads, are the sole memorials of a once great populace. But tradition, with wonderful tenacity, clings to its legends. Even from the dross of nameless nations, some golden deed shines forth, with a lustre antiquity cannot tarnish. So among the supernatural songs of the Iroquois we find a living parable.

Long before the coming of the pale-faces, there was a great warrior of the Onondaga-Iroquois, by name "The Big Papoose." He had a round, small, smooth face, like that of a child, but his arms were long, and his shoulders broad and powerful as the branches of an oak. At the council fires he spoke not, at hunting parties he was indolent, and of the young squaws none could say, "he loves me." But if he spoke not at the council fires, the people knew the scalps in his wigwam were numerous as the cones upon the pine tree; and if he cared not for hunting, yet he wore a triple collar made of the claws of three grizzly bears, and the old braves loved to sing of the great elk he had pursued and killed with a blow of his stone axe, when his feet were as the wings of a swallow. True it was, the love that is so common to man, the love of woman, was not in his breast; but the brightest and boldest maiden's eyes dropped in his presence, and many a time the bosoms of the young squaws would heave —just a little. Yet the Big Papoose was the friend of children. Who bound the tiny, flint arrow-heads to the feathered shafts, and strung the little bow with the sinews of deer, and practised the boy-warriors of the tribe in mimic warfare, and taught them to step with the foot of the sparrow, and to trap the fox, the rabbit, and the beaver, and to shout the death-whoop, the *sa sa kuan?* Who was it, but the Big Papoose lying yonder, face downward, on the frozen crust of the lake, his head covered with skins, and around him a score of boy-warriors, lying face downward too, watching the fish below, through the holes in the ice, that they might strike them with the pointed javelin, the *aishkun?* Yes, he was the friend of children, the Big Papoose!

There was then a very old brave of the Onondaga tribe; his hair was like the foam of the waterfall, and his eyes were deep and dark as the pool beneath it. He was so old that he could lay his hand upon the head of a hundred years and say—" boy!"

He it was who had found, far in the north, under the uttermost stars, the sacred pieces of copper; he it was who had seen the great fish, so large that a single one could drink up the lake at a mouthful, and the great Thunder Water he had seen—*Niagara!* and the cavern, big enough to contain all the Indian tribes, the Iroquois and the Algonquins; and the stone arch that held up the skies, the sun, and moon, and the clouds he had stood beneath, and he had seen it.

He was called The White Cloud, and sometimes, when the summer's heat had been too powerful upon the earth, and the green leaves of the maize drooped too much, he would bring forth the magic red pipe, and smoke, and blow the smoke towards the west, and then the vapors would rise up from the great lake Ontario, and approach him, and overshadow him, and the rain would fall, and the leaves rise up refreshed, and the little birds would sing loudly in the wet forest. Then, too, would the Big Papoose sit on the same log with the White Cloud, and ask him to tell of the mysteries of the skies, and the Sachem would chant of the White Rabbit of the North, the Queen of the Heavens, that holds dominion over the uttermost stars, and the snows of winter; that hides in the summer, when the sun is powerful, that she may rival his brightness in the season of frost.

One day the Big Papoose said to the old chief—"Why, oh White Cloud, do you ever blow the smoke of the calumet towards the west; is there not rain too in the east?" Then the white-haired answered—"Because I like not the visions I see when I blow the smoke towards the east. As the smoke from the calumet moves westward, I behold in it nations of red men, moving, and ever moving, towards the caverns of the sun. But when I blow the smoke towards the east, I see the red men no more, but the glitter of mighty waters, and winged canoes, in size like the lofty hemlocks of the forest, and potent arrows of fire, that dart forth with clouds and thunderings. And further and further towards the east, I see more and more of the winged canoes, in number like the leaves that are blown by the winds of autumn, and the winged canoes bear many nations, and in the approaching nations I see not one red man." "I have dreamed," replied the young warrior, "of a maiden whose eyes were in color like yonder lake, and whose skin was beautiful as the snow at sunset." "Do you not think of her often; more than of the women of the Onondagas?" said the White Cloud. The young warrior bowed his head. "The time will come," said the old chief, "when the woman with blue eyes will think of the young chief of the Onondagas." "When?" said the listener, eagerly. The White Cloud touched with his finger a young pine, whose stem was not thicker than a stalk of maize one moon old, and replied, "When this trunk shall have grown so a man may stretch his arms around it, and yet his right hand cannot meet his left, then will the young chief of the Onondagas live in the thoughts of the maiden with the skin like the flush of sunset on the snow." "You speak truth," answered the young chief, "so, too, have I dreamed." "Tell me," continued the white-haired prophet, "whom do you envy of living men?" "Not one," replied the young warrior. "Whom of the dead do you envy?" "The warriors who are dead in battle, and yet live famousest in the songs of the Iroquois." "Look!" said the prophet. A volume of smoke arose from the red pipe, and the old man blew it gently towards the east. The Iroquois saw it spread into a plain, variegated with hills and rivers, and the villages of his tribe. Then it passed beyond the boundaries of his nation, and he recognized the habitations of the Algonquins; he saw their burial-places, and the stretched skins with the accursed totems of his hereditary enemies; he saw, too, the noted warriors of their tribes, the women, the medicine-men, and the children. Then the cloud rose up over a mountain, and he looked from its level summit down upon a sparkling river, broader than the rivers of his own country, and beyond, on the opposite side, villages of Algonquin tribes, the wigwams of the Nepperhans. And he was standing on the brink of gigantic cliffs, whose vast shadows lay midway across the sparkling river; and, as he looked, his foot touched a fragment of rock, and it fell sheer down from the summit of the precipice to its base, and struck nothing as it fell. And just beyond him was a shelf of rock hanging over a terrible shore—huge splinters of stone below, under his feet, and as his eyes wandered up and down the sparkling river, far as his vision reached, the great shadow of the precipices, and the savage walls of stone, and the fragmentary shore went on unending. Then the sparkling river grew dimmer, and the rocks faded from view, and he saw only the blue sky, and the clouds, and high up in the east, an eagle. "My son," said the white-haired, "you have seen it. To-morrow night, loosen the thongs of your moccasins beyond the wigwams of the Iroquois. In the country of the Algonquins, are those wondrous precipices, and before seven days you will see the eastern sun rising over the sparkling river. Take with you this bag of pigments and painting implements. On the bare rocks, above the platform you have seen, inscribe the totem of your tribe, and the record of your achievements. Go! I say no more."

Then the White Cloud put the tube of the calumet to his lips, and as the smoke arose from the kinikinic, the bowl of the red pipe expanded wider and wider, and the blue vapor spread out like the mist that rises from a lake in a midsummer morning. Then there came a powerful wind from the east, and the smoke rolled away before it, and was driven, with inconceivable swiftness, over the Lake Ontario, until it grew red under the sinking sun, and passed to the far off hunting-grounds of the Dacotahs. The young chief watched until it vanished, and then turned to his companion. There was nothing near him but the green grass and the slender pine the White Cloud had touched with his finger.

Then the Big Papoose took the bag of pigments to his wigwam, and prepared for the journey. Around his broad chest he drew the folds of a gorgeous hunting-shirt, decorated with many-hued barbs of the porcupine, and secured it with a gaudy belt of wampum. His leggings were fringed with the hair of scalps, and Indian beads and shells of various colors, and his moccasins were wrought with quills, tinted like flowers of the prairie. Then he took from the notched poles of the wigwam his tufted bow, and a sheaf of arrows tipped with brilliant feathers, and he thrust the stone axe through his belt of wampum, and shook once more the slender spear-staff, with its ponderous head of pointed flint. And as he passed on beyond the wigwams of his tribe, the young squaws gazed after him with wondrous dark eyes, and the old women said, "Perhaps he will bring with him, when he returns, a Chenango woman, or a squaw from the blue Susquehanna."

Twice the moon rose, and he saw the maize fields

of the Algonquins. Later and later she glittered over his solitary path by the rocky gorges of the Delaware. Then he saw in the north the misty mountains of Shawangonk, and lodges of hostile tribes without number, and other maize fields, and at night the camp-fires of a great people. Then he came to shallow rivers dotted with canoes, but the streams were less broad than the river of the Oswegos. And then he saw before him a sloping upland, and just as the moon and the dawn were shining together, he stood under tall trees on the summit, and beneath him was the platform of rock, and the waters of the sparkling river.

"My dear," said Mrs. Sparrowgrass, "I am sorry to interrupt you, but is not that our boat out there, going up the river?" "Yes," added Mr. Sumach, suddenly leaping up with energy, "and my flute too, I believe." "It cannot be," I replied, "for I fastened the boat with an iron grapnel," and, as I did not like to be interrupted when I was reading, told Mr. Sumach, very quietly, but severely, he would find his *bassoon* just back of our stone table. The explanation being satisfactory, I was allowed to proceed with the legend.

There was a pathway to the platform, as it might be, a channel for the heavy rains that sometimes pour from the table-lands of the precipice to the ravine, and tumble, in a long, feathery torrent over its rocky breast. It was a narrow passage, with walls of stone on either side, and ended just a few feet south of the jutting ledge, so that the young chief had to leap from the brink of the gorge to the edge of the platform. Then he looked around, and behind him rose up the flat surface of thunder-split rock. Then he walked to the further end of it, and laid upon the ground his tufted bow and sheaf of arrows, loosened his belt of wampum, cast down his terrible stone axe, and leaned his pointed spear against the vast wall of the terrace. Then he took from the bag the pigments and the painting implements, and before mid-day he had sketched upon the rocky back-ground the vast outlines of his picture.

It was at the moment when he had completed the totem of his tribe, when he was nearest the gorge and furthest from his weapons, that a fawn darted from the chasm to the plateau, gathered up its affrighted form at sight of him, and then sprang sheer over the brink. The next instant an Algonquin warrior leaped upon the ledge. A startled look at the Iroquois—a contemptuous glance at the pictograph—two panther bounds—and the hereditary foes were struggling in a death-grapple upon the eaves of the precipice. Sometimes they leaned far over the brink, and then unitedly bent back, like twin pine trees over-blown. Both were unarmed, for the Algonquin had not suspected an enemy in a place where the foot of Iroquois had never trod, and the weapons of his adversary were distant from them a bow-shot. So, with terrible strength, and zeal, and skill, each sought to overthrow the other, until in the struggle they fell, still clutched together, upon the rocky floor of the battle-ground. There, with tremendous throes and throbs of anger, they lay, until the shadows of the cliffs had stretched far over the bosom of the sparkling river.

"Let us rise," said the Algonquin. The warriors rose to their feet and stood gazing at each other.

There they were upon that terrible brink, within reach of each other. A touch of the hand would have precipitated either upon the fragmentary shore below.

"Let us not perish," said the Algonquin, "like

the raccoon and the fox, starving in the death-lock, but let us die like braves."

The Iroquois listened.

"Do you go," continued the Algonquin, "tell the warriors of my tribe to come, that they may witness it, and I will leap with you from this ledge upon the death below."

The Iroquois smiled.

"Stay," added the Algonquin, "I am a child. Do I not know the fate of an Iroquois who would venture within the camp of my people? Remain you, until my return, that the history of my deed may be inscribed with that you have pictured upon these rocks."

The Iroquois smiled again, and said, "I wait."

The Algonquin bounded from the parapet and was gone.

Left to himself, the Iroquois collected together his painting implements, and filled with brilliant colors the outlines he had sketched upon the wall. Then he cast his spear far into the sparkling river, and sent the stone axe circling though the air until it splashed far out in the stream, and he broke the tufted bow with his powerful arms, and snapped his feathered arrows one by one. Then he girded on his gorgeous belt of wampum, and waited. Of whom was he dreaming as he sat beneath the shadow of the pictograph? Was it not of the blue-eyed maiden with cheeks like the flush of sunset on the snow?

The Iroquois waited. Then he heard a murmur, as of the wind stirring the leaves, then the rush of rapid footsteps, and, as he started to his feet, the cliffs above him were thronged with Algonquin warriors. There was silence for an instant, and then an hundred bows were bent, an hundred bow-strings snapped, an hundred arrows converged through the air and struck him! But as he turned to hurl defiance at his enemies, a lithe form bounded upon the parapet—it caught the figure studded with arrows and tottering upon the brink in its arms—and screamed into the dying ears—"I am here, oh, Iroquois!" and then, except the pictograph, nothing human remained upon the platform of the Palisades!

When I had finished the legend, Mr. Sumach startled the echoes with a burst of fluting that defies description. So I set to work resolutely to pack up the basket, for I thought such a place as the one we were visiting did not require the aid of art to make it interesting. After the packing was finished, we started off for the boat, Mr. Sumach tooting over the rocks in a marvellous manner, until we came to the place where some climbing was necessary, and there I had the satisfaction of seeing the flute dislocated and cased, and then it fell in the water, when Mr. S. had some trouble to get at it. When we got to the place of anchorage, we found the tide had risen and the grapnel under water, but no boat; so I suppose the other end of the rope had not been tied to the ring in the bow. We had a pretty walk, though, to Closter, and hired another boat. As our boat was brought home next day it was no great matter; but I wished the person who found it for us had found also the oars and the thole pins.

CHAPTER XIII.

The Children are sent to School—Old Soldiers—An Invitation, and Cruel Disappointment—Our Eldest begins to show Symptoms of the Tender Passion—Poetry—The Melodies of Mother Goose—Little Posterity by the Wayside—A Casualty—*The Drowning of Poor Little Tommy.*

WE have sent the children to school. Under the protecting wing of Mrs. Sparrowgrass, our two eldest boys passed in safety through the narrow channel of orthography, and were fairly launched upon the great ocean of reading before a teacher was thought of. But when boys get into definitions, and words more than an inch long, it is time to put them out, and pay their bills once a quarter. Our little maid, five years old, must go with them, too. The boys stipulated that she should go, although she had never gone beyond E in the alphabet before. When I came home from the city in the evening, I found them with their new carpet-satchels all ready for the morning. There was quite a hurrah! when I came in, and they swung their book-knapsacks over each little shoulder by a strap, and stepped out with great pride, when I said, "Well done, my old soldiers." Next morning we saw the old soldiers marching up the garden-path to the gate, and then the little procession halted; and the boys waved their caps, and one dear little toad kissed her mitten at us—and then away they went with such cheerful faces. Poor old soldiers! what a long, long siege you have before you!

Thank Heaven for this great privilege, that our little ones go to school in the country. Not in the narrow streets of the city; not over the flinty pavements; not amid the crush of crowds, and the din of wheels: but out in the sweet woodlands and meadows; out in the open air, and under the blue sky—cheered on by the birds of spring and summer, or braced by the stormy winds of ruder seasons. Learning a thousand lessons city children never learn; getting nature by heart—and treasuring up in their little souls the beautiful stories written in God's great picture-book.

We have stirring times now when the old soldiers come home from school in the afternoon. The whole household is put under martial law until the old soldiers get their rations. Bless their white heads, how hungry they are. Once in a while they get pudding, by way of a treat. Then what chuckling and rubbing of little fists, and cheers, as the three white heads touch each other over the pan. I think an artist could make a charming picture of that group of urchins, especially if he painted them in their school-knapsacks.

Sometimes we get glimpses of their minor world —its half-fledged ambitions, its puny cares, its hopes and its disappointments. The first afternoon they returned from school, open flew every satchel, and out came a little book. A conduct-book! There was G. for good boy, and R. for reading, and S. for spelling, and so on; and opposite every letter a good mark. From the early records in the conduct-books, the school-mistress must have had an elegant time of it for the first few days, with the old soldiers. Then there came a dark day; and on that afternoon, from the force of circumstances, the old soldiers did not seem to care about showing up. Every little reluctant hand, however, went into its satchel upon requisition, and out came the records. It was evident, from a tiny legion of crosses in the books, that the mistress's duties had been rather irksome that morning. So the small column was ordered to deploy in line of battle, and, after a short address, dismissed—without pudding. In consequence, the old soldiers now get some good marks every day.

We begin to observe the first indications of a love for society growing up with their new experiences. It is curious to see the tiny filaments of friendship putting forth, and winding their fragile tendrils around their small acquaintances. What a little world it is—the little world that is allowed to go into the menagerie at half price! Has it not its joys and its griefs; its cares and its mortifications; its aspirations and its despairs? One day the old soldiers came home in high feather, with a note. An invitation to a party, "Master Millet's compliments, and would be happy to see the Masters, and Miss Sparrowgrass to tea, on Saturday afternoon." What a hurrah! there was, when the note was read; and how the round eyes glistened with anticipation; and how their cheeks glowed with the run they had had. Not an inch of the way from school had they walked, with that great note! There was much chuckling over their dinner, too; and we observed the flush never left their cheeks, even after they were in bed, and had been asleep for hours. Then all their best clothes had to be taken out of the drawer and brushed; and the best collars laid out; and a small silk apron, with profuse ribbons, improvised for our little maid; and a great to-do generally. Next morning I left them, as I had to go to the city; but the day was bright and beautiful. At noon, the sky grew cloudy. At two o'clock, it commenced raining. At three, it rained steadily. When I reached home in the evening, they were all in bed again; and I learned they had been prevented going to the party on account of the weather. "They had been dreadfully disappointed," Mrs. Sparrowgrass said; so we took a lamp and went up to have a look at them. There they lay—the hopeful roses of yesterday, all faded; and one poor old soldier was sobbing in his sleep.

We begin to think our eldest is nourishing a secret passion, under his bell-buttons. He has been seen brushing his hair more than once, lately; and, not long since, the two youngest came home from school, crying, without him. Upon investigation, we found our eldest had gone off with a school-girl twice his size; and, when he returned, he said he had only gone home with her, because she promised to put some bay-rum on his hair. He has even had the audacity to ask me to write a piece of poetry about her, and of course I complied.

TO MY BIG SWEETHEART.

My love has long brown curls,
  And blue forget-me-not eyes ;
She's the beauty of all the girls—
  But I wish I was twice my size ;
Then I could kiss her cheek,
  Or venture her lips to taste ;
But now I only reach to the ribbon
  She ties around her waist.

Chocolate-drop of my heart!
  I dare not breathe thy name ;
Like a peppermint stick I stand apart
  In a sweet, but secret flame :
When you look down on me,
  And the tassel atop of my cap,
I feel as if something had got in my throat,
  And was choking against the strap.

I passed your garden and there,
  On the clothes-lines, hung a few
Pantalettes, and one tall pair
  Reminded me, love, of you ;

And I thought, as I swung on the gate
  In the cold, by myself alone,
How soon the sweetness of hoarhound dies,
  But the bitter keeps on and on.

It was quite touching to see how solemnly the old soldiers listened, when this was being read to them; and when I came to the lines:—

"I feel as if something had got in my throat,
  And was choking against the strap"—

Ivanhoe looked up with questioning eyes, as if he would have said, "how did you know that?"

It is surprising how soon children—all children—begin to love poetry. That dear old lady—Mother Goose! what would childhood be without her? Let old Mother Goose pack up her satchel and begone, and a dreary world this would be for babies! No more "Pat-a-cake baker's man;" no more "Here sits the Lord Mayor;" no more "This little pig went to market;" no more "Jack and Jill," going up the hill after that unfortunate pail of water; no more "One, two, buckle my shoe;" and "Old Mother Hubbard," who had such an uncommonly brilliant dog; and "Simple Simon," who was not quite so simple as the pieman thought he was; and "Jacky Horner," whose thumb stands out in childhood's memory like Trajan's legended pillar; and the royal architecture of "King Boggin; and the peep into court-life derived from the wonderful "Song of Sixpence:"—what would that dear little half-price world do without them? Sometimes, too, the melodious precepts of that kind old lady save a host of rigid moral lessons—"Tell-tale-tit," and "Cross-patch, draw the latch," are better than twenty household sermons. And then those golden legends: "Bobby Shaftoe went to sea;" and "Little Miss Muffitt, who sat on a tuffit;" and the charming moon-story of "Little Bo Peep with her shadowless sheep;" and the capital match Jack Sprat made, when he got a wife "who could eat no lean;" and the wisdom of that great maxim of Mother Goose:—

"Birds of a feather flock together."

What could replace these, should the priceless volume be closed upon childhood for ever?

When we think of the great world, and its elaborate amusements—its balls, and its concerts; its theatres and its opera-houses; its costly dinners, and toilsome grand parties: its clanging pianos, and its roaring convival songs; its carved furniture, splendid diamonds, rouge, and gilding; its hollow etiquette, and its sickly sentimentalities, what a poor, miserable show it makes beside little Posterity, with his toils and pleasures; his satchel, and scraps of song, sitting by his slender pathway, and watching with great eyes the dazzling pageant passing by. Little Posterity! Sitting in judgment by the wayside, and only waiting for a few years to close, before he brings in his solemn verdict.

What delicate perceptions children have, lively sympathies, quick-eyed penetration. How they shrink from hypocrisy, let it speak with never so soft a voice; and open their little chubby arms, when goodness steps into the room. What a sad-faced group it was that stood upon our bank, the day little Tommy was drowned.

There is a smooth sand beach in front of our house, a small dock, and a boat-house. The railroad track is laid between the bank and the beach, so that you can look out of the car-windows and see the river, and the Palisades, the sloops, the beach, and the boat-house. One summer afternoon, as the train flew by the cottage (for the station is beyond it a short walk), I observed quite a concourse of people on one side of the track—on the dock—and sat down by the water's edge. So when the cars stopped, I hurried back over the iron track I had just passed, and on my way met a man, who told me a little boy was drowned in the water in front of my house. What a desperate race Sparrowgrass ran that day, with the image of each of his children successively drowned, passing through his mind with the rapidity of lightning flashes! When I got in the crowd of people, I saw a poor woman lying lifeless in the arms of two other women; some were bathing her forehead, some were chafing her hands, and just then I heard some one say, "It is his mother, poor thing." How cruel it was in me to whisper, "Thank God!" but could I help it? To rush up the bank, to get the boat-house key, to throw open the outside doors, and swing out the davits, was but an instant's work; and then down went the boat from the blocks, and a volunteer crew had pushed her off in a moment. Then they slowly rowed her down the river, close in shore; for the tide was falling, and every now and then the iron boat-hook sank under the water on its errand of mercy.

Meanwhile we lashed hooks to other poles; and along the beach, and on the dock, a number of men were busy with them searching for the body. At last there was a subdued shout—it came from the river, a little south of the boat-house—and the men dropped the poles on the dock, and on the beach, and ran down that way, and we saw a little white object glisten in the arms of the boatmen, and then it was laid tenderly, face downward, on the grass that grew on the parapet of the railway. Poor little fellow! He had been bathing on the beach, and had ventured out beyond his depth in the river. It was too late to recall that little spirit—the slender breath had bubbled up through the water half an hour before. The poor women wrapped up the tiny white death in a warm shawl; and one stout fellow took it in his arms, and carried it softly along the iron road, followed by the concourse of people.

When I came up on the bank again, I thanked God, for the group of small, sad faces I found there—partly for their safety—partly for their sympathy. And we observed that afternoon, how quiet and orderly the young ones were; although the sun went down in splendid clouds, and the river was flushed with crimson, and the birds sang as they were wont to sing, and the dogs sported across the grass, and all nature seemed to be unconsciously gay over the melancholy casualty; yet our little ones were true to themselves, and to humanity. They had turned over an important page in life, and were profiting by the lesson.

CHAPTER XIV.

Winter once more—Mr. Sparrowgrass feels as if he would like to Chirp a little—Thomas Fuller, D.D.—The Good Wife—Old Dockweed again—A Barrel of Cider—News of the Saddle and Bridle—Superior Tactics of the Village Teamster—Christmas—Great Preparations—Christmas Carols and Masques—A Suggestion of Mrs. Sparrowgrass.

"THE first flurry of snow," said I, making a show of shaking off a few starry flakes from my hat, "the first sky-signals of winter." It is a good thing to have winter in the country. There is something cheery in the prospect of roaring fires; and Christmas trees, glittering with tapers—and golden eggs—and sugar-hearts—and wheels—and harps of sparry sweets; and pipes and tabors; and mince pies; and ringing sleigh-bells; and robes of fur, and reeking horses; and ponds with glassy floors, alive with, and rattling under the mercurial heels of skaters. We love to watch the snow shaking down from the clouds; and to rise up some bright morning, when its fine woof is folded over the backs of mountains, and in the laps of valleys, like a web; and to pass through the colonnaded woods, where the gaunt old trees are feathered to the uttermost twigs; and to drink from the cold spring-water, that trickles over a beard of icicles, and pours, with a summer sound, in the rusty tin-cup, that belongs to the old saw-mill in the glen. It is pleasant to think how soon the birds will be about us once more, not birds of summer, but snow-birds; and with what glee those wily freebooters—crows, will croak forth their gratulations that the winter has come, and with it the privilege of picking up an honest livelihood, in spite of Lazarus in the frozen corn-field, with his hat like a pod of cotton. All the poets love winter, why should not everybody?

> "Winter's the time to which the poet looks
> For hiving his sweet thoughts, and making honey-books."

"I feel as if I would like to chirp a little this evening, Mrs. SparrowG. What shall we have? Lamb? Let me read you 'Dream Children,'. or, perhaps, Fuller would be newer—old Fuller! Here he is; the ancient and venerable D. D. Now, my dear, 'The Good Wife.' Mrs. Sparrowgrass bridled up, and was all smiles. Then I read:

"St. Paul to the Colossians (iii. 18), first adviseth women to submit themselves to their husbands, and then counselleth men to love their wives. And sure it was fitting that women should have their lesson given them, because it was hardest to be learned, and, therefore, they need have the more time to con it."

"H'm!" said Mrs. Sparrowgrass, "St. Paul! He was a wise man (ironically). Read on."

"She keeps house if she have not her husband's company (*that* you always have), or leave, for her patent, to go abroad."

Mrs. Sparrowgrass wished to know what "patent" meant, in that sense. "My dear," said I, "'patent' is a writ or privilege, given or granted." Then I continued:

"For the house is the woman's centre. It is written: 'The sun ariseth; man goeth forth unto his work and to his labor until the evening' (Psalm civ. 22); but it is said of the good woman: 'She riseth while it is yet night' (Prov. xxxi. 15). For man in the race of his work starts from the rising of the sun, because his business is without doors, and not to be done without the light of heaven; but the woman hath her work within the house, and, therefore, can make the sun rise by lighting of a candle."

"Was Dr. Fuller married?" quoth Mrs. S. "Yes, my dear, probably two hundred years ago." "H'm!" said Mrs. Sparrowgrass. "She was a model wife, my dear," said I. "Who? Mrs. Fuller!" "No, Monica." Then I read the beautiful story from the book, and afterwards took down old, gilt Boccaccio, and repeated the still more beautiful story of Griselda—the pearl of the Decameron. This latter story pleased Mrs. Sparrowgrass very much; so it grew to be exceedingly pleasant in-doors, what with the wood fire and the candles; while the cold, the white snow, and the moonshiny river, made it harmonious out of the window; and I was just about saying, I meant to read all Dickens' Christmas Stories over, and Thackeray's Rose and the Ring, and Bracebridge Hall, and the Sketch Book, before the holidays; when we heard something like wheels cheeping through the snow outside, and a muffled crumping, and then a knock at the front-door.

Upon opening the door, whom should we see

but old Dockweed, in a very short overcoat, with duck-legs, attached to a shadow of supernatural proportions, that folded over the side steps of the porch, and ran out to, and up the trunk of a tree, with wonderful sharpness of outline. And there was his swart wagon, with ebony spokes, and a very spectre of a horse: and high up in the wagon, a ghastly barrel, with icy hoops, and chime of silver, and all under the moon—oh! Then we knew the cider had come from Binghamton!

It is a good thing to have a friend in Broome County.

Then I told old Dockweed, who had aroused all the small-fry in their beds, cribs, and cradles, with his voice, to take his horse and wagon to the back of the house; and after some heaving and tilting, we got the barrel down in the snow, and rolled it, with purple fingers, safely into the cellar. Then I put my hand in my pocket to pull out the customary amount, but old Dockweed laid his mitten upon my elbow, with a familiarity that might be excusable in a small village, but which was by no means respectful in a village so extensive as our village. "Sparrygrass," said he, "how's yer hos?" I replied that he seemed to be doing well. "Sparrygrass," continued he, "I got somethin' to tell you now, that'll please yer; I got your saddle and bridle, and what's more, I got the fellow that stole yer hos—all right—up at White Plains, in the lock-up—and nothin' to do but just to go there and appear agin him, and send him to Sing-Sing.

"Don't you know," he continued, "some time ago I asked you how yer hos was gettin' on, and you said 'purty well?'" I replied that I remembered it. "Well, then, I knowed then where your hos was, but thinks I, if Sparrowgrass is a-goin' to keep his head shet up about losin' his hos, I can keep my head shet up about findin' on him. 'Taint my business, you know. I always think that when anybody puts confidence into me, that I ought to put confidence into them, and not without." This just distribution of relative duties inspired me with such a feeling of respect for old Dockweed and his principles, that if any person had been just then pushing him into the river I should not have interfered. "So you knew that he was in the pound," said I. "Yes," he replied, "and knowed about him bein' stolen afore that. You see one night my wife says to me, says she, 'Is that the cars a-comin'?' I says 'No,' but wasn't sure. You see my wife she heard it first, because she sleeps on the side of the bed that's nighest to the window; well, we heard it a comin', and by and by it got up close to our house, and then says my wife, 'Did you ever hear such awful whistling?' Says I, 'No, but I know what it is,' says I; 'that is Sparry-grasses hos.'" "Why didn't you try to stop him, then," said I, "if you knew it was my horse?" "Well," replied Dockweed, "how did I know that you wasn't a-top of him? Well, next morning it was all out, and the hos was took into custody and pounded; and so I told the boys not to say nothing about it until I see you, and then you see, when I see you, you wouldn't let on, and I wouldn't let on." "And pray," said I, "how did you find the bridle and saddle, and the thief?" "Well," continued the veteran teamster, "you see I had to carry a bag of potatoes up for a colored woman; she lives way up t'other side of the aquaduck, and when I took the bag into the kitchen, I see a little end of the girt and a buckle just peeking out under the bed, so I said nothin', but thinks I, wherever there's a girt there's a saddle, and what are they doin' with a saddle when they ain't got no horse? says I; so I told my wife, and she told me to tell the squire, and so he sent up the constable and took the man and the things, and now he's up at White Plains."

I immediately thanked old Dockweed for this kind effort on his part, which would cost me a week's time at least, waiting upon the court as witness, to say nothing of expenses of wagon-hire to get there, and hotel bills when I got there; besides, if there ever were a case of horse-thieving that merited my approval, over which I had chuckled in golden chuckles, and satirically approved and forgiven, this was one. "Dockweed," said I, "I feel much obliged to you for your kind attentions, and as a public spirited individual—as one to whom the community owes a debt of gratitude, permit me to make a slight present in acknowledgment of your eminent services. This oration being in concord with the mind of old Dockwood, he took off his mitten, and held out his hand. "I do not intend," said I, "to offer you money, but something more pleasing to you, something you will watch over, and guard with tender care; something that will constantly remind you of yourself as a conservator of public morals." Here old Dockweed doffed his rabbit-skin cap, and dropped into the deepest deep of humility. "I intend," said I, "to present you with my horse!" I never saw so wild and withered a look as the old teamster's, when these awful words broke upon his two credulous ears. "Well," he replied, slowly drawing on his mitten, his eyes still cast down, "well, as to that, I ain't got stable room just now, and—and it's too much—it's a lettle too much, to give away yer hos—jist for that—but (in great perplexity) now—I'll tell you what I'll do—I won't touch yer hos—it's too much, but I'll call it square, *and take the saddle and bridle!*" With that he hooked on his rabbit-skin cap, collected his fee for bringing the cider, and put himself in his wagon without further delay. I watched the old rogue as he stood up under the moon, and envied him his ride home. "Well, my dear," said I to Mrs. S., after I had told her the whole story, "I suppose it will be a pleasant thing to go to White Plains; it will enable me to give you an account of it, its scenery, its people, its manners and customs, its population, its geology, and above all, its court-house. I hope the snow will hold, so that at least there will be good sleighing.

"After all Christmas is coming—a fig for subpœnas! Merry Christmas, and in the country! I wish some of the rare old sports remained of picturesque ages. We certainly must do something; a boar's head for instance, and a lemon; snap-dragon, and some chirping old songs—

> 'Now does jolly Janus greet your merriment;
> For since the world's creation,
> I never changed my fashion;
> 'Tis good enough to fence the cold:
> My hatchet serves to cut my firing yearly,
> My bowl preserves the juice of grape and barley:
> Fire, wine, and strong beer, make me live so long here,
> To give the merry New-Year a welcome in.'

"A Christmas tree we must have, and some masque, or pantomime for the children. Let us look up some good old carols, for the morning, and rouse the small world with gun-fire and blare of bugle. There will be stockings to fill, and we will get colored candles to light the toy-table before cock-crow. I wish we could have a yule clog for the hearth, but the chimney flue is too small; at all events, we can brew a pitcher of mulled wine, and stick sprigs of evergreens all around the room. That will make some show and jollity. Holly, bay, and mistletoe, so common in the Southern

States, are not plants of this region, but we can borrow some ivy leaves and make out as we may.

'Sing holly, go whistle and ivy!'

"Come, we must have old Misrule with his yellow ruff, and Carol with his robe and flute, and Mistress Mince Pie, and Mumming, in his mask, and ancient Wassail, with his brown bowl.

'And we will drink from the barrel, my boys,
A health to the barley mow!
The barrel, half-barrel, firkin, half-firkin, gallon, half-gallon,
quart, pint, half-pint, nipperkin—
AND THE BROWN BOWL!
A health to the barley mow!'

And I mean to read to the young-ones, Robert Southwell's pretty carol:

'As I in hoarie winter's night
Stood shivering in the snow,
Surprized I was with sudden heat,
Which made my heart to glow;
And lifting up a fearefull eye
To view what fire was neere,
A pretty babe, all burning bright,
Did in the aire appeare.'

"There, now, and if the snow holds, we will have a snow statue—say Santa Claus, with his arms stuck full of toys, and his cold cheeks blown out with a penny trumpet.

'Santa Claus, goed heilig man.'

Santa Claus, good, holy man; and then we can make a martyr of him, afterwards, with snow-balls. And in the evening we will have the masque and the brown bowl-a; 'the nipperkin, and the brown bowl!'

'Next crowne the bowle full
With *gentle* lamb's-wool;
Add sugar, nutmeg, and ginger,
With store of ale too,
And thus ye must doe,
To make the wassaile a SWINGER!'

"I wish we had suitable music for the day, Mrs. Sparrowgrass—harps and pipes; but who could play harp and pipe, if we had them? I think, though, we can get a drum.

'A drum, a drum, a sheepskin drum,
Or tabor rubbed with a rousing thumb,
Or a cholicky bagpipe's blowsy hum,
To show my master's †mas's come!'

Anything noisy and cheerful will do. I suppose it will be necessary to write off some lines to speak in the masque for Christmas evening; so, Mrs. S.,

I want you to get the dresses, and everything ready, and I will do all the rest. Have you any red ribbons, my dear?" Mrs. Sparrowgrass replied she had not. "Well, then, we must get some; and we want a few feathers, and spangles, and a high-peaked hat or two, and some ruffs made, and rosettes, and a red petticoat, and a wimple, and some swords, and red paint, and trunk hose, doublets, and mantles, and white shoes, and a velvet cap, and some hoops and bells, and torches, and masks—

> ——'To present,
> With all its appurtenances,
> A right Christmas, as of old it was,
> To be gathered out of the dances.'"

"I think," said Mrs. S., who was very busy making a little cap, "it will please the children quite as well if you buy them a magic lantern, and put up a white sheet to exhibit it on. It seems to me this Christmas masque will cost a world of labor." "Capital!" said I. "You have a wise little head of your own, Mrs. S., and when I buy the lantern, I mean to buy a big one!

> 'Christmas comes but once a year,
> Once a year,
> Once a year!'"

CHAPTER XV.

An offer for the Horse—Difficulty of Shipping him according to the Terms of Bill of Lading—Anticipations—Marine Sketch—Mrs. Sparrowgrass buys a Patent Bedstead—An essay on Mechanical Forces, and Suggestions in regard to a Bronze Legislature—The New Bedstead is tried and found—" not available."

"MRS. SPARROWGRASS," said I, during one of the remarkably bland evenings we have had lately; "there is, at last, an offer for our horse." This good news being received with an incredulous look, I pulled from my pocket the *Louisville Journal*, and read therein as follows:

"The admirers of 'Mr. Sparrowgrass' will be pleased to learn, that he bargained for a horse. After detailing his experiences with the animal, Mr. Sparrowgrass thus posts him: 'Does anybody want a horse at a low price? A good, stylish-looking animal, close-ribbed, good loin, and good stifle, sound legs, with only the heaves, and the blind staggers, and a slight defect in one of his eyes?" We can put Mr. S. in the way of a trade. We know a physician, who feeds his horse well, who pays more for horsewhips than for provender. He would trade for any animal that has a thin skin and a good memory."

"Well," said Mrs. Sp., "what of that? What can you do in relation to the matter? You have not seen the other horse." "True," I replied, "but that need not prevent me SHIPPING MINE! And you may depend upon it, if ever I get him on board ship, and the bill of lading is in my pocket, no earthly power can make me take him back again. I shall say to the captain, 'My dear sir; that horse is not accustomed to going, but, if he has any go in him, he will have to go now.'" This play upon words, so entirely original, struck me as being pretty fair; whereupon, I sat down quite complacently to read the rest of the paper. "But," continued Mrs. Sparrowgrass, smoothing her hair with both hands, "suppose, after they get him on board the vessel, they should find out what kind of a horse he was, and suppose, then, they should refuse to take him, how could you help it?" "Why, my dear," replied I, "if I have a bill of lading, they must take him. A bill of lading is a certificate or contract signed by the captain and owners of the vessel, in which they agree to carry such and such goods from the port where they receive them, to the port to which the vessel is bound. A bill of lading reads something like this: 'Shipped in good order, and well-conditioned' "——

"How does it begin?" said Mrs. S., with the first word in the key of C sharp.

"Shipped in good order, and well-conditioned," I responded, but my voice was in the key of F minor. For here, at the very threshold of my hope, was a barrier. The terms of the bill of lading itself would prevent me shipping him. How could I say he was "in good order and well-conditioned?"

To my mind, there is nothing so common in life as disappointments. Let any man take his happiest day, and see if it be not somewhat flecked and flawed with them. I think the most favored could count twenty balks to one success in his past days. The human mind is apt to anticipate the end before the beginning has begun. Tom Ailanthus hears he has fallen heir to an estate worth one hundred thousand dollars, and before he sleeps, buys a house near Fifth Avenue, furnishes it, gets married, presents his wife with a splendid set of diamonds, invests forty thousand as special partner in some safe concern, makes another fortune, does the tour of Europe, gets back, marries off his daughters, moves into the country, builds a villa, with lawns, fish-ponds, conservatories, hot and cold graperies, and circulates around his domains, the Sir Roger de Coverly of the neighborhood. But when the estate comes to be settled, and its value established, Tom Ailanthus, who before never had kept a dollar long enough in his company to get thoroughly acquainted with it, finds himself a poor man, with only fifty thousand. His anticipations have presented him with fifty thousand disappointments. So we go:

> "The space between the *ideal* of man's soul
> And man's *achievement*, who hath ever past?
> An ocean spreads between us and that goal,
> Where anchor ne'er was cast!"

We are born to disappointments as the sparks fly upward. See, now, how my anticipations were balked. I had imagined everything when I read that paragraph. Look upon the picture:

THE HORSE—HIS EXODUS.

Livery-stable keeper hears he's going to Kentucky-ho!
Whoa! (Tableau.)
A crowd of idle Nepperhanners cluster at the steamboat wharf,
To see him g' off.

Steamboat struggles down the river (panorama—Palisades)
Country fades—
Town approaches—churches, cabmen, steamboats, stenches, streets, and slips,
Lots of ships!
GANG-PLANK SCENE—Old ladies, baskets—*land him!* "g' up!" won't budge a bit.
'P'leptic fit!
Orange-woman bankrupt, crazy! (horse has smashed her tropic fruit).
Pay the woman—have to do't.
Reach the N' Orleans packet (racket), horse is hoisted up in slings,
Pegasus! (no wings.)
Skipper signs the bill of lading! horse is lowered down below.
"Whose horse is't?" "Don't know."
Steam-tug Ajax 'long-side packet—lugs her, tugs her down the bay;
(S'pulchral neigh!)
SEA SCENE!—Narrows—Staten Island—horsep't'l—light-house—Sandy Hook—
Captain—cook.
Morning—dawning—lighthouse fainting—at the anchor heaves the crew.
Horse heaves too!
And ship goeth over the ocean blue!

SCENE II.

GULF-SCENE—Tempest—inky water—Norther! (strikes one like a blow).
Squalls (with snow).

Midnight—lighthouse sinks, a star now!—"Captain?" "Yes, we run from shore."

"Captain—pshaw!"

Trunks philander round the cabin—state-rooms getting sick and sicker.

"I say—Ick-ah!"

Morning—sunbeams—fair winds—billows—sandy beaches—stunted trees;

Hail Balize!

Pilot—river—rushing current—yellow water—crooks and bends:

Sickness ends.

Dinner—sunset—N' Orleans City—Crescent—Levee—Lafayette.

"Not there yet!"

SCENE III.

Horse re-shipped—high-pressure steamboat—pipes alternate puff and cough.

There—he's off!

"Up the river!"—drift-wood—moonlight—L'wesiana glorious—great

Sugar state!

Level country—white-washed villas, negro cabins, fences, hedges,

Skirt the edges.

Baton Rouge is passed, and then, for long, long days and nights, he sees

Cotton trees!

Ever, ever, growing, growing, sunlight, moonlight, near and far,

There they are.

Natchez—Vicksburgh—Memphis! Each one stands upon a separate bluff,

Bold and rough!

Cairo—flat-boats—fiddling — dancing — gambling—wharf-boats—
on we go.
Ohio!
'Past we glide" (see Robert Browning), up *that* river on we
glide.
(We say—" slide.")
Past Paducah—past Shawneetown—till (Ah! stop—my trembling
quill),
LOUISVILLE!!!

"Now, Mrs. Sparrowgrass, I had *imagined* all of that panorama; and here we are, with the horse upon our hands, just because bills of lading begin in the way they do. I believe I shall have to make him a present to some bone-boiling establishment." "That is a cruel thought," said Mrs. S. "By the way," said I, "what do you think of my poetry, my dear?" Mrs. Sparrowgrass answered she had not heard any poetry, except now and then a rhyme, which seemed to come in the prose very well. "Prose," said I, "*prose?* Do you not know the verse is octameter catalectic, alternating with lines of a trochee and a half, sometimes irregulated in order to give scope to my fancy?" Mrs. Sparrowgrass said it did not strike her in that way. "Then if it did not strike you it cannot be poetry. Of course not. Poetry to be poetry *must strike.* If it do not, then it is not poetry, but, Mrs. Sp. it may be (excuse me) werse."

I have bought me a new patent bedstead, to facilitate early rising, called a "wake-up." It is a good thing to rise early in the country. Even in the winter time it is conducive to health to get out of a warm bed by lamp-light; to shiver into your drawers and slippers; to wash your face in a basin of ice-flakes; and to comb out your frigid hair with an uncompromising comb, before a frosty looking-glass. The only difficulty about it lies in the impotence of human will. You will deliberate about it, and argue the point. You will induge in specious pretences, and lie still with only the tip end of your nose outside the blankets; you will pretend to yourself that you *do* intend to jump out in a few minutes; you will tamper with the good intention, and yet indulge in the delicious luxury. To all this the "wake-up," is inflexibly and triumphantly antagonistic. It is a bedstead with a clock scientifically inserted in the head-board. When you go to bed, you wind up the clock, and point the index-hand to that hour on the dial, at which you wish to rise in the morning. Then you place yourself in the hands of the invention, and shut your eyes. You are now, as it were, under the guardianship of King Solomon and Doctor Benjamin Franklin. There is no need to recall those beautiful lines of the poet's—

> "Early to bed, and early to rise,
> Will make a man healthy, wealthy, and wise."

Science has forestalled them. The "wake-up" is a combination of hard wood, hinges, springs, and clock-work, against sleeping late o' mornings. It is a bedstead, with all the beautiful vitality of a flower—it opens with the dawn. If, for instance, you set the hand against six o'clock, in the morning, at six, the clock at the bed's head solemnly strikes a demi-twelve on its sonorous bell. If you pay no attention to the monitor, or idly, dreamily endeavor to compass the coherent sequence of sounds, the invention, within the succeding two minutes, drops its tail-board, and lets down your feet upon the floor. While you are pleasantly defeating this attempt upon your privacy, by drawing up your legs within the precincts of the blankets, the virtuous head-board, and the rest of the bed, suddenly rise up in protest; and the next moment, if you do not instantly abdicate, you are launched upon the floor by a blind elbow that connects with the crank of an eccentric, that is turned by a cord, that is wound around a drum, that is moved by an endless screw, that revolves within the body of the machinery. So soon as you are turned out, of course, you waive the balance of the nap, and proceed to dress.

"Mrs. Sparrowgrass," said I, contemplatively, after the grimy machinists had departed, "this machine is one of the most remarkable evidences of progress, the ingenuity of man has yet developed. In this bedstead we see a host of cardinal virtues made practical by science. To rise early, one must possess courage, prudence, self-denial, temperance, and fortitude. The cultivation of these virtues, necessarily attended with a great deal of trouble, may now be dispensed with, as this engine can entirely set aside, and render useless, a vast amount of moral discipline. I have no doubt, in a short time we shall see the finest attributes of the human mind superseded by machinery. Nay, more, I have very little doubt that, as a preparatory step in this great progress, we shall have physical monitors of cast-iron and wheel-work to regulate the ordinary routine of duty in every family."

Mrs. Sparrowgrass said she did not precisely understand what I meant. "For instance," said I, in continuation, "we dine every day; as a general thing, I mean. Now sometimes we eat too much, and how easy, how practicable it would be to regulate our appetites by a banquet-dial. The subject, having had the superficial area of his skull, and the cubic capacity of his body worked out respectively by a licensed craniologist, and by a licensed coporalogist, gets from each a certificate, which certificates are duly registered in the county clerk's office. From the county clerk he receives a permit, marked, we will say, ten." "Not ten pounds, I hope," said Mrs. S. "No, my dear," I replied, "ten would be the average of his capacity. We will now suppose the chair, in which the subject is seated at dinner, rests upon a pendulous platform, over a delicate arrangement of levers, connected with an upright rod, that runs through the section of table in front of his plate, and this rod, we will suppose, is toothed into a ratchet-wheel, that moves the index of the banquet-dial. You will see at once, that, as he hangs balanced in this scale, any absorption of food would be instantly indicated by the index. All then, he is called upon to do, is to watch the dial, until the hand points to 'ten,' and then, stop eating." "But," said Mrs. Sparrowgrass, "suppose he shouldn't be half through?" "Oh," said I, "that would not make any difference. When the dial says he has had enough, he must quit." "But," said Mrs. Sparrowgrass, "suppose he *would not* stop eating?" "Then," said I, "the proper way to do would be to inform against him, and have him brought immediately before a justice of the peace, and if he did not at once swear that he had eaten within his limits, fine him, and seize all the victuals on his premises." "Oh," said Mrs. S., "you would have a law to regulate it, then?" "Of course," said I, "a statute—a statutory provision, or provisionary act. Then, the principle once being established, you see how easily and beautifully we could be regulated by the simplest motive powers. All the obligations we now owe to society and to ourselves, could be dispensed with, or rather transferred to, or vested in, some superior machine to which we would be accountable by night and day. Nay, more than that, instead of sending representatives to legislate for us, how easy it would be to construct a legislature of bronze and wheel-work—an incorruptible legislature. I would suggest a hydraulic or pneumatic congress, as being less liable to explode, and more easily graduated than one propelled by steam simply. All that would be required of us then would be to elect a state engineer annually, and he, with the assistance of a few underlings, could manage the automata as he pleased." "I do not see," replied Mrs. Sparrowgrass, "how that would be an improvement upon the present method, from all I hear." This unexpected remark of Mrs. S. surprised me into silence for a moment, but immediately recovering, I answered that a hydraulic or pneumatic legislature would at least have this advantage—it would construct enactments for the State at, at least, one fifthieth part of the present expense, and at the same time do the work better and quicker.

"Now, my dear," said I, as I wound up the ponderous machinery with a huge key, "as you are always an early riser, and as, of course, you will be up before seven o'clock, I will set the indicator at that hour, so that you will not be disturbed by the progress of science. It is getting to be very cold, my dear, but how beautiful the stars are to-night. Look at Orion and the Pleiades! Intensely lustrous, in the frosty sky."

The sensations one experiences in lying down upon a complication of mechanical forces, are somewhat peculiar, if they are not entirely novel. I once had the pleasure, for one week, of sleeping directly over the boiler of a high-pressure Mississippi steamboat; and, as I knew, in case of a blow-up, I should be the first to hear of it, I composed my mind as well as I could under the circumstances. But this reposing upon a bed of statics and dynamics, with the constant chirping and crawling of wheel-work at the bed's head, with a thought now and then of the inexorable iron elbow below, and an uncertainty as to whether the clock itself might not be too fast, or to slow, caused me to be rather reflective and watchful, than composed and drowsy. Nevertheless, I enjoyed the lucent stars in their blue depths, and the midnight moon now tipping the Palisades with a fringe of silver fire, and was thinking how many centuries that lovely light had played upon those rugged ridges of trap and basalt, and so finally sinking from the reflective to the imaginative, and from the imaginative to the indistinct, at last reached that happy state of half-consciousness, between half-asleep and asleep, when the clock in the machine woke up, and suddenly struck eight! Of course, I knew it was later, but I could not imagine why it should strike at all, as I presumed the only time of striking was in the morning, by way of signal. As Mrs. S. was sound asleep, I concluded not to say anything to her about it; but I could not help thinking what an annoyance it would be if the clock should keep on striking the hours during the night. In a little while the bed-clothes seemed to droop at the foot of the bed, to which I did not pay much attention, as I was just then engaged listening to the drum below, that seemed to be steadily engaged in winding up its rope, and preparing for action. Then I felt the upper part of the patent bedstead rising up, and then I concluded to jump out, just as the iron elbow began to utter a cry like unto the cry of a steel katy-did, and did jump, but was accidentally preceded by the mattress, one bolster, two pillows, ditto blankets, a brace of threadbare linen sheets, one coverlid, the baby, one cradle (over-turned), and Mrs. Sparrowgrass. To gather up these heterogeneous materials of comfort required some little time, and, in the meanwhile, the bedstead subsided. When we retired again, and were once more safely protected from the nipping cold, although pretty well cooled, I could not help speaking of the perfect operation of the bedstead in high terms of praise, although, by some accident, it had fulfilled its object a little earlier than had been desirable. As I am very fond of dilating upon a pleasing theme, the conversation was prolonged until Mrs. Sparrowgrass got sleepy, and the clock struck nine. Then we had to turn out again. We had to turn out every hour during the long watches of the night, for that wonderful epitome of the age of progress. When the morning came, we were sleepy enough, and the next evening we concluded to replace the "wake-up," with a common, old-fashioned bedstead. To be sure, I had made a small mistake the first night, in not setting the "*indicator*," as well as the *index* of the dial. But what of that? Who wants his rest, that precious boon, subjected to contingencies? When we go to sleep, and say our prayers, let us wake up according to our natures, and according to our virtues; some require more sleep, some less; we are not mere bits of mechanism after all; who knows what world we may chance to wake up in? For my part, I have determined not to be a humming-top, to be wound up, and to run down, just like that very interesting toy, one of the young Sparrowgrassii has just now left upon my table, minus a string.

CHAPTER XVI.

Casualties will occur—Ice and ice-houses—A hint from the Flowery Nation—Baldwin's Pond—Skaters—Our horse gets into business and is launched upon an ice island—A Derrick—The result thereof.

CASUALTIES will occur; there is no providing against the infinite chapter of accidents. We have met with a misfortune. Our country horse is dead. Much as we grieved over him living, still we cannot help brooding over his untimely fate. After all, sympathy, pity, tenderness, are inexplicable virtues; why should such a loss cast its little cloud over our domestic sun, when greater, more pitiable events, fail to affect us? Our horse is dead! Well, he was not worth his fodder, yet we sorrow for him. The loss of fifty thousand Russians at Kars or Erzeroum, would not, could not, touch us so nearly. This is a strange instrument—the human heart! An organ with unaccountable stops—a harp of a thousand strings, many of them, I fear me, deplorably short.

In the winter time, when the frost builds its transparent flooring over the ponds, it is customary to fill the ice-houses in the country. It is a good thing to have an ice-house in the country. You keep your summer Sunday dinner, your milk, and your butter, in great perfection, if you have such a frigid tabernacle. Sometimes, on a sultry day, it is pleasant to descend to its cool depths—to feel a winter atmosphere in the heart of the dog-days—to enjoy a sparry arctic in the midst of a flowery tropic. To build a good ice-house, you must have foresight, and a capable carpenter. In China they rear them above ground; say a circle of bamboo poles lashed together; at the top, thatched over with straw, and a few feet of earth thrown up around the base; these keep the ice, even until the next year. Here, where ornate architecture is a necessity, ice-houses are more elaborately structured. What with a cupola, and a bracketted roof, knobs, and balls, and bells, a very pretty temple can be made of pagoda pattern, but then, it must be conceded, not so well calculated to resist a heavy thaw in July, as others of plainer mould.

Our ice-house, however, is not of the ornate kind; nor is it of the conservative species. In style, it is of the super-and-sub-terranean order of architecture, and really holds its own quite comfortably—except in very hot weather. We fill it usually in December, and this season our horse was brought forth in all his harness, to draw the clear blue blocks from Baldwin's haunted pond, upon a strong sled;—we supposed he could perform that duty with credit to himself. So we thought, "Alas poor Yorick!"

Baldwin's pond is a vast sheet of water, in truth it is *The Nepperhan River* dammed up; and around its legended brink there are villas, and gardens, and noble trees, and wild vines, and a couple of hat factories, and, just below it, a waterfall, and, in the distance, Chicken Island, and beyond that a bridge, and further on a gate, with a broad arch above it, through which you enter the village. In the summer time its sweet seclusion would enchant Kensett; in winter its picturesqueness would arrest Gignoux. The pond in December is a mine of wealth to the teamsters, as there are scores of ice-houses to be filled in the village; and from the transparent clearness of its waters, it makes pure, *blue* ice, valuable to pack, and to keep, and to use. "Alas poor Yorick!"

Just above it is 'The Glen,' which in autumn is the wildest and grandest place imagination can conceive of, with its proud abundance of foliage in such profusion of color, that nature's opulence itself seems to be there exhausted in tints. As you stand upon its western shore, and look across the pond, you see opposite, THE HOUSE WITH THE STONE CHIMNEY, nestled down among the frowzy willows, and just beyond that again, is the road that skirts the river, and if you follow that for a short distance you will come to the upper pond, over which hangs the double arch of the aqueduct.

The pond is a great resort for skaters in the winter, and sometimes of a moonlight evening, its white floor is a scene of enchantment, with the phantom-like crowd, whirling and shifting, in a maze of light and shadow. To and from this pond our poor old horse, with his rude sled, had been travelling all day, really earning his feed, and establishing a reputation for himself of the most creditable nature, when it chanced, towards nightfall, there befell him an accident.

In getting out the blocks of ice, the men had worked down towards the dam, making a sort of basin of water, which reached from the centre of the frozen sheet to the brink of the fall, and projecting into this tiny bay was a tongue, or peninsula of ice, connected with the main sheet over the upper, or northern part of the pond. Upon this narrow peninsula the sled was backed, with the rear end close to the open water, our poor horse standing with his back towards it also; unconscious of the fate which was awaiting him. In this position he had stood hour after hour, as block after block had been hauled up from the water, until his load was completed, and then straining at his cracking harness until the half-frozen runners of the sled slipped from their icy grooves, away he would go with his crystal freight, to fill up the ice-house. It seems, however, that, by reason of the continued cold weather, the blocks of ice were unusually thick, and heavy, so that hauling them out of the basin by hand labor, was very severe upon the men, but, as it chanced, there came a good Samaritan to the pond, towards the close of the day, who seeing the men so hard at work, bethought him of a remedy which was in the village, in the shape of a "derrick." Now a derrick is an instrument well known upon our coasts, and in our larger cities, but not so common in the country. It is a frame-work of timber that stands up upright, sometimes upon two legs, sometimes upon three or four, and at the top of the upright beams there is a long cross-piece, like the mizen yard of a ship, and at the end of the yard-arm, a block and tackle. Of course it would be quite easy with this engine to raise the largest lumps from the water, so some of the men went to bring it to the pond upon a sled, while others ceased hauling the ice, and gave up working until it arrived to assist them. In a short time the men returned, and at once they were hard enough at work, raising the derrick upright on the unbroken sheet of ice, just over against, and parallel with, the peninsula, upon which our poor horse, with his empty sled was standing, patiently waiting for his load. Once or twice he was seen to give the huge instrument an ominous glance, so that one of the men walked up to hold his head, for fear he would take fright and run away from it. Pity he had not. Up it rose portentous in the air, got almost to its place, stood for a moment straight up, then leaned over the other side, slipped upon the ice—there was a cry " Get out of the way !"—and down rushed the derrick with a thunderous blow that broke off our poor horse's peninsula, and launched him and his sled on an ice-island, in the midst of the basin of water. For a short time he kept his footing upon the island, but the end upon which he was standing gradually sank into the water, until he slid into the cool element, and then, instead of swimming towards the unbroken ice, where he would have found assistance, he turned down stream, and towing his sled behind him, reached at last the edge of the mill-dam. There, after some struggles, he managed to get one fore leg over the brink, and so hung, in spite of all persuasion, his nostrils throbbing with terror, his neck smoking with cold, and his one pitiful eye looking wistfully toward the crowd that had betrayed him. Had there been a boat he might have been saved, but there was none near, except a skiff, both filled with, and bedded in, a solid mass of ice, near the shore. The water was pouring over the dam, so that no one could approach him from below, nor could living man walk upon its slippery edge. They tried to throw a slip-noose over his neck, but without success; they held a sieve of oats in the most tempting way towards him, but he shook his head. At last, when all efforts to save him proved unavailing, an old sea-captain who had commanded a Nepperhan sloop in the last war, and had seen service, was touched with pity; he sent for his gun. The old fellow's hand shook as he loaded it, but he loaded it deliberately, took excellent aim, fired, and, amid a thousand echoes, the head of our poor old horse was thrown up in the air for a moment, and then it dropped upon the brink of the dam. There it lay, in the midst of the waters—stirring from side to side with the ripples that poured over the edge—so life-like in its motions, that some said "he must yet live;" but it was not so, and the next morning it was firmly set in an icy collar, and to this day he may be seen looking over the mill-dam, as you approach Baldwin's pond, from the south, by way of Chicken Island, or as you come up the road, hard by THE HOUSE WITH THE STONE CHIMNEY.

FEBRUARY, 1856.

CHAPTER XVII.

The great Snow-storm—A quotation from Samuel—Recollections of Town—What we then thought—A Song—Scraps in a Commonplace-book—An old epistle—And anticipations.

THIS has been a great snow-storm. Since we have lived in the country we have had two *great* snow-storms. A snow-storm in the city, with its motley panorama, is a curious spectacle, but a snow-storm in the country is sublime. The harmony of a winter landscape always inspires me with a sweet and melancholy gravity, exceeding, in its profound tranquillity, any emotion derived from a mere transitory flush of joy. The soul rests amid the hush and calm. Nature itself,—restless, industrious nature—at last reposes, in a sort of frozen rapture.

One does not wish to hear, at all hours, the pleasant jargon of sleigh-bells, let them ring never so melodiously: it is good, sometimes, to shut out the noisy carnival, to enjoy the broader winter of tho country, with feelings akin to those the hardy navigator experiences amid the strange solitudes of the Arctic. Look at the crags opposite, muffled breast high in snow, and the broad river with its myriad ice-islands. Look at the leagues of coldness, stretching northward until the vision rests upon the crescent line of hills glowing like sunset-clouds upon the borders of the Tappan-Zee. Look up at the bright sun of winter in his cerulean dome above, and at the fair country around us, within the horizon's blue ring, and say, if it be not a good thing to have a snow-storm in Westchester County. Thou ancient Dorp of Yonkers! I love thee with a love passing the love of women.

The ambiguity of this last expression gave rise to a novel train of ideas in the mind of Mrs. Sparrowgrass, upon which I immediately turned to the twenty-sixth verse of the first chapter of Samuel II., and read therefrom the exquisite lines I had so happily quoted.

"It is a good thing to live in the country," said I; "this is something different from what we had surmised in the little back parlor in Avenue G, Mrs. Sparrowgrass. Do you not remember how we used to anticipate rural felicity?" Mrs. Sparrowgrass replied, she remembered it very well. "It is not precisely what we had pictured to ourselves, is it?

"When a little farm we keep,
And have little girls and boys,
With little pigs and sheep,
To make a little noise,
Oh what happy, happy days we'll see,
With the children sitting, sitting on our knee."

"Not precisely," echoed Mrs. S., "but still I like it as it is. To think of going back to the city now, is to think of moving into a prison. Yet there was something cheerful in the little house in town, too. There was a gas-lamp in front of the door, that even in stormy weather threw out its friendly ray, and I used to think it good company to have it always burning before the window, and shining up through the blinds. Then your library was quite a jewel in its way, with the brilliant jet of light over the table—and the rows of gilt books—and the pictures on the walls—and the brackets, niches, and busts, and statuettes, and pieces of armor, and bows, and spears, and stag-horns, all looking so bright and pleasant. I do not think this one lights up so well as that did." "Not with two candles and a wood fire?" said I. "No," replied

Mrs. S., "it is not so bright as that little town library." "Then," said I, "permit me to substitute, my dear, the word '*cosy*,' as suggestive of the impression one has in entering this bookery." "That will do very well," replied Mrs. S., "I am not making comparisons, but you must remember we were very happy in that little house in town. We had a great many friends there." "So we had." "A great many friends, and a great many pleasant days, and pleasant evenings, especially in winter, when we had little pop visits from our neighbors." "Yes, Mrs. S.," remarked I, "but if I remember truly, there was one winter which of all others seems to me the brightest and the cheerfullest." "Which one was that?" said Mrs. S. "The last one we passed in town," I replied, with great impressiveness of manner, "the winter of anticipations—when we were laying out our plans for living in the country."

To this Mrs. Sparrowgrass answered by smoothing her hair with her thimble, and putting on an expression of wonderful contentment. "I wish," said she, after a pause, "I could remember all we talked about in those days, and all we had pictured to ourselves about it. I know that when anybody came in it was the constant topic of conversation, and I know when we were alone, how much you were engaged with your plans for the new house. And then, too, whenever you wrote a letter, there was always something to say about leaving town, and whenever you received a letter, there was always a great deal of congratulation, and a great deal of advice, and a great many inquiries as to whether there was any fever and ague in the district. Then, too, you had a little song which you sang once or twice to the children, which I have never heard you sing since, and which I have forgotten, and which I would not have remembered but for your speaking of our little house in town, where we were certainly very, very happy."

"What," said I, "forgotten my song, Mrs. Sparrowgrass? Forgotten my song? Then I mean to sing it if I have any voice left." So after a few preliminary attempts I commenced it. But, alas! my memory gave out with the first two lines, so I had to take down my old commonplace book where I found these reminiscent lines.

OH, A COUNTRY HOME FOR ME!

Air—JEANETTE AND JEANNOT.

Oh, a country home for me! where the clover blossoms blow;
And the robin builds his nest in the old cherry bough;
Where the roses, and the honey-buds are clinging to the wall,
Each a perfumed cup of jewels when the rain-drops fall.
Where the leaves and lights are blending,
And the swallows soar and sing,
And the iron chain and bucket drips
Above the silver spring:
Oh, a country home for me! etc.

When the sun is in the west, and the winds are lulled to rest,
And the babe sleeps on its mother's arm, the robin in her nest;
When the cottage taper twinkles through the lattice, and the gloom
Of the dusky trellis roses, and the woodbine's bloom:
When the moon is on the wave,
And the shadows in the grove,
How sweet to wander side by side
With those we dearly love:
Oh, a country home for me! etc.

"I am so glad you have found it," said Mrs. S. "It quite reminds me of old times. But it seems to me in a few places the lines might be improved; for instance,

"Where the swallows soar and sing."

"True," said I, interrupting further criticism,

"that line could never have been written in the country; swallows soar not, neither do they sing, but still we will let the lines remain, as they shadow forth the idea of what we thought of the country, when we lived in town. Here," I continued, turning over some yellow paper, and tumbling out a wilderness of scraps that were lying perdue between the pages," here are a few more scraps of anticipation, odds and ends of hope, minutes of dead-reckoning. Look now at that list of climbing plants! It was certainly my intention to get each and every one, and if I had, what a gorgeous show the cottage would have made by this time: the bower of roses, "by Bendemeer's stream," would have been nothing to it. Then look here; another list! Rural ornaments for gardens, rustic vases, hanging flower-pots, urns, sun-dials, kiosks, arbors, terrace-work, rock-work, and as I live a fountain! Think of it; a fountain, with a pool of goldfish below to catch the shredded silver—

> "And in the midst, fresh whistling through the scene,
> A lightsome fountain starts from out the green,
> Clear and compact, till, at its height o'er-run,
> It shakes its loosening silver in the sun."

"How beautiful that would have been, viewed

through a vista of stately trees, with a grand arched gate at the end, and a pair of stone lions after Canova—one on either side." "All fancy," said Mrs. S. "All fancy," I echoed, "and not all fancy." Here are more scraps of the same kind. Memoranda, Downing's Rural Architecture, Landscape Gardening—a few hints from Lord Bacon. Mem. "*have a bed of Shakspeare flowers*,"

—Daisies pied, and violets blue,
And lady-smocks all silver-white,
And cuckoo buds of yellow hue.

Those I mean to have, and rosemary for remembrance! and 'pansies for thoughts,' and columbines." "That would be charming." "Charming? so it would. And now look at this practical bundle of hints cut from newspapers—the careful gleanings from the harvests of the Evening Post—the articles marked, "Agricultural," in that excellent paper. "There Mrs. S., I have read everything in that bundle religiously, and if I had an estate, twice the size of this county, it would be scarcely large enough to cultivate turnips in, according to the various methods proposed by those agricultural articles, and as for the potato, I will venture to say the Greeks and Trojans around the dead body of Protoclus, could scarcely vie in zeal with the champions of the Evening Post that contest the palm around that famous root. True? It is true; in our more modern days, such a contest here might, perhaps, be limited to the un-warlike columns that muster under the editorial Generalissimo, but, nevertheless, it is likewise true that there is enough partisan spirit displayed in those antagonistic paragraphs, marked 'potato,' to breed a rebellion in Ireland, Mrs. Sparrowgrass, in twenty-four hours."

"Whew! look here, another relic of the past. A draft of a letter to a friend h'm—h'm—

"For my part, I begin to weary of artificial life, and sigh for the Great Mother (this is from the city you know, to a friend in the country). I see the waving of trees, but they are rooted in a church-yard (St Mark's) or grow up between flag-stones: I hear the melody of birds, but they are pewter canaries at sixpence apiece. I am tired of water 'running up and down and through my lady's chamber,' I want to see it rise like a naiad dripping from a well. I am weary of stone steps, and have a sort of green sickness for rustic porches clambered over with vines; I sigh for flowers other than artificial; and do much desire to look upon the rain, not as an inconvenience, but as a blessing to the crops,

THEREFORE

I'd kind o'like to have a cot
Fixed on some sunny slope ; a spot
  Five acres more or less ;
With maples, cedars, chesnut trees,
And poplars whitening in the breeze.

'Twould suit my taste, I guess,
To have the porch with vines o'erclung,
With pendant bells of woodbine swung,
  In every bell a bee ;
And round my latticed window spread
A clump of roses, white and red.

  To solace mine and me,
I kind o'think I should desire
To hear about the lawn a choir
  Of wood-birds singing sweet;
And in a dell, I'd have a brook
Where I might sit and read my book.

  Such should be my retreat;
Far from the city's crowds and noise
Where I could rear my girls and boys,—
  I have some two or three,

And if kind Heaven should bless my store
With five, or six, or seven more,
  How happy I would be.

"There, Mrs. S., take those papers and put them away with the old love-letters, and the rest of the bye-gones. Some day you will take them out again; perhaps, to read to another generation—¿Quien sabe?"

CHAPTER XVIII.

A Conference in the Library—Mr. Sparrowgrass writes an Essay—Life in Town and Life in the Rural Districts—Mrs. Sparrowgrass continues the theme—Two Pictures from Nature—and the Last Word.

"HERE we are, Mrs. Sparrowgrass, just on the eve of retiring to private life. We must shake hands with our friends, and say 'good-bye.' This is to be the last paper—'to-morrow to fresh fields and pastures new.'" Mrs. Sparrowgrass smiled a little smile, and sighed a little sigh; then it became very still, but the clock ticked loudly on the library mantel, and the wood-fire chirped, and the sound of thread and needle tugging through a stiff piece of linen, were quite audible. "I think," said Mrs. S., after a long pause, "I think there is a great deal to be said about living in the country; a great deal yet to be said."

"True," I replied, "but I believe, Mrs. S., I have said my say about it. I begin to feel that the first impressions, the novelty, the freshness, incident to the change from city to country are wearing away."

"Do you think so?" said Mrs. Sparrowgrass.

"Yes," I replied, "I think so; in truth I am very sure of it. Do you not see it with very different eyes from those you first brought with you out of the city?"

Mrs. Sparrowgrass said, "She did not know but that she did."

"Of course you do," I continued, "the novelty of the change is gone; we have become used to our new life—custom has made every part of it familiar."

"Not to me," answered Mrs. S., brightening up; "not to me; every day I see something new, every day the country seems to grow more beautiful; there are a thousand things to attract me, and interest me here, which I never could have seen in the city; even the winters seem to be brighter, and the days longer, and the evenings pleasanter; and then I have so much to be thankful for, that the children are so strong and hardy; that we keep such good hours; and that you have grown to be so domestic."

This compliment made me smile in turn, but I pretended to be very busy with my writing. The smile, however, must have been seen, I think, for Mrs. S. repeated, very softly, "You *have* grown to be more domestic, and that alone is enough to make me happy here."

"So, my dear," said I, after a pause, "you believe that, among other things, a domestic turn of mind can be better cultivated in the country than in the city?"

Mrs. Sparrowgrass assented by nodding like a crockery Chinese lady.

"Then," said I, "the fact is worth publishing, and it shall be, for the benefit of all concerned. And now let me read to you a short essay I have been writing on country life, seen in a twofold aspect—that is, as we had imagined it, and as we have found it."

Mrs. Sparrowgrass placed the candles nearer the desk and resumed her needlework. Now then—

"To one who has been long in city pent,
'Tis very sweet to look into the fair
And open face of heaven, to breathe a prayer
Full in the smile of the blue firmament.
Who is the more happy, when, with heart's content,
Fatigued he sinks into some pleasant lair
Of wavy grass, and reads a debonair
And gentle tale of love and languishment."

There are very few persons insensible to the tender influence of nature; few who do not feel at times a yearning to exchange a limited life, held in common with the vast multitude, for one of more generous boundaries, where the soul can repose amid contemplation, and the mind rest from its labors, and even the languid pulse thrill with an inspiration that is independent of excitement. It is this feeling that lends a crowning grace to works of fiction, that adds enchantment to narrative, that makes every virtue conceivable, that echoes into music, and blossoms into song. It is this feeling that leads us to prefer Sir Roger de Coverly to Sir Andrew Freeport; it is this that transports us with delight as we wander with Robinson Crusoe; this that weaves a spell of fascination around the loves of Paul and Virginia.

But we may leave the kingdom of books and pass from their royal domains into the broader commons of every-day life, and if yonder laborer, trudging along the dusty high road, far from the pitiless pavements, could give expression to his thought, he would affirm that this early, summer, Sunday morning is, to him, an idyl full of poetic beauty and tenderness.

Take, too, the city school-boy and his mates, and see them with uncontrollable instincts pouring forth from the avenues of the town to revel in the ragged grass of the suburbs, to sit, haply, beneath the shadow of a tree, or to bathe in waters that dimple over beaches of sand, instead of beating against piers of weedy timber. Take the school-boy, and if he tell you truly, he will confess that, even amid the discipline of the school, his mind was truant to his hard arithmetic, and his dry grammar; that while he was seemingly plodding through his lessons, he was really dreaming of green fields, and sunny air, tremulous with the murmur of brooks, and fragrant with the odor of lilacs.

Nor is this feeling limited to certain classes of men, nor is it incident only to our earlier years. It is the prospect of some ideal home in the country, that often binds the merchant to the town, in order that he may win a competency to retire with; binds him to his desk until his head begins to silver over, and habit has made the pursuit of wealth a necessity. It is this ideal future that often haunts the statesman with pictures scarcely less seductive than ambition itself, with prospective hopes, which he promises himself some day shall be realized—some day, when his labors are over, and the nation is safe. It is this that passes like a vision before the eyes of the soldier in the solitary fortress; this that lulls and cradles the mariner to sleep, in his oaken prison; this that leads the angler into the depths of the solemn woods; this that depopulates cities in the sweet summer time.

Most natural then as this wish may be, to those accustomed to the life of a city, there are certain seasons only when the desire throbs in the veins with an impulse not to be resisted—as during the feverish dog-days, or in the dewy mornings of early spring—

> "The Spring is here, the delicate-footed May,
> With its slight fingers full of buds and flowers,
> And with it comes a wish to be away,
> Wasting in wood-paths the voluptuous hours."

At such times the heart, instinctively led by its own happiness, revels in, anticipation of, winding woodpaths, and green glades and quiet nooks, and streams, and the twitter of birds, and the voluptuous breathing of flowers, and the murmur of insects in the holiday fields.

But when the winter comes, the bright city, with its social populace, presents a striking contrast to the dreary, solitary country, with its lonely roads, dark plains, and desolate woods, so that the very thought itself is suggestive only of gloom and discomfort.

There are other considerations, too, sympathies that may not be readily, nor rudely divorced—actualities by which we are strongly, though almost imperceptibly, bound to a city life, such as customary habits, familiar acquaintances, and communion with old, time-honored friends. These, in themselves, are often potent enough to prevent us. Separation is the saddest word in the book of humanity.

Then again come other actualities—little actualities of two, and four, and six years old, with preternatural eyes, and feverish lips, and wasted arms, mutely imploring us to follow the doctor's advice, and give them a change of air—not for a few weeks, but for a few years, and these have their influence. For I pity the parent who does not feel the welfare of his little ones nearest his heart. So that at last, after gravely weighing all arguments on either side, the great word is spoken—

"We will move into the country." Once settled as a fixed fact, once established as a thing no longer debatable, the idea of living in the country speedily invests itself with its old and happiest colors, puts on cap and kirtle, and cottages the future in an Eden of lattice-work, and lawn. Thenceforth every grass-plat in the city becomes an object of interest, every tree a study, every market vegetable a vital topic. Anticipation can scarcely wait upon fluent time; weeks and months seem narrow and long, as the streets we traverse. At last the period of thraldom over, for such it seems, the May day of moving comes, and then, with all the silver in a basket, and all the children in a glow, and all the canary birds in a cage, we depart from the city, its houses, and its streets of houses, its associations, and its friendships. We depart from the city, not forgetful of its benevolence, its security, its protection. Sorrow be to him who would launch a Parthian arrow at his own birth-place, wherever, or whatever that may be!

It must be confessed, that the realization of a hope is sometimes not so beautiful as the hope itself. It must be confessed that turnpike roads are not always avenues of happiness; that distance, simply contemplated from a railroad depot, does not lend enchantment to the view of a load of furniture travelling up hill through a hearty rainstorm; that communion with the visible forms of nature, now and then, fails to supply us with the requisite amount of mild and healing sympathy; that a rustic cottage may be overflowing with love, and yet overflowed with water; that, in fine, living in the country rarely fulfils at once the idea of living in clover. To one accustomed to the facile helps of a great city, its numerous and convenient stores, its limited distances, its ready attentions, and its easy means of information and communication, the slow and sleepy village presents a contrast, which, upon the whole, can scarcely be considered as favorable to the latter. Plumbers are very slow in the country; carpenters are not swift; locksmiths seldom take time by the forelock; the painter will go off fishing; the grocer on a pic-nic; the shoemaker to the menagerie:

> "The butcher, the baker, the candlestick maker,
> And all of them gone to the fair,"

strikes harshly upon the nice, civic sense of one accustomed to the prompt exactitudes of the town.

Say, however, that by the driving wheel of perseverance, the customary, inside economy moves on regularly as usual, yet are there new sources of disquiet; the chickens will walk into the kitchen, the dogs will get into the parlor, and the children will march into the dining-room with an incalculable quantity of mud. This last is the most grievous trouble of all, for how can we keep the children in, or keep them out? Then, too, there are other little matters; the well will dry up, or the chimney will smoke, or the dogs will dig immense holes in the garden-beds, or somebody's wagon will take a slice off the turf border of the grass-plat, or the garden-gate will fracture one of its hinges, or something or other of some kind will happen, in some way, to disturb the serenity of the domestic sky. And let it be remembered also, that although a green hedge is a very pretty object, it requires to be trimmed; that peas must be supplied with bushes from infancy; that lima beans when they want poles, have to be indulged in that weakness; that tomatoes get along best on crutches; that corn and potatoes, being very courteous plants, require a little bowing and scraping at times, with a hoe; that garden vegetables of all conditions seem rather fond of leading a ragged, vagabond life, and therefore should be trained by themselves, and not suffered to grow up in a rabble of weeds.

Let it then be fairly and candidly confessed, that living in the country does not exempt from care and laborious patience, those, who build their habitations beneath its halcyon skies. There are many things which should have been thought of, and which one never does think of as accessories in the ideal picture. The first effort of rural simplicity is to disabuse the mind of these fallacies. Once understood that life in the country does not imply exemption from all the cares and business of ordinary life; that happiness, here as elsewhere, is only a glimpse between the clouds; that there are positive disadvantages incurred by living out of town; and that anticipation must succumb to the customary discount; once understood, and carefully weighed in a just balance, life in the country becomes settled on a firm basis and puts on its pleasantest aspect.

Then a well-ordered garden presents manifold charms to the eye, whether it be when the first green shoots appear, or in the ripened harvest;

then every bud that blows bears in its heart a promise or a memory; then rain-storms are fountains of happiness; then the chirping of early birds is sweeter than the cunning of instruments; then the iterated chorus of insects in the fields is pleasanter than a pastoral poem; then the brown, unbroken soil has an earthy smell no thing can match; and the skies, the river, the mountains, with a thousand touches, illustrate the bounty, the tenderness, the wondrous providence of the Creator.

Furthermore, the very toil, which at first seems like a hardship, betimes, carries with it a recompense. As the frame becomes disciplined by the additional duties imposed upon it, the labor grows lighter, and more attractive; not only that, the blood circulates with renewèd life, the eye becomes brighter, the muscles more elastic, cheerfulness begins to ring out its bells in the clear air, and sleep falls upon the lids, gentle as a shadow.

If you have little ones, think what a blessing such discipline is to them. Just look at the boys, and their red-blown cheeks, and their sled out in the snow there! Listen; did you ever hear such a Christmas carol in the streets?

Not the smallest item in the account is this, that for want of other pleasures, parents are prone, in the country, to turn their attentions to the little ones, to enter more familiarly into their minor world, to take a part in its pageants, to read more carefully its tiny history, to become developed by its delicate sympathies, so that in time one gets to be very popular there, and is hailed as a comrade and good fellow —one of the elected—and eligible to receive all the secret grips and pass-words of the order. And this is not to be lightly considered either, for how can we expect our children will make us their choicest companions when we are old, if we make them not our friends when they are young? And as a child is often like a star in the house, why should not the father and mother be nearest to its light. Jean Paul Richter somewhere says of children, "The smallest are nearest God, as the smallest planets are nearest the sun." Therefore, it is a good thing not to be on the outside of their planetary system.

Take it all in all, then, we may rest assured, that although our first experiences do not fulfill the ideal images we had raised, yet when the fibres become familiar to the soil, and spread, and strengthen, we soon overcome the shock of transplantation. Then our new life burgeons and blossoms, like a tree, that in more open ground spreads forth its happy leaves to catch the sunshine and the rain, the air and the dews; and ever and ever growing and growing, its harmonious proportions are uplifted nearer and nearer to that harmonious Heaven, which God has hung with clouds and studded with stars, as types and symbols, only, of the glories of that which lies still further beyond.

"Is that all you have to say?" said Mrs. Sparrowgrass. "That is all, my dear," I replied, and then very composedly lighted a cigar. The clock ticked loudly again, the wood-fire chirped, and the thread and needle tugged its way through the linen with a weary note, like a prolonged sigh with the bronchitis.

"For my part," said Mrs. S., after a pause of fifteen minutes' duration by the library clock, "I think you have not done justice to the country. You do not speak at all of the pleasant neighbors we know, of the pleasant visits we have had, and the parties on the river, and the beach in front of the house, where the children go in bathing during the summer months, and the fishing, and crabbing, and the delightful drives and rides, and the interest we take in planting, and the pleasure of picking off the early peas, and the quiet of our Sabbaths, and 'the charm of seclusion,' which you so often allude to in your library, when you sit down at a pile of books."

"True."

"And although it may be a trifling matter, yet it is a very pleasant thing to own a boat, and to have a hammock swung under the trees for the children to play in, or to read and smoke in, when you are tired; and to keep poultry, and to watch a young brood of chickens, and to have eggs fresh laid for breakfast."

"I know it."

"And even if we do meet with mishaps, what of them? I never do expect to pass through life without some disappointments; do you?"

"Certainly not."

"And then you have scarcely alluded to the country in winter time: why nothing can compare with it; I could not have believed that it would have been so beautiful, if I had not seen it and known it."

(Three puffs of smoke in rapid succession.)

"And then to walk through a green, winding lane, with daisies and roses all along on both sides, as we often do towards evening, in summer, is a thing worth remembering."

"Worth remembering? It is a poem in itself."

"And the pleasant note of a cow-bell at nightfall, or in the wood by day, is a pretty sound."

"It is a wonder the golden chime of that bell has not been rolled out in melodious lines by somebody." (two puffs and a half.)

"And, although it may make you smile, there is something very musical to me, in the bullfrog's whistle. I love to hear it, in early spring."

"After that we may expect blue-birds."

"Yes," said Mrs. S., "ah, how fond the children are of blue-birds."

"Yes, and how thankful we should be that they have such innocent loves."

"I think," said Mrs. S., "children can scarcely develop their natural affections in the city. There is nothing for them to cling to, nothing to awaken their admiration and interest there."

"Except toy-stores, which certainly do wake up an immense amount of admiration and interest in the small fry, Mrs. S."

"True, but they are better off with a few occasional presents. I know how happy they are for a short time with them; but I fear me the excitement is not productive of good. Toys produce more strife among the little ones than all the pleasure is worth. For my part, I almost dread to see them come into the house, although I do feel gratified in witnessing the surprise and delight with which they are received by the children."

"That is a clear case."

"If you want to see a picture," continued Mrs. S., full of the theme, and putting down her sewing, "I think I can show you one worth looking at."

(One short puff, and one eye shut, expressive of an anxious desire to see the picture.)

Mrs. Sparrowgrass rolled back the library window-shutters, and the flood of white light that poured into the room fairly dimmed the candle on the table. There was the pure white snow; and the round, full moon; and the lustrous stars; and the hazy line of the Palisades; and the long reach of river glistening with a thousand brilliants. For from every point of ice there shone a nebulous light, so that the river seemed a galaxy studded with magnificent planets; and as we stood gazing upon this wondrous scene, we heard the sound of an approaching train, and then, suddenly reddening through the stone arch in the distance, there darted forth into the night, the Iron Meteor with its flaming forehead, and so flying along the curve of the road, thundered by, and was presently heard no more.

I think Mrs. Sparrowgrass rather surpassed herself when she conjured up this splendid vision, for she became very grave and silent.

"This beautiful scene," said I, "this glistening river, reminds me of something, of a scientific fact, which, although true in itself, sounds like the language of oriental fable. Did you know, my dear, that those vast Palisades yonder, rest upon beds of jewels?"

"Beds of jewels?" echoed Mrs. Sparrowgrass.

"Yes, my dear, beds of jewels; for these are basaltic rocks of volcanic birth, and at some time were spouted up, from the molten caverns below the crust of the earth, in a fluid state; then they spread out and hardened on the surface; so that if we go to, or a little below, low-water mark, we shall find the base of them to be the old red sandstone, upon which they rest.

"I thought," replied Mrs. S., "they went down very deep in the earth—that they were like all other rocks."

"No," I answered, "they are not *rooted* at all, but only rest upon the top of old red sandstone. Well, in the crevices between the basaltic and sandstone rocks, the mineralogists find the best specimens of amethysts, onyxes, sapphires, agates, and cornelians. And that this is the case with the Palisades, has been often proved at Fort Lee, where the cliffs begin. There the sandstone is visible above ground, and there the specimens have been found imbedded between the strata."

"You are sure the idea is not imaginary?" said Mrs. S.

"All true, my dear."

"Then I shall never think of them in future, without remembering their old jewels; I wonder, if they were to tumble down now and expose their riches, whether the amethysts and onyxes would compare with the brightness of those frozen gems?"

"Certainly not." (Shutters close.)

"And now," continued Mrs. Sparrowgrass, "I want to show you another picture;" and with that she lifted the candle and walked softly up stairs before me into the nursery; there were five little white-heads, and ten little rosy-cheeks, nestled among the pillows, and I felt a proud, parental joy in gazing upon their healthy, happy faces, and listening to their robust breathings.

"These," said Mrs. S., in a whisper, as she shaded the light, "*are my jewels.*"

"And mine too, Mrs. Sparrowgrass," said I.

"Yes," whispered Mrs. S., very seriously, "and if ever I should be taken away from them, I want you to promise me one thing."

"Tell me what it is," said I, very much determined that I would do it, whatever it might be.

"Promise me," said Mrs. S., "that while they are growing up you will keep them from the city—that their little minds and bodies may be trained and taught by these pure influences, that, so long as they are under your direction, you will not deprive them of the great privilege they now enjoy—that of living in the country."

THE

REDOUBTABLE ACHIEVEMENTS

OF

CAPTAIN DAVIS

AND

CAPTAIN BELGRAVE.

CAPTAIN DAVIS:

A CALIFORNIAN BALLAD.

THE sources of the following ballad are to be found in the California papers of December, 1854. It appears from letters published in the *Mountain Democrat* (extra) and the *Sacramento Statesman*, (extra) that a party of miners were encamped near Rocky-Cañon, a deep and almost inaccessible, uninhabited, rocky gorge, near Todd's Valley; and it happened that some of them were out hunting near the cañon, in which they saw "three men quietly following the trail to prospect a mine of gold-bearing quartz in the vicinity. Suddenly, a party of banditti sprang out of a thicket, and commenced firing at the three who were prospecting. James McDonald. of Alabama, was killed at the first shot.

Dr. Bolivar A. Sparks, of Mississippi, fired twice at the robbers, and fell, mortally wounded. Captain Jonathan R. Davis, of South Carolina, then drew his revolvers and commenced shooting at the enemy—every ball forcing its victim to bite the dust. He was easily distinguished from the rest by his white hat, and from his being above the medium height. The robbers then made a charge upon him with their knives and one sabre. Captain Davis stood his ground firmly until they rushed up *abreast* within four feet of him. He then made a spring upon them with a large Bowie-knife, and gave three of them wounds which proved fatal." Afterwards he killed all the rest, and then tore up his shirt to bind the wounds of the survivors. The party of spectators then came down. It seems they had been prevented joining in the fight from a sense of etiquette: as the letter of one party expresses it—"Being satisfied that they were *all strangers*, we hesitated a moment before we ventured to go down." When they got down, they found eleven men stretched on the ground, with some others in a helpless condition. They then formed a coroner's jury, and held an inquest over twelve dead bodies. Captain Davis was the only living person left in the Rocky-Cañon. One letter says: "Although we counted twenty-eight bullet holes through Captain Davis' hat and clothes (seventeen through his hat and eleven through his coat and shirt), he received but two very slight flesh-wounds."

The ballad was written, during intervals of severe occupation, upon the backs of business-letters and scraps of cartridge-paper, in railroad cars, and on the Hoboken ferry-boat. This will be obvious to the skillful, upon perusal. The object of the writer was to preserve, in the immortal KNICKERBOCKER Magazine, a record of the 'Battle of Rocky-Cañon,' for fear the story might be lost in the perishable pages of the daily press:

Ye Battail of Rocky Canyon.

ALL the heroes that ever were born,
Native or foreign, bearded or shorn,
From the days of Homer to Omar Pasha
Who mauled and maltreated the troops of the Czar,
And drove the rowdy Muscovite back,
Fin and Livonian, Pole and Cossack,
From gray Ladoga to green Ukraine,
And other parts of the Russian domain
With an intimation exceedingly plain,
That they'd better cut! and not come again!

All the heroes of olden time
Who have jingled alike in armor and rhyme,
Hercules, Hector, Quintus Curtius,
Pompey, and Pegasus-riding Perseus,
Brave Bayard, and the brave Roland,
  Men who never a fight turned backs on;
Charles the Swede, and the Spartan band,
  Coriolanus, and General Jackson,
Richard the Third, and Marcus Brutus,
And others, whose names won't rhyme to suit us,
Must certainly sink in the dim profound
When Captain Davis's story gets round.

Know ye the land where the sinking sun
Sees the last of earth when the day is done?
Where the course of empire is sure to stop,
And the play conclude with the fifth-act drop? *
Where, wonderful spectacle! hand in hand
The oldest and youngest nations stand?
Where yellow Asia, withered and dry,
Hears Young America, sharp and spry,
With thumb in his vest, and a quizzical leer,
Sing out, "Old Fogie, come over here!"

  Know ye the land of mines and vines,
  Of monstrous turnips and giant pines,
  Of monstrous profits and quick declines,
  And Howland and Aspinwall's steamship lines?
Know ye the land so wondrous fair?
  Fame has blown on his golden bugle,
From Battery-place to Union-square,

See Berkeley.

Over the Park and down McDougal;
Hither, and thither, and everywhere,
In every city its name is known;
There is not a grizzly Wall-street bear
That does not shrink when the blast is blown:
There Dives sits on a golden throne,
With Lazarus holding his shield before,
Charged with a heart of auriferous stone,
And a pick-axe and spade on a field of *or*,
Know ye the land that looks on Ind?
There only you'll see a pacific sailor,
Its song has been sung by Jenny Lind,
And the words were furnished by Bayard Taylor.

Seaward stretches a valley there,
Seldom frequented by men or women;
Its rocks are hung with the prickly-pear,
And the golden balls of the wild persimmon;
Haunts congenial to wolf and bear,
Covered with thickets, are everywhere;
There's nothing at all in the place to attract us,
Except some grotesque kinds of cactus;
Glittering beetles with golden wings,
Royal lizards with golden rings,
And a gorgeous species of poisonous snake,
That lets you know when he means to battle
By giving his tail a rousing shake,
To which is attached a muffled rattle.

Captain Davis, (Jonathan R.,)
With James McDonald, of Alabama,
And Dr. Bolivar Sparks were *thar*,
Cracking the rocks with a miner's hammer;

Of the valley they'd heard reports
"That plenty of gold was there in quartz:"
Gold in quartz they marked not there,
But p'ints enough on the prickly pear,
As they very soon found
When they sat on the ground,
  To scrape the blood from their cuts and scratches;
For a rickety cactus had stripped them bare,
  And cobbled their hides with crimson patches.
Thousands of miles they are from home,
  Hundreds from San Francisco city;
Little they think that near them roam
  A baker's dozen of wild banditti;
Fellows who prowl, like stealthy cats,
In velvet jackets and sugar-loaf hats,
Covered all over with trinkets and crimes,
  Watches and crosses, pistols and feathers,
Squeezing virgins and wives like limes,
  And wrapping their legs in unpatented leathers:
Little they think how close at hand
Is that cock of the walk—"the Bold Brigand!"

And here I wish to make a suggestion
  In regard to those conical, sugar-loaf hats,
I think those banditti, beyond all question,
  Some day will find out they 're a parcel of flats;
For if that style is with them a passion,
And they stick to those hats in spite of the fashion,
Some Tuscan Leary, Genin, or Knox,
Will get those brigands in a —— bad box;
For the Chief of Police will send a "Star"
To keep a look-out near the hat bazaar:

And when Fra Diavolo comes to buy
  The peculiar mode that suits his whim,
He may find out, if the Star is spry,
  That instead of the hat they've ironed him!

Captain Davis, and James McDonald,
  And Doctor Sparks together stand;
Suddenly, like the fierce Clan Ronald,
  Bursts from the thicket the Bold Brigand,
Sudden, and never a word spoke they,
But pulled their triggers and blazed away.

"Music," says Halleck, "is everywhere;"
  Harmony guides the whole creation;
But when a bullet sings in the air
So close to your hat that it moves your hair,
To enjoy it requires a taste quite rare,
  With a certain amount of cultivation.
But never music, homely or grand,
Grisi's "Norma" or Gungl's band,
The distant sound of the watch-dog's bark,
  The coffee-mill's breakfast-psalm in the cellar,
"Home, Sweet Home," or the sweet "Sky-lark,"
  Sung by Miss Pyne, in "Cinderella;"
Songs that remind us of days of yore,
  Curb-stone ditties we loved to hear,
"*Brewers' yeast!*" and "*Straw, oat straw!*"
  "*Lily-white corn, a penny an ear!*"
  Rustic music of chanticleer,
  "Robert the Devil," by Meyerbeer,
  Played at the "Park" when the Woods were here,
Or any thing else that an echo brings
From those mysterious vibrant strings,

That answer at once, like a telegraph line,
To notes that were written in "*Old Lang Syne*;"
Nothing, I say, ever played or sung,
Organ panted, or bugle rung,
Not even the horn on the Switzer Alp,
  Was half so sweet to the Captain's ear
As the sound of the bullet that split his scalp,
  And told him a scrimmage was awful near.

Come, O Danger! in any form,
"The earthquake's shock or the ocean-storm;"
Come, when its century's weight of snow
The avalanche hurls on the Swiss chateau;
Come with the murderous Hindoo Thug,
Come with the Grizzly's fearful hug,
With the Malay's stab, or the adder's fang,
Or the deadly flight of the boomerang,
But never come when carbines bang
That are fired by men who must fight or hang.

On they came, with a thunderous shout
  That made the rocky-cañon ring:
("Cañon," in Spanish, means tube, or spout,
  Gorge, or hollow, or some such thing.)
On they come, with a thunderous noise;
Captain Davis said, calmly, "Boys,
I've been a-waiting to see them chaps;"
And with that he examined his pistol-caps;
Then a long, deep breath he drew,
Put in his cheek a tremendous chew,
Stripped off his waist-coat and coat, and threw
Them down, and was ready to die or do.

Had I Bryant's belligerent skill,
  Wouldn't I make this a bloody fight?
Or Alfred Tennyson's crimson quill,
  What thundering, blundering lines I'd write!
I'd batter, and hack, and cut, and stab,
And gouge, and throttle, and curse, and jab;
I'd wade to my ears in oaths and slaughter,
Pour out blood like brandy and water;
Hit 'em again if they asked for quarter,
  And clinch, and wrestle, and yell, and bite.
But I never could wield a carnivorous pen
Like either of those intellectual men;
I love a peaceful, pastoral scene,
With drowsy mountains, and meadows green,
Covered with daisies, grass, and clover,
  Mottled with Dorset or South-down sheep—
Better, than fields with a red turf over,
  And men piled up in a Waterloo heap.
But, notwithstanding, my fate cries out:
"Put Captain Davis in song and story!
That children hereafter may read about
  His deeds in the Rocky-Cañon foray!"

James McDonald, of Alabama
  Fell at the feet of Doctor Sparks;
Doctor," said he, "I 'm as dead as a hammer,
  And you have a couple of bullet marks.
This," he gasped, "is the end of life."
"Yes," said Sparks, "'t is a mighty solver;
Excuse me a moment—just hold my knife,
  And I'll hit that brigand with my Colt's revolver."

Then through the valley the contest rang,
Pistols rattle and carbines bang;

Horrible, terrible, frightful, dire
Flashed from the vapor the foot-pads' fire,
Frequent, as when in a sultry night
Twinkles a meadow with insect-light;
But deadlier far as the Doctor found,
  When, crack! a ball through his frontal bone
Laid him flat on his back on the hard-fought ground,
  And left Captain Davis to go it alone!

Oh! that Roger Bacon had died!
Or Schwartz, the monk, or whoever first tried
Cold iron to choke with a mortal load,
To see if saltpetre wouldn't explode.
For now, when you get up a scrimmage in rhyme,
The use of gunpowder so shortens the time,
That just as your Iliad should have begun,
Your epic gets smashed with a Paixhan gun;
And the hero for whom you are tuning the string
Is dead before 'arms and the man' you sing;
  To say nothing of how it will jar and shock
  Your verses with hammer, and rammer, and stock,
  Bullet and wad, trigger and lock,
  Nipple and cap, and pan and cock;
But wouldn't I like to spread a few pages
All over with arms of the middle ages?
Wouldn't I like to expatiate
On Captain Davis in chain or plate?--
  Spur to heel, and plume to crest,
  Visor barred, and lance in rest,
  Long, cross-hilted brand to wield,
  Cuirass, gauntlets, mace, and shield;
Cased in proof himself and horse,
From frontlet-spike to buckler-boss;

Harness glistering in the sun,
Plebeian foes, and twelve to one!
I tell you now there's a beautiful chance
To make a hero of old romance;
But I'm painting his picture for after-time,
And don't mean to sacrifice truth for rhyme.

Cease, Digression; the fray grows hot!
Never an instant stops the firing;
Two of the conical hats are shot,
And a velvet jacket is just expiring:
Never yields Captain Davis an inch,
For he didn't know how, if he wished, to flinch;
Firm he stands in the Rocky Gorge,
Moved as much by those vagrom men
As an anvil that stands by a blacksmith's forge
Is moved by the sledge-hammer's "ten-pound-ten!"
Firm, though his shirt, with jag and rag,
Resembles an army's storming-flag:
Firm, till sudden they give a shout,
Drop their shooters and clutch their knives;
When he said: "I reckon their powder's out,
And I've got three barrels, and that's three lives!

One! and the nearest steeple-crown
Stood aghast, as a minster spire
Stands, when the church below is on fire,
Then trembles, and totters, and tumbles down.
Don Pasquale the name he bore,
Near Lecco was reared his ancestral cot,
Close by Lago Como's shore,
For description of which, see "Claude Melnotte."

Two! and instantly drops, with a crash,
An antediluvial sort of moustache;
Such as hundreds of years had grown,
When scissors and razors were quite unknown.
He from that Tuscan city had come,
Where a tower is built all out of—plumb!
Puritani his name was hight—
A terrible fellow to pray or fight.

Three! and as if his head were cheese,
  Through Castadiva a bullet cut;
Knocked a hole in his os unguis,
  And bedded itself in the occiput.
Daily to mass his widow will go,
  In that beautiful city a lovely moaner,
Where those supernatural sausages grow,
  Which we mis-pronounce when we style "Bellona!"

As a crowd, that near a depot stands
  Impatiently waiting to take the cars,
Will "clear the track" when its iron bands
  The ponderous, fiery hippogriff jars,
Yet the moment it stops don't care a pin,
But hustle and bustle and go right in;
So the half of the band that still survives,
Comes up with long moustaches and knives,
Determined to mince the Captain to chowder,
So soon as it's known he is out of powder.

Six feet one, in trowsers and shirt,
Covered with sweat, and blood, and dirt;

Not very much scared (though his hat was hurt,
And as full of holes as a garden-squirt);
Awaiting the onslaught, behold him stand
With a twelve-inch "Bowie" in either hand.
His cause was right, and his arms were long,
His blades were bright, and his heart was strong;
All he asks of the trinketed clan
Is a bird's-eye view of the foremost man;
But shoulder to shoulder they come together,
Six sugar-loaf hats and twelve legs of leather:—
Fellows whose names you can't rehearse
Without instinctively clutching your purse:
  Badiali and Bottesini,
  Fierce Alboni and fat Dandini,
  Old Rubini and Mantillini,
  Cherubini and Paganini:
(But I had forgot the last were shot;
No matter, it don't hurt the tale a jot.)

Onward come the terrible crew!
  Waving their poignards high in air,
But little they dream that seldom grew
  Of human arms so long a pair
As the Captain had hanging beside him there,
  Matted, from shoulder to wrist, with hair;
  Brawny, and broad, and brown, and bare.

Crack! and his blade from point to heft
Has cloven a skull, as an egg is cleft;
And round he swings those terrible flails,
Heavy and swift, as a grist-mill sails;

Whack! and the loftiest conical crown
  Falls full length in the Rocky Valley;
Smack! and a duplicate Don goes down,
  As a ten-pin falls in a bowling-alley.

None remain but old Rubini,
Fierce Alboni, and fat Dandini:
Wary fellows, who take delight
In prolonging, as long as they can, a fight,
To show the science of cut and thrust,
  The politest method of taking life;
As some men love, when a bird is trussed,
  To exhibit their skill with a carving-knife:
But now with desperate hate and strength,
They cope with those arms of fearful length.

A scenic effect of skill and art,
A beautiful play of tierce and carte,
A fine exhibition it was, to teach
The science of keeping quite out of reach.
But they parry, and ward, and guard, and fend,
  And rally, and dodge, and slash, and shout,
In hopes that from mere fatigue in the end
  He either will have to give in or give out.

Never a Yankee was born or bred
Without that peculiar kink in his head
By which he could turn the smallest amount
Of whatever he had to the best account.
So while the banditti cavil and shrink,
It gives Captain Davis a chance TO THINK!
And the coupled ideas shot through his brain,
As shoots through a village an express-train;

And then! as swift as the lightning flight,
When the pile-driver falls from its fearful height,
He brings into play, by way of assister,
His dexter leg as a sort of ballista;
Smash! in the teeth of the nearest rogue,
He threw the whole force of his hob-nailed brogue!
And a horrible yell from the rocky chasm
  Rose in the air like a border slogan,
When old Rubini lay in a spasm,
  From the merciless kick of the iron brogan.

As some old Walton, with line and hook,
Will stand by the side of a mountain-brook,
Intent upon taking a creel of trout,
But finds so many poking about
Under the roots, and stones, and sedges,
In the middle, and near the edges,
Eager to bite, so soon as the hackle
Drops in the stream from his slender tackle,
And finally thinks it a weary sport,
To fish where trout are so easily caught;
So Captain Davis gets tired at last
Of fighting with those that drop down so fast,
And a tussle with only a couple of men
Seems poor kind of fun, after killing-off ten;
But just for the purpose of ending the play
He puts fierce Alboni first out of the way,
And then to show Signor Dandini his skill,
He splits him right up, as you'd split up a quill;
Then drops his Bowie, and rips his shirt
To bandage the wounds of the parties hurt;
An act, as good as a moral, to teach
"That none are out of humanity's reach,"

An act that might have produced good fruit,
Had the brigands survived, but they didn't do it.

Sixteen men do depose and say,
"That in December, the twentieth day,
They were standing close by when the fight occurred,
And are ready to swear to it, word for word,
That a bloodier scrimmage they never saw;
That the bodies were sot on, accordin' to law;
That the provocation and great excitement
Wouldn't justify them in a bill of indictment;
But this verdict they find against Captain Davis,
That if ever a brave man lived—he brave is."

CAPTAIN BELGRAVE.

I.

"My eyes make pictures when they are shut.

In one of those villages peculiar to our Eastern coast, whose long lines of pepper-and-salt stone-fences indicate laborious, if not profitable farming, and where the saline breath of the ocean has the effect of making fruit-trees more picturesque than productive, in a stone chunk of a house, whose aspect is quite as interesting to the geologist as to the architect, lives Captain Belgrave.

The Captain, as he says himself, "is American clean through, on the father's side, up to Plymouth Rock, and knows little, and cares less, of what is beyond that." To hear him talk, you would suppose Adam and Eve had landed there from the May Flower, and that the Garden of Eden was located within rifle distance of that celebrated land-mark. His genealogical table, however, stands upon unequal legs; for, on his mother's side he is part German and part Irishman. I mention this for the benefit of those who believe that certain qualities in men are hereditary. Of course it will be easy for them to assign those of Captain Belgrave to their proper source.

The house is square, and would not be remarkable but for a stone turret on one corner. This, rising from the ground some forty feet, embroidered with ivy, and pierced with arrow-slits, has rather a feudal look. It stands in a by-lane, apart from the congregated village. On the right side of the road is a plashy spring, somewhat redolent of mint in the summer. Opposite to this, in a clump of oaks, surrounded with a picket-fence, is the open porch, with broad wooden benches, and within is an ample hall, looking out upon well-cultivated fields, and beyond — blue water! This is the "Oakery," as Captain Belgrave calls it. Here he lives with his brother Adolphus—bachelors both.

His title is a mystery. There is a legend in the village, that during the last war Belgrave was enrolled in the militia on some frontier. One night he was pacing as sentinel on a long wooden piazza in front of the General's quarters. It was midnight; the camp was asleep, and the moon was just sinking behind a bank of clouds. Belgrave heard a footstep on the stairs at the foot of the piazza. "Who goes there?" No answer. Another step. "Who goes there?" he repeated, and his heart began to fail him. No answer—but another step. He cocked his musket. Step! step! step! and then between him and the sinking moon appeared an enormous head, decorated with diabolical horns. Belgrave drew a long breath and fired. The next instant the spectre was upon him; he was knocked down; the drums beat to arms; the guard turned out, and found the sentinel stretched upon the floor, with an old he-goat, full of defiance and odor, standing on him. From that time he was called "Captain."

No place, though it be a paradise, is perfect without one of the gentler sex. There is a lady at the Oakery. Miss Augusta Belgrave is a maiden of about—let me see; her age was formerly inscribed on the fly-leaf of the family Bible between the Old and New Testaments; but the page was torn out, and now it is somewhere in the Apocrypha. No matter what her age may be; if you were to see her, you would say she was safe over the breakers. Two unmarried brothers, with a spinster sister, living alone: it is not infrequent in old families. The rest of the household may be embraced in Hannah, the help, who is also "a maiden all forlorn," and Jim, the stable-boy. Jim is a unit, as well as the rest. Jim has been a stable-boy all his life, and now, at the age of sixty, is only a boy ripened. His chief pride and glory is to drive a pair of bob-tailed bay trotters that are (traditionally) fast! Adolphus, who has a turn for literature, christened the off-horse "Spectator;" but the near horse came from a bankrupt wine-broker, who named him "Chateau Margaux." This the Captain reduced to "Shatto," and the village people corrupted to "Shatter."

There was something bold and jaunty in the way the Captain used to drive old Shatter on a dog-trot through the village (Spectator rarely went with his mate except to church on Sundays), with squared elbows, and whip depending at a just angle over the dash-board. "Talk of your fast horses!" he would say. "Why, if I would only let *him* out," pointing his whip, like a marshal's baton, toward Shatter, "you would see *time!*" But he never lets him out.

The square turret rises considerably above the

house roof. Every night, at bed-time, the villagers see a light shining through its narrow loop-holes. There are loop-holes in the room below, and strong casements of ordinary size in the rooms adjoining. In the one next to the tower Miss Augusta sleeps, as all the village knows, for she is seen at times looking out of the window. Next to that is another room, in which Adolphus sleeps. He is often seen looking out of that window. Next, again, to that is the vestal chamber of Hannah, on the south-west corner of the house. She is sometimes seen looking out of the window on either side. Next to that again is the dormitory of Jim, the stable-boy. Jim always smells like a menagerie, and so does his room, no doubt. He never looks out of his window except upon the Fourth of July, when there is too much noise in the village to risk driving Spec and Shat. No living person but the occupants has ever been in that story of the house. No living person understands the mystery of the tower. The light appears at night through the loop-holes in the second story, then flashes upward, shines again through the slits in the lofty part of the turret, burns steadily half an hour or so, and then vanishes. Who occupies that lonely turret?

Let us take the author-privilege and ascend the stairs. First we come to Jim's room; *we pass through that* into Hannah's apartment. There is a bolt on the inside of her door; we pass on into the room of Adolphus; it, too, has a bolt on the inside. Now all the virtues guide and protect us, for we are in the sleeping-apartment of the spinster sister! It, too, has a bolt on the inside; and here we are in the tower: the door, like the rest, is bolted. There is nothing in the room but the carpet on the floor; no stair-case, but a trap-door in the ceiling. It is but a short flight for fancy to reach the upper story. The trap is bolted in the floor; there is a ladder standing beside it; here are chairs, a bureau, a table, with an extinguished candle, and the moonlight falls in a narrow strip across the features of Captain Belgrave, fast asleep, and beside him a Bible, and an enormous horse-pistol, loaded.

Nowhere but in the household of some old bachelor could such discipline exist as in the Oakery. At night the Captain is the first to retire; Miss Augusta follows with a pair of candle-sticks and candles; then metaphysical Adolphus with his mind in a painful state of fermentation;

then Hannah, the help, with a small brass candlestick; then Jim, the stable-boy, who usually waits until the company is on the top-stair, when he makes a false start, breaks, pulls himself up, and gets into a square trot just in time to save being distanced at the landing. Adolphus and Jim are not trusted with candles. Miss Augusta is rigorous on that point. She permits the Captain to have one because he is careful with it; besides he owns the house and everything in it; the land and everything on it; and supports the family; therefore his sister indulges him. We now understand the internal arrangement of the Oakery. It is a fort, a castle, a citadel, of which Augusta is the scarp, Jim the glacis, Hannah the counter-scarp, and Adolphus the ditch. The Captain studied the science of fortification after his return from the wars.

The Belgraves are intimate with only one family in the village, and they are new acquaintances—the Mewkers. There is Mr. Mewker, Mrs. Mewker, Mrs. Lasciver, formerly Miss Mewker, and six or seven little Mewkers. Mewker has the reputation of being a good man, but unfortunately his appearance is not prepossessing. He has large bunchy feet, with very ineffectual legs, low shoulders, a sunken chest, a hollow cavity under the waistcoat, little, weak eyes that seem set in bladders, straggling hair, rusty whiskers, black, and yellow teeth, and long, skinny, disagreeable fingers; beside, he is knock-kneed, shuffling in gait, and always leans on one side when he walks. Uncharitable people say he leans on the side where his interests lie, but Captain Belgrave will not believe a word of it. Oh! no; Mewker is a different man from that. He is a member of the church, and sings in the choir. He is executor of several estates, and of course takes care of the orphans and widows. He holds the church money in trust, and of course handles it solely to promote *its* interests. And then he is so deferential, so polite, so charitable. "Never," says the Captain, "did I hear him speak ill of anybody, but he lets me into the worst points of my neighbors by jest teching on 'em, and then he excuses their fibles, as if he was a kind o' sorry for 'em; but I keeps my eye onto 'em after the hints he give me, and he can't blind me to *them.*"

Harriet Lasciver, formerly Miss Mewker, is a widow, perfectly delicious in dimples and dimity, fond of high life and low-necked dresses, music, birds, and camelias. Captain Belgrave has a great fancy for the charming widow. This is a secret, however. You and I know it, *and so does Mewker.*

II.

It is Sunday in Little-Crampton—a summer Sunday. The old-fashioned flowers are blooming in the old-fashioned gardens, and the last vibration of the old rusty bell in the century-old belfry seems dying off, and melting away in fragrance. Outside, the village is quiet, but within the church there is an incessant plying of fans and rustling of dresses. The Belgraves are landed at the porch, and Spec and Shat whirl the family carriage into the grave-yard. The Mewkers enter with due decorum. Adolphus drops his hymn-book into the pew in front, as he always does. The little flatulent organ works through the voluntary. The sleek head of the Rev. Mr. Spat is projected toward the audience out of the folds of his cambric handkerchief; and after doing as much damage to the simple and beautiful service as he can by reading it, flourishes through the regular old Spatsonian sermon; its tiresome repetitions and plagiarisms, with the same old rising and falling inflections, the same old tremulous tone toward the end, as if he were crying; the same old recuperative method by which he recovers his lost voice in the last sentence, when it was all but gone; and the same old gesture by which the audience understand that his labors (and theirs) are over for the morning. Then the congregation departs with the usual accompaniments of dresses rustling, and pew-doors slamming; and Mr. Mewker descends from the choir and sidles up the aisle, nursing his knobs of elbows in his skinny fingers, and congratulates the Rev. Mr. Spat upon the excellent discourse he had delivered, and receives the customary *quid pro quo* in the shape of a compliment upon the excellent singing in the choir. This account adjusted, Mr. Mewker shuffles home beside the lovely widow; and Mrs. Mewker and the small fry of members follow in their wake.

"I have looked into the records in the county clerk's office," Mewker says in a whisper, to his sister, "and the property is all right. That old Thing, (unconscious Augusta Belgrave, rolling home behind Spec and Shat, do you hear this?)

that old Thing, and that old fool of a book-worm (Adolphus) can be packed off after the wedding, and then we can arrange matters between us. Spat understands me in this, and intends to be hand and glove with Belgrave, so as to work upon him. He will, he *must* do it, for he knows that his remaining in this church depends upon me." Here Mr. Mewker was interrupted by one of the young Mewkers, who came running up, hat in hand. "Oh! pa, look there! see those beautiful climbing roses growing all over that old tree!" "Jacob," said Mewker, catching him by the hair, and rapping his head with his bony knuckles until the tears came, "haven't I told you not to speak of such trivial things on the Sabbath? How dare you (with a repetition of raps) think of climbing roses so soon after church? Go (with a fresh clutch in the scalp of Mewker, Junior), go to your mother, and when I get home I will punish you." Mr. Mewker resumed the whispered conversation. "Belgrave is ruled entirely by his sister, but between Spat and me, she can be blinded, I think. If she should suspect, now, she would interfere, of course, and Belgrave would not dare to disobey her. But if we can get him committed once in some way, he is such a coward that he would be entirely in my power. Dear," he said aloud to Mrs. M., "how did you like the sermon?" Angelic," replies Mrs. Mewker. "That's my opinion, too," responds Mewker. "Angelic, angelic. Spat is a lovely man, my dear. What is there for dinner?"

If there were some feminine meter by which Harriet Lasciver's soul could be measured, it would indicate "good" pretty high up on the scale. Yet she had listened to this after-church discourse of her brother not only with complacency, but with a full and unequivocal assent to all he had proposed. So she would have listened, so assented to anything, no matter what, proposed by him; and all things considered, it was not surprising. Even as continued attrition wears the angles of the flint until it is moulded into the perfect pebbles, so had her nature been moulded by her brother. He had bullied her in her childhood and in her womanhood, except when there was a purpose in view which he could better accomplish by fawning; and her natural good disposition, so indurated by these opposed modes of treatment, had become as insensible to finer emotions as her heart was callous to its own impulses. There was one element in his composition which at times had cast a gloss upon his actions. It was his piety! God help us! that any one should allude to that but with reverence and love! Nor do I here speak of it but as a profession, an art, or specious showing forth of something that was not real, but *professed*, in order to accomplish other ends. What profited her own experience, when Harriet Lasciver was so far imposed upon as to believe her brother's professions sincere? What though all his life he had been a crooked contriver and plotter, malicious in his enmity, and false in his friendship; *and she knew it?* Yet, as she could not reconcile it with his affected sanctity, she could not believe it. That wonderful power which men seldom, and women never analyze—hypocrisy, held her entangled in its meshes, and she was his instrument to be guided as he chose. Every noble trait true woman possesses—pity, tenderness, love, and high honor—were commanded by an influence she could not resist. Her reason, nay, her feelings were dormant, but her faith slept securely upon her brother's religion!

In this instance there was another consideration

—a minor one, it is true, but in justice to the widow, it must be added. She really admired the Captain; but that makes no great difference. A widow must love somebody. Those delicate tendrils of affection which put forth with the experiences of the young wife, die not in the widow, but survive, and must have some support. Even if the object be unworthy or unsightly, as it happens sometimes, still will they bind, and bloom, and cling, and blossom around it, like honeysuckles around a pump.

III.

The windows at the Oakery are open, and the warm air of a Sunday summer evening pours in, as Augusta pours out the tea. The Captain burns his mouth with the first cup, turns the tea into the saucer, blows it to cool it, drinks it off hastily, takes a snap at the thin, white slice of bread on his plate, takes another snap at a radish somewhat overcharged with salt, wipes his mouth, goes to the window and calls out "Jim!" Jim appears at the stable-door with a wisp of straw and a curry-comb. "Put in the hosses!" Jim telegraphs with the curry-comb, "All right, Sir!" Augusta stares at Adolphus, and Adolphus brushes the metaphysical films from his eyes, and, for once, seems wide awake. The Captain takes his seat and a fresh snap at the bread. Augusta looks at him steadily. "Why, brother, where are you going with the horses on Sunday afternoon?" The Captain squints at the bread, and answers, "To Mewker's." "Mewker's!" repeats Augusta; "Mewker's! why, brother, you're crazy; they never receive company on Sunday. You know how strictly pious Mr. Mewker is, and he would look at you with amazement. To see you riding, too! why—I—never!"

The Captain, however, said nothing, but waited, with some impatience, until Spec and Shat turned out with the carriage from the stable. Then he took the ribbons, stopped, threw them down, went up into the tower, came back with a clean shirt on, climbed into the seat, and drove off.

"He'll come back from there in a hurry, I guess," said Augusta to the wondering Adolphus.

But the Captain did not return until eleven that night, and then somewhat elevated with wine. "Augushta," said he, as the procession formed as usual on the stairs, "that Mucous 'sha clever feller, heesha clever feller, heesha dev'lish clever feller; heesh fond of talking on church matters, and sho 'mi. His shister, sheesha another clever feller, she's a chump! I asked 'em to come to-morrow to tea, and shaid they would."

"Why, brother, to-morrow is Monday, washing-day!" replied the astonished spinster.

"Tha 's a fac, Gushta, fae," answered the Captain, as he took the candle from his sister at the tower-door; "but, wash or no wash, musht come. When I ask 'em to come, musht come. Goo-ni!"

The bolts are closed on the several doors, scarp and counterscarp, ditch and glacis are wrapped in slumber; but the Captain lies wide awake, looking through the slits in the tower casement at the Great Bear in the sky, and thinking rapturously of the lovely Lasciver.

Never did the old family carriage have such a polishing as on that Monday morning. Never did Jim so bestir himself with the harness as on that day under the eye of Belgrave. The Captain neglects to take his accustomed ride to the village in the morning, that Spec and Shat may be in condition for the afternoon. At last the carriage rolls down the road from the Oakery, with Jim on the box, and the Captain retires to dress for company. In due course the carriage returns with Spec and Shat somewhat blown with an over-load; for all the young Mewkers are piled up inside, on the laps of Mrs. Mewker and the lovely Lasciver. Then Augusta hurries into the kitchen to tell Hannah, the help, to cut more bread for the brats; and Adolphus is hurried out into the garden to pull more radishes; and the young Mewker tribe get into his little library, and revel in his choice books, and quarrel over them, and scatter some leaves and covers on the floor as trophies of the fight. Then the tea is brought on, and the lovely Lasciver tries in vain to soften the asperity of Augusta; and then Mewker takes her in hand, and does succeed, and in a remarkable degree, too. Meanwhile the ciphers of the party, Mrs. Mewker and Adolphus, drink and eat in silence. Then they adjourn to the porch, and Mewker sits beside Augusta, and entertains her with an account of the missions in Surinam, to which she turns an attentive ear. Then Mrs. Mewker says it is time to go, "on account of the children," at which Mewker darts a petrifying look at her, and turns with a smile to Augusta, who, in the honesty of her heart, says "she, too, thinks it *is* best for the young ones to go to bed early. Then Jim is summoned from the stable, and Spec and Shat; and the Mewkers take leave, and whirl along the road again toward home.

It was long before the horses returned, for Jim drove back slowly. There was not a tenderer heart in the world than the one which beat in the bosom of that small old boy of sixty. He sat perched upon the box, calling out, "Gently, soho!" to Spec and Shat, when they advanced beyond a walk, and held a talk with himself in this wise: "I don't want to carry that old carcase agin. He gits in and praises up the Cap'n so as *I* can hear him, and then asks me if I won't lay the whip on the hosses. Says I, 'Mr. Mewker, them hosses has been druv.' Says he, 'Yes, James, but you can give 'em a good rubbin' down when you get to hum, and that will fetch 'em all right.' Now, I want to know if you take a man, and lay a whip onto him, and make him travel till he's sore, whether rubbin' down is a-goin' to make him all right? No, Sir. Then he calls me James. I don't want no man to call me James; my name's Jim. There was old Midgely; he called me James; didn't he coax out of me all I'd saved up for more'n twenty years, and then busted? There was Deacon Cotton; didn't he come in over the Captain with that pork? He called me James, too. And there was that psalm-singin' pedlar that got Miss Augusty to lend him the colt; *he* called me James. Did he bring the colt back? No, Sir; at least not yit, and it's more'n three years ago. When a man calls me James, I take my eye and places it onto him. I hearn him when he tells Miss Mewker not to give beggars nothin'. *I* hearn him. He sez they may be impostors! Well, 'spose they be? When a feller-creetur' gits so low as to beg, haven't they got low enough? Aint they ragged, dirty, despised? Don't they run a chance of starvin', impostors or not, if every body drives 'em off? And what great matter is it if they do get a-head of you, for a crumb or a cent? When I see a feller-creatur' in rags, beggin', I say human natur' has got low enough; it's in rags! it begs! it's 'way down, and it don't make much difference if it's actin' or not. Them aint impostors that will do much harm. Them aint impostors like old Midgely, and Deacon Cotton, and that old psalm-singin' pedlar that borrowed the colt; at least they don't cut it so fat. But 'spose they don't happen to be impostors, arter all? Whar's that account to be squared? I guess I'd raythe be the beggar than the other man when that account is squared. I guess when that account is squared, it will kind a-look as if the impostor wasn't the one that asked for the stale bread, but the one that wouldn't give it. Seems as if I've heard 'em tell about a similar case somewhere."

A good rubbing down, indeed, for Spec and Shat that night, and a well-filled manger too. When Jim picked up his stable-lantern, he gave each horse a pat on the head, and a parting hug, and then backed out, with his eyes still on them. "Spec!" said he at the door. Spec gave a whinny in reply. "Shat!" Shat responded also. "Good-night, old boys! Old Jim aint a-goin' to lay no whip onto you. If old Jim wants to lay a whip onto something, it won't be onto you, that's been spavined and had the bots, and he's cured 'em, and they know it, hey! No, Sir. His 'tipathy works outside into another quarter. Is my name James? Well, it aint. It's Jim, isn't it? Yes, Sir!"

IV.

From that night, however, the halcyon days of Spec and Shat were at an end. The Mewkers loved to ride, but they had no horses: the only living thing standing upon four legs belonging to Mr. Mewker was an ugly, half-starved, cross-grained, suspicious looking dog, that had the mange and a bad reputation. Of course, the Captain's horses were at their service, for rides to the beach, for pic-nics in the woods, for shopping in the village, or, perchance, to take Mr. Mewker to some distant church-meeting. And not only were the horses absent at unusual times; there seemed to be a growing fondness in the Captain for late hours. The old-style regularity of the Oakery, the time-honored habits of early hours to bed, the usual procession up the stairs, formal but cheerful, were, in some measure, broken into; not but what these were observed as formerly; not but what every member of the family waited and watched until the Captain returned, no matter how late; but that sympathetic feeling which all had felt when the hour of bed-time came, had ceased to be, and in its place was the dreary languor, the tiresome, tedious feeling that those experience who sit up and wait and wait, for an absent one, waiting and asking, " Why tarry the wheels of his chariot?" There was an increasing presentiment, a gloomy foreshadowing of evil, in Miss Augusta's mind at those doings of the Captain: and this feeling was heightened by something, trifling in itself, yet still mysterious and unaccountable. Somebody, almost every day, cut off a tolerably large piece from the beef or mutton, or whatever kind of meat there chanced to be in the cellar. And nobody knew anything about it. Hannah was fidelity itself; Jim was beyond suspicion; Adolphus never went into the cellar, scarcely out of the library, in fact. The Captain! could it be her brother? Miss Augusta watched. *She saw him do it!* She saw him covertly draw his jack-knife from his pocket, and purloin a piece of beautiful rump-steak, then wrap it in paper, put it in his pocket, and walk off whistling, as if nothing had happened. "The widow is at the bottom of this!" was the thought that flashed through the mind of Augusta. She was indirectly correct. The widow was at the bottom of the theft, and I will tell you how. I have mentioned a large mangy dog, of disreputable character, Mr. Mewker's property, and "Bose" by name. Whenever the Captain drove up the path to the house of his friend, there, beside the step of the wagon, from the time it passed the gate until it reached the porch, was this dog, with a tail short as pie-crust, that never wagged; thick, wicked eyes, and a face that did not suggest fidelity and sagacity, but treachery and rapine, dead sheep, and larceny great or small. And although the Captain was a stout, active, well-framed man, with a rosy cheek, a bright eye, and a sprightly head of hair, yet he was afraid of that dog. And therefore the Captain, to conciliate Bose, brought him every day some choice morsel from his own kitchen; and as he did not dare to tell Augusta, the same was abstracted in the manner already described.

Here I must mention a peculiarity in Captain Belgrave's character. He never saw a dog without thinking of hydrophobia; he never bathed on the beautiful beach in the rear of his house without imagining every chip in the water, or ripple on the wave, to be the dorsal fin of some voracious shark. When he drove home at night, it was with fear and trembling, for an assassin might be lurking in the bushes; and if he passed a sick neighbor, he walked off with small-pox, measles, typhoid, and whooping-cough trundling at his heels. In a word, he was the most consummate coward in Little-Crampton. It was for this reason he had built and slept in the tower; and what with reading of pirates, buccaneers, Captain Kidd, and Black Beard, his mind was so infected that no sleeping-place seemed secure and safe, but his own turret and trap-door, scarp, counter-scarp, ditch, and glacis, through which all invaders had to pass before they encountered him with his tremendous horse-pistol.

It was not the discovery of the theft alone that had opened the eyes of Augusta in regard to her brother's motions. Although he had told her, again and again, that he merely went to Mewker's to talk over church matters, yet she knew intuitively, as every woman would, that, a widow so lovely as Harriet Lasciver could not but have great attractions for such an old bachelor as her brother. In fact, she knew, if the widow, as the phrase is, "set her cap for him," the Captain was a lost man. But to whom could she apply for counsel and assistance? Adolphus? Adolphus had no more sense than a kitten. Hannah? There was something of the grand old spinster-spirit about Augusta that would not bend to the level of Hannah, the help. Jim? She would go to Jim. She would see that small boy of sixty, and ask his advice. And she did. She walked over to the stable in the evening, while her brother was making his toilet for the customary visit to the Mewkery, and without beating around the bush at all, reached the point at once. "Jim," said she, "the Captain is getting too thick with the Mewkers, and we must put a stop to it, How is that to be done?"

Jim paused for a moment, and then held up his forefinger. "I know *one* way to stop him a-goin' there; and, if you say so, Miss Augusta, then old Jim is the boy to do it."

Augusta assented in a grand, old, towering nod. Jim, with a mere motion of his forefinger, seemed to reiterate, "If you say so, I'll do it."

"Yes."

"Then, by Golly!" responded Jim, joyfully, "arter this night he'll never go there ag'in."

Augusta walked toward the house with a smile, and Jim proceeded to embellish Shatter.

By-and-by the Captain drove off in the wagon, and old Jim busied himself with Spectator, fitting a mouldy saddle on his back, and getting him ready for action.

V.

There was a thin cloud, like lace, over the moon that night; just enough to make objects painfully distinct, as Captain Belgrave turned out from Mewker's gate, and took the high road toward home. He jogged along, however, quite comfortably, and had just reached the end of Mewker's fence, when he saw a figure on horseback, emerging from the little lane that ran down, behind the garden, to the pond at the back of the house. The apparition had a sort of red cape around its shoulders; a soldier-cap, with a tall plume (very like the one the Captain used to wear on parade), was upon its head; in its hand was a long, formidable-looking staff; and the horse of the spectre was enveloped in a white saddle-cloth, that hung down almost to the ground. What was remarkable, Old Shatter, as if possessed with the devil, actually drew out of the road toward the stranger, and gave a whinny, which was instantly responded to in the most frightful tones by the horse of the spectre. Almost paralyzed, the Captain suffered the apparition to approach him. What a face it had! Long masses of hair, like tow, waved around features that seemed to have neither shape nor color. Its face seemed like a face of brown paper, so formless and flat was it, with great hideous eyes and a mouth of intolerable width. As it approached, the figure seemed to have a convulsion—it rolled so in the saddle; but, recovering, it drew up beside the shaft, and, whirling its long staff, brought such a whack upon Shatter's flank, that the old horse almost jumped out of his harness. Away went the wagon and the Captain, and away went the spectre close behind; fences, trees, bushes, dust, whirled in and out of sight; bridges, sedges, trout-brooks, mills, willows, copses, plains, in moonlight and shadow, rolled on and on; but not an inch was lost or won; there, behind the wagon, was the goblin with his long plume bending, and waving, and dancing, and his staff whirling with terrible menaces. On, and on, and on, and ever and anon the goblin steed gave one of those frightful whinnies that seemed to tear the very air with its dissonance. On, and on, and on! The Captain drove with his head turned back over his shoulder, but Shat knew the road. On, and on, and on! A thought flashes like inspiration through the mind of the Captain, "The horse-pistol!" It is under the cushions. He seizes it nervously, cocks it, and—bang! goes the plume of the goblin. "By gosh!" said a voice under the soldier-cap, "I didn't cal'late on that;" and then, "I vum ef old Shat hain't run away!" Sure enough, Shatto has run away; the wagon is out of sight in a turn of the road; the next instant, it brings up against a post; off goes Shat, with shafts and dislocated fore-wheels; and old Jim soon after finds the remains of the wagon, and the senseless body of his master, in a ditch, under the moon, and a willow. To take the red blanket from his shoulders, which he had worn like a Mexican poncho by putting his head through a hole in the middle, is done in an instant; and then, with big tears rolling down his cheeks, the old boy brings water from a spring, in the crown of the soldier-cap, to bathe the face of the Captain. The report of the pistol has alarmed a neighbor; and the two, with the assistance of the hind wheels and the body of the wagon, carry poor Belgrave through the moonlit streets of Little-Crampton, to the Oakery.

When the Captain opened his eye (for the other was under the tuition of a large patch of brown paper, steeped in vinegar), he found himself safe at home, surrounded and fortified, as usual, by Augusta, Adolphus, Hannah, the help, and Jim, in picturesque attitudes. How he came there, was a mystery. Stay; he begins to take up the thread: Mewkers, fence, the figure, the race for life, and the pistol! What else? Nothing—blank—oblivion. So he falls into a tranquil state of comfort, and feels that he does not care about it. No getting up that steep ladder to-night! Never mind. It is a labor to think, so he relapses into thoughtlessness, and finally falls asleep. There was a stranger in the room behind the bed's head, a tall, astringent-looking man, Dr. Butternuts, by whom the Captain had been let blood. If Belgrave had seen him, he would have fainted. "No injuries of any consequence," says the doctor, departing and waving his brown hand. "Terribly skart, though," Augusta responds, in a whisper. "Yes, he will get over that; to-morrow he will be better;" and the doctor waves himself out. Adolphus retires, and then Hannah, the help; but Augusta and Jim watch by the bedside until morning. The Captain, every now and then, among the snowy sheets and coverlet, turns up a side of face that looks like a large, purple egg-plant, at which Jim sighs heavily; but Augusta whispers soothingly, "Never mind, Jim, it's for his good; I'm glad you skart him; you skart him a leetle too much this time, that's all; next time you'll be more careful, won't you, and not skear him so bad?"

That Captain Belgrave had been thrown from his wagon, and badly hurt, was known all over Little-Crampton, next morning. Some said he had been shot at by a highwayman; some said he had shot a highwayman. The story took a hundred shapes, and finally was rolled up at the door of the Rev. Melchior Spat, who at once took his wagon, and drove off to the Mewkery. There the rumor was unfolded to Mr. Mewker, who, enjoying it immensely, made so many funny remarks thereon, that the Rev. Melchior Spat was convulsed with laughter, and then the two drove down to the Oakery to condole with the sufferer. On the way there, the Rev. Melchior was so wonderfully facetious, that Mewker, who never enjoyed any person's jokes but his own, was actually stimulated into mirth, and had it not been for happily catching a distant sight of the tower, would have so forgotten himself as to drive up to the door with a pleasant expression of countenance. As it was, they both entered grave as owls, and inquired, in faint and broken voices, how the Captain was, and whether he was able to see friends. Augusta, who received them, led them up to the room, where the Captain, with his face like the globe in the equinox, sitting propped up in bed, shook both feebly by the hand, and then the Rev. Melchior proposed prayer, to which Mewker promptly responded by dropping on his knees, and burying his face in the bottom of an easy chair. This was a signal for Adolphus to do likewise; and the Captain, not to be behind, struggling up into a sitting posture, leaned forward in the middle of the coverlet, with his toes and the end of his shirt deployed upon the pillows. Then the Rev. Melchior, in a crying voice, proceeded according to the homœopathic practice—that is, making it short and sweet as possible—touched upon the excellent qualities of the sufferer, the distress of his beloved friends, and especially of the anxiety which would be awakened in the bosom of one now absent, "whose heart was only the heart of a woman, a heart not strong and able to bear up against calamity, but weak, and fragile, and loving, and pitiful, and ten der; a heart that was so weak, and loving, and pitiful, and tender, and fragile, that it could not bear up against calamity; no, it could not; no, it could not; it was weak, it was pitiful, it was loving, it was tender, it was fragile like a flower, and against calamity it could not bear up."

So great was the effect of the Rev. Melchior Spat's eloquence, that the Captain fairly cried, so as to leave a round wet spot in the middle of the coverlet, and Mr. Mewker wiped his eyes frequently with his handkerchief, as he rose from the chair. And although the voice of the Reverend Melchior had been heard distinctly, word for word, by Jim, in the far-off stable, yet it sank to the faintest whisper when he proceeded to inquire of the Captain how he felt, and what was this dread ful story. And then the Captain, in a voice still fainter, told how he was attacked by a man of immense size, mounted on a horse of proportionate dimensions, and how he had defended himself, and did battle bravely until, in the fight, "Shatto got skeared, and overset the wagon, and then the man got onto him, and pounded the life out of him, while he was entangled with reins." Then Mr. Mewker and the Rev. Mr. Spat took leave with sorrowful faces, and as they drove home again, renewed the jocularity which had been interrupted somewhat by the visit to the Oakery.

To say that Mr. Mewker neglected his friend, the Captain, during his misfortunes, would be doing a great injustice to that excellent man. Every day he was at the Oakery, to inquire after his health; and rarely did he come without some little present, a pot of sweetmeats, a bouquet, or something of the kind, from the lovely Lasciver. How good it was of him to buy jelly at two shillings a pound at the store, and bring it to the Captain, saying, "This little offering is from Harriet, who thought some delicacy of the kind would be good for you." Was it not disinterested? Hiding his own modest virtues in a pot of jelly, and presenting it in the name of another! The truth is, Mewker's superior tactics were too profound for Augusta to contend against; she felt, as it were, the sand sliding from under her feet. Nor was Mewker without a powerful auxiliary in the Reverend Melchior Spat, who, by his prerogative, had free access to the house at all times, and made the most of it, too. Skillfully turning to common topics when Augusta was present, and as skillfully returning to the old subject when she retired, he animated the Captain with such desire for the lovely widow, that, had it not been for his black eye, he would assuredly have gone off and proposed on the spot. This feeling, however, subsided when the Rev. Melchior was gone; the Captain did not think of marrying; he was a true old bachelor, contented with his lot, and not disposed to change it even for a better; besides, he was timid.

VI.

At last our hero was able once more to go about, and Jim drove him down slowly to the Mewkery. Such a noise as Bose made when he saw the carriage approaching! But there was no present from the hand of his friend this time; so Bose contented himself with growling and snapping angrily at his own tail, which was not longer than half a cucumber. What a blush spread over the face of the Captain when he saw the widow, all dimples and dimity, advancing to meet him in the familiar back-parlor! How the sweet roses breathed through the shaded blinds as he breathed out his thanks to the widow for many precious favors during his confinement. They were alone; the Captain sat beside her on the sofa; one of her round, plump, white, dimpled hands was not far from him, resting upon the black hair-cloth of the sofa bottom. He looked right and left; there was no one near; so he took the hand respectfully, and raised it to his lips, intending to replace it of course. To his dismay, she uttered a tender "O!' and leaned her head upon his shoulder. What to do, he did not know; but he put his arm around her bewitching waist, to support her. Her eyes were closed, and the long, radiant lashes heightened, by contrast, the delicious color that bloomed in her cheeks. The Captain looked right and left again; no one was near; if he could venture to kiss her? He had never kissed a pretty woman in all his life! The desire to do so increased; it seemed to grow upon him; in fact, drawn toward her by an influence he could not resist, he leaned over and touched those beautiful lips, and then—in walked Mr. Mewker.

Had Mewker not been a genius, he might have compromised everything by still playing the humble, deferential, conscientious part; but hypocrisy on a low key was not his cue now; he knew his man too well for that, and besides, familiar as this branch of art had been, there was another still more natural to him; he was wonderful in the sycophant, but matchless in the bully! Those little, weak, bladdery eyes seemed almost to distil venom, as, wrapping his knobby arms in a knot, he strode up to the astonished Belgrave, and asked him "how he dared invade the privacy of his house, the home of his wife and children, and the sanctuary of his sister? How he dared trespass upon the hospitality that had been extended toward, nay, that had been lavished upon him? Was not the respectability of the Mewker family, a family related to the wealthy Balgangles of Little-Crampton, and connected by marriage with the Shellbarques of Boston, a sufficient protection against his nefarious designs? And did he undertake, under the mask of friendship," and Mewker drew up his forehead into a complication of lines like an indignant web, "to come, as a hypocrite, a member of the church (O Mewker!) with the covert intention of destroying the peace and happiness of his only sister?"

Belgrave was a man who never swore; but on this occasion he uttered an exclamation: "My grief!" said he, "I never had no such idee."

"What, then, are your intentions?" said Mewker, fiercely.

"T' make it all straight," replied the Captain.

"How?"

Belgrave paused, and Mewker shuffled rapidly to and fro, muttering to himself. At last he broke out again:

"How, I say?"

"On that p'int I'm codjitatin'."

"Do—you—mean—" said Mewker, with a remarkable smile, placing his hand calmly on the Captain's shoulder, "to—trifle—with—me?"

"No," replied poor Belgrave, surrendering up, as it were, what was left of him; "I'm ready to be married, if that will make it all straight, provided," he added, with natural courtesy, turning to the lovely widow, "provided this lady does not think me unworthy of her."

Mewker drew forth a tolerably clean handkerchief, and applied it to his eyes: a white handkerchief held to the eyes of a figure in threadbare black is very effective. The lovely Lasciver remained entirely passive; such is discipline.

Here, at last, was an opportunity to beat a retreat. The Captain rose, and shaking Mewker's unemployed hand, which, he said afterwards, "felt like a bunch of radishes," left the room without so much as a word to the future Mrs. Belgrave. So soon as the door closed upon him, Mr. Mewker raised his eyes from the handkerchief, and smiled sweetly upon his sister. The thing is accomplished.

As some old bear, who had enjoyed freedom from cubhood, feels, at the bottom of a pit dug by the skillful hunter, so feels Captain Belgrave, as he rides home sorrowfully. His citadel, after all, is not a protection. Into its penetralia a subtle spirit has at last found entrance. The air grows closer and heavier around him, the shadows broader, the bridges less secure, the trout-brooks blacker and deeper. How shall he break the matter to Augusta? "No hurry, though; the *day* hasn't been app'inted yit;" and at this suggestion the clouds begin to break and lighten. Then he sees Mewker, threadbare and vindictive; his sky again is overcast, but filaments of light stream through as he conjures up the image of the lovely widow, the dimpled hand, the closed eyes, the long radiate lashes, cheeks, lips, and the temptation which had so unexpected a conclusion. Home at last; and, with some complaint of fatigue, the Captain retires, to his high tower to ruminate over the past and the future.

The future! yes, the future! A long perspective stretched before his eyes; and, at the end of the vista, was a bride in white, and a wedding. It would take some months to gradually break the subject to his sister. Then temperately and moderately, the courtship would go on, year by year, waxing by degrees to the end.

VII.

Mr. Mewker altered the focus of Belgrave's optics next morning, by a short note, in which he himself fixed the wedding-day at two weeks from the Captain's declarations of intentions. This intelligence confined the Captain two days in the tower, "codjitating," during which time everybody in Little-Crampton was informed that Widow Lasciver and he were engaged to be married. The news came from the best authority—the Rev. Melchior Spat. On the evening of the second day, a pair of lead-colored stockings, a fustian petticoat, a drab short gown, and a bright bünch of keys, descended the steep step-ladder from the trap in the tower, and walked into the room adjoining. Then two hands commenced wringing themselves, by which we may understand that Augusta was in great tribulation. The rumor, rife in Little-Crampton, had reached her ears, and her brother had confirmed its truth. The very means employed to keep him out of danger had only assisted the other party to carry him off. This should be a warning to those who interfere with affairs of the heart. But what was her own future? Certainly her reign was at an end; a new queen-bee was to take possession of the hive; and then — what then? kings and kaisers, even, are not free from the exquisite anguish which, in that hour, oppressed the heart of Augusta Belgrave. It was but a step; but what a step? from mistress to menial, from ruler to subordinate. She knelt down heavily by the bedside, and there prayed; but oh! the goodness of woman's heart!—it was a prayer, earnest, sincere, truthful and humble; not for herself, but for her brothers. Then her heart was lightened and strengthened; and as she rose, she smiled with a bitter sweetness, that, considering everything, was beautiful.

Great preparations now in Little-Crampton for

the weding. Invitations were out, and needles, scissors, flowers, laces, ribbons, and mantua-makers, at a premium. The Captain took heart of grace, and called upon his lovely bride, but always managed to get past *that lane* before night-fall. Hood & Wessup the fashionable tailors of Little-Crampton, were suborned to lay themselves out night and day upon his wedding-suit. He had set his heart upon having Adolphus dressed precisely like himself on the occasion. Two brothers dressed alike, groom, and groomsman, look remarkably well at a wedding. But to his surprise, Adolphus refused to be dressed, and would not go to the wedding—"*positively.*" Neither would Augusta. Brother and sister set to work packing up, and when the expected night arrived there was all their little stock and store in two, blue, wooden trunks, locked, and corded, and ready for moving, in the hall of the Oakery.

VIII.

It was a gloomy night outside and in, for the rain had been falling all day, and a cold rain-storm in summer is dreary enough. But cheerful bars of light streamed across the darkness from the tower windows, lighting up a green strip on a tree here and there, a picket or two in the fence, and banding with an illuminated ribbon the side and roof of the dripping barn. The Captain was making his toilet. White ruffled shirt, with a black mourning pin containing a lock of his mother's hair; white Marseilles waistcoat, set off with an inner vest of blue satin (suggested by Hood & Wessup); trowsers of bright mustard color, fitting as tight as if his legs had been melted and poured into them; blue coat, cut brass buttons, end of handkercher' sticking out of the pocket behind; black silk stockings and pumps; red check-silk neck-cloth, and flying-jib collars. Down he came, and there sat brother and sister on their corded trunks in the hall, portentous as the Egyptian statues that overlook the Nile from their high stone chairs. Not a word was said; but the Captain opened the door and looked out. "Why, it rains like fury. Jim!"

Jim, who was unseen in the darkness, and yet within three feet of the door, answered cheerily, "Aye, aye, Sir!"

"All ready, Jim?"

"All ready, Capt'in."

"Wait till I get my cloak;" and as the Captain wrapped himself up, his sister silently and carefully assisted him; not on account of his plumage, but to keep him from catching cold.

Off goes Shatter, Jim, and the Captain; off through the whistling rain and the darkness. The mud whirled up from the wheels and covered the cloak of the bridegroom, so he told Jim "to drive keerful, as he wanted to keep nice." It was a long and dreary road, but at last they saw the bright lights from Mewker's windows, and with a palpitating heart the Captain alighted at the porch.

Old Bose, who had been scouring the grounds and barking at every guest, started up with a fearful growl, but the Captain threw off his travel-stained cloak, and exhibited himself to the old dog in all his glory. The instant Bose recognized his friend and benefactor he leaped upon him with such a multitude of caresses that the white Marseilles vest and mustard-colored trowsers were covered with proofs of his fidelity and attachment. "Hey, there! hey! down, Bose!" said Mewker at the door: "Why, my dear brother!"

The Captain, with great gravity, was snapping with his thumb and finger the superfluous mud with which Bose had embellished his trowsers.

"Come in here," said Mewker, chuckling and scratching his chin. "I'll get you a brush. No hurry. Time enough before the ceremony."

The Captain walked after him through the hall, and caught a glimpse of the parlors, radiant with wax-lights, and crowded with such a display of company as was rarely seen in Little-Crampton.

"Come in here," said Mewker, still chuckling, as he opened the door. "This is your room;" and he winked, and gave the bridegroom such a nudge with his knobby elbow as almost tumbled him over the bed. "Your room—understand? *The bridal-chamber!* Wait here, now; wait here till I get a brush."

The Captain, left alone, surveyed the apartment. The pillow-cases were heavy with lace. Little tasteful vases filled with flowers, made the air drunk with fragrance; a white, worked pin-cushion was on the bureau, before an oval glass, with his own name wrought thereon in pins' heads. The astral lamp on the mantel shed a subdued and chastened light over the whole. Long windows reached to the floor, and opened on the piazza;

light Venetian blinds were outside the sashes, without other fastenings than a latch. The Captain tried the windows, and they opened with a touch of his thumb and fore-finger. He had not slept in so insecure a place for more than twenty years. Then he thought of the phantom-horseman, and the deep pond behind the house. He shivered a little, either from cold or timidity. The window was partially raised, so he throws it up softly, touches the latch; the blinds are open; he walks out on the piazza, and then covertly steals around to the front of the house, where he finds Shatter and the wagon, with old Jim peering through the blinds, to see the wedding come off.

"Jim," he says, in a hoarse whisper, "take me hum. I ain't a-goin' to sleep in such a room as that, no how."

The old boy quietly unbuckled the hitching-strap, and when Mewker got back with the brush, Shatter was flying through the mud toward the Oakery, at a three-minute gait. Two or three quick knocks at his own door, and it is opened by Augusta, who, with her brother, had kept watch and ward on their corded trunks. The Captain took the candle from the table without saying a word, ascended the stairs, passed through scarp, counterscarp, glacis, and ditch, mounted his ladder, drew it up after him, bolted the trap in the floor, and cocked his pistol.

"Now," said he, "let 'em come on! They ain't got me married this time, anyhow!"

THE END.

THE HIDDEN PATH.

A NOVEL.

BY MARION HARLAND.

AUTHOR OF "ALONE."

12mo. Price $1 25.

"High as has been the reputation acquired by the many authoresses of our country, we shall be mistaken if the writer of 'Alone' and of 'The Hidden Path' does not take ere long, place and precedence. She combines as many excellences with as few faults as any one we can at the present writing call to mind. There is an originality in her thinking which strikes one with a peculiar force, and he finds himself often unconsciously recurring to what has had such a powerful effect upon him. She is emphatically an authoress not to be forgotten; her works are no short-lived productions, for they have in them a genius, a power and a purpose."—*Boston Evening Gazette.*

"It forms a series of delightful home pictures, changing from place to place, but chiefly confined to Virginia, the writer's native State, and she paints its beauties with a master hand. She loves her native State, and has paid it no mean tribute in her book. We congratulate the young and gifted authoress for having produced a work so remarkable for its delicacy, purity and general worth, and prophesy for her a brilliant and successful career in the world of letters."—*Old Colony Memorial, Plymouth, Mass.*

"It will every way sustain the praise so worthily won by the author's first effort. It exhibits the same healthful sentiment and beautiful feeling, the same truthful simplicity and yet charming elegance, the same just appreciation of different phases of social and domestic life. The tale is one of American life, and is most aptly and gracefully wrought."—*N. Y. Courier and Enquirer.*

"'The Hidden Path' is a work of originality and genius, full of striking thoughts, beautiful descriptions, and graceful conversation, and just interesting enough as a story to carry the reader through a volume from the perusal of which one rises better at heart and with a more genial, kindly feeling toward humanity in general."—*Boston Daily Journal.*

We have read 'The Hidden Path' with unmingled pleasure. It is one of the best novels of the day. The promise given by Miss Harland in her 'Alone' has been fully met. She takes rank among the best writers of fiction of this age. The story is interesting; the language pure, often eloquent; the plot natural and interesting; and the mora excellent."—*New York Daily News.*

"We take the liberty of confidently commending it to our readers as one of those gentle, earnest books which will be found acceptable to all pure hearts, and become, we sincerely trust, an especial favorite with the women readers of America."—*Philadelphia Evening Bulletin.*

"Home, sincerity and truth, are invested with most attractive charms, and their value enhanced by painful contrasts. While engaging the imagination by its well-conceived plot, it makes all submit to its moral impression, and enlists the reader's approbation exclusively with the virtuous and true."—*New York Evangelist.*

"Its great charm, like that of 'Alone,' consists in the sincerity which pervades it, and in the delicate sentiments of love and friendship which, in all their unadulterated sweetness, throw a magic grace over the whole volume."—*New York Day Book.*

THE LIFE AND SAYINGS OF MRS. PARTINGTON,

AND OTHERS OF THE FAMILY.

BY B. P. SHILLABER.

1 elegant 12mo., 43 Illustrations. Price $1 25.

"'Hang the books!' said an appreciative examiner, to whom we handed a copy for inspection, 'I can't afford to buy them, but I can't do without this;' and laughing until the tears ran, he drew forth the purchase-money. It is just so, reader; you can't do without this book. It is so full of genial humor and pure human nature that your wife and children must have it, to be able to realize how much enjoyment may be shut up within the lids of a book. It is full of human kindness, rich in humor, alive with wit, mingled here and there with those faint touches of melancholy which oft-times touch Mirth's borders."—*Clinton Courant.*

"She has caused many a lip to relax from incontinent primness into the broadest kind of a grin—has given to many a mind the material for an odd but not useless revery—has scooped out many a cove on the dry shores of newspaper reading, and invited the mariner reader to tarry and refresh himself. 'Ruth Partington' is a Christian and a patriot. Such a book will go everywhere—be welcomed like a returned exile—do good, and cease not."—*Buffalo Express.*

"If it is true that one grows fat who laughs, then he who reads this book will fat up, even though he may be one of Pharaoh's 'lean kine.' That it does one good to laugh, nobody doubts. We have shook and shook while running through this charming volume, until it has seemed as though we had increased in weight some fifty gounds, more or less." -*Massachusetts Life Boat.*

"A regular Yankee institution is Mrs. Partington, and well deserves the compliment of a book devoted to her sayings and doings. She is here brought before the public, which is so greatly indebted to her unique vocabulary for exhaustless stores of fun, in a style worthy of her distinguished character."—*N. Y. Tribune.*

"There is a world of goodness in her blessed heart, as there is a universe of quiet fun in the book before us. 'A gem of purest ray serene' glitters on almost every page. Everybody should buy the book; everybody, at least, who loves genial, quiet wit, which never wounds, but always heals where it strikes."—*Independent Democrat.*

"It is crammed full of her choicest sayings, and rings from title page to 'finis' with her unconscious wit. It is just the book for one to read at odd moments—to take on the cars or home of an evening—or to devour in one's office of a rainy day. It is an excellent antidote for the blues."—*Oneida Herald.*

"Housewives who occasionally get belated about their dinner, should have it lying round. It will prevent a deal of grumbling from their 'lords,' by keeping them so well employed as to make them forget their dinner."—*New Hampshire Telegraph.*

"Her 'sayings' have gone the world over, and given her an immortality that will glitter and sparkle among the records of genius wherever wit and humor shall be appreciated." —*Worcester Palladium.*

"IT IS A LOVE TALE OF THE MOST ENTRANCING KIND."
Boston Daily Traveller.

"WHO IS THE AUTHOR? WE GUESS A LADY."—*N. Y. Life Illustrated.*

ISORA'S CHILD.

1 large 12mo. volume. Price $1 25.

"It is one of those few books of its class that we have read quite through—for we found it to have the requisites of a good book, namely, the power of entertaining the reader to the end of the volume. The story is not complex, but is naturally told; the characters are drawn with sharp delineation and the dialogue is spirited. It is something to add, in the present deluge of bad books with pleasant names, both the morals and 'the moral' of the work are unexceptionable. It is understood to be the production of a lady whose name is not unknown to the reading public; and we congratulate her on the increase of reputation which 'Isora's Child' will bring her when her present incognito shall be removed."—*Burlington* (Vt.) *Sentinel.*

"This book starts off with its chapter first, and introduces the reader at once to the heroes and incidents of the really charming story. He will speedily find himself interested as well by the graceful style and the skill with which the different scenes are arranged, as by the beauty of the two principal characters, and the lessons of loving faith, hope, and patience, which will meet him at the turning of almost every leaf. This is one of the best productions of its kind that has been issued this season, and promises to meet with warm approval and abundant success."—*Detroit Daily Democrat.*

"Another anonymous novel, and a successful one. There is more boldness and originality both in its conception and in its execution than in almost any work of fiction we have lately read. Its characters are few, well delineated, and consistently managed. There is no crowding and consequent confusion among the *dramatis personæ.* There are two heroines, however, Flora and Cora, both bewitching creatures, and, what is better, noble, true-hearted women, especially the former, Isora's child—the dark-eyed and passionate, but sensitive, tender, and loving daughter of Italy. The work will make its mark. Who is the author? We guess a lady, and that this is her first book."—*Weekly Life Illustrated.*

"Its incidents are novel and effectively managed; and its style possesses both earnest vigor and depth of pathos, relieved by occasional flashes of a pleasing and genial humor. Among the crowd of trashy publications now issued from the press, a work as true to nature, and as elevated and just in its conceptions of the purposes of life, as this is, is all the more welcome because it is so rare. We have no doubt it will be as popular as it is interesting."—*Albany Evening Journal.*

"We have seldom perused a work of fiction that gave us more real pleasure than this. From first to last page, it enchains the attention, and carries your sympathies along with the fortunes of the heroine. The descriptive powers of the unknown authoress are of the loftiest order, and cannot fail of placing her in the first ranks of authorship.', —*Cincinnati Daily Sun.*

"A story which perpetually keeps curiosity on the alert, and as perpetually baffles it till it reaches its dénoûment, is certainly a good one."—*Buffalo Commercial Advertiser.*

JACK DOWNING'S NEW BOOK!

'WAY DOWN EAST;

OR, PORTRAITURES OF YANKEE LIFE.

BY SEBA SMITH, ESQ.

Illustrated, 12mo. Price $1.

"We greet the Major, after a long interval, with profound pleasure and respect. Well do we remember how, years ago, we used to pore over his lucubrations on the events of the time—how he enlightened us by his home-views of the Legislature's doings, of the Gineral's intentions, and of the plans of ambitious Uncle Joshua. Here was the 'spot of his origin,' and around us were the materials from which he drew his stores of instructive wit. Therefore we, of all the reading public, do the most heartily greet his reappearance. We find him a little more artistic than of old, more advanced in grammar and orthography, but withal displaying the same intimate knowledge of Down Eastdom, and retaining the same knack of genuine Yankee humor. In fact, taking all things together, no other writer begins to equal him in the delineation of the live Yankee, in the points where that individual differs from all the 'rest of mankind.' This is his great merit as an author, and one which the progress of manners will still further heighten—for it is only in some portions of our own State that the real Yankee can now be found.

"The present book has sixteen chapters devoted to home-stories. They are racy and humorous to a high degree."—*Portland Daily Advertiser.*

"It is now generally conceded that Seba Smith is the ablest, and at the same time the most amusing delineator of Yankee life who has hitherto attempted that humorous style of writing—not excepting even Judge Haliburton himself. This is no rash expression, for there is not a passage in 'Sam Slick' so graphic, funny and and comical, but we find equalled if not surpassed in the sensible and philosophic, although ludicrous epistles, of 'Major Jack Downing'—epistles of which we defy the most stupid to glance at a paragraph without reading the whole."—*Philadelphia News.*

"This is a book of real Yankee life, giving the particulars of character and incidents in New England, from the Pilgrim fathers and their generations, Connecticut Blue Laws, and the civic and religious rules, customs, &c., from the Nutmeg State away down East, as far as Mr. Jones ever thought of going. It is a very laughable affair, and every family in all Yankeedom will enjoy its perusal."—*Hingham (Mass.) Journal.*

"There are few readers who do not desire to keep up an acquaintance with the original Major Jack Downing, whose peculiar humor, while it is irresistible in its effects, is never made subservient to immorality. But these stories are an improvement on those originally given by the author, as they are illustrative of Yankee life and character in the good old times of the Pilgrim Fathers."—*Christian Advocate and Journal.*

"The stories are the most humorous in the whole range of Yankee literature, full of genuine wit, rare appreciation of fun, and giving an insight into human motive which shows the close observation and keen relish of life, of a good-humored philosopher."—*Saturday Evening Mail.*

"A charmingly interesting book, this, for all who hail from Down East, or who like to read good stories of home life among the Yankees."—*Salem Register*

EXTRAORDINARY PUBLICATION!

MY COURTSHIP AND ITS CONSEQUENCES.

BY HENRY WIKOFF.

A true account of the Author's Adventures in England, Switzerland, and Italy, with Miss J. C. Gamble, of Portland Place, London. 1 elegant 12mo. Price, in cloth, $1 25.

The extraordinary sensation produced in literary circles by Mr. Wikoff's charming romance of real life, is exhausting edition after edition of his wonderful book. From lengthy reviews, among several hundred received, we extract the following brief notices of the press:

"We prefer commending the book as beyond question the most amusing of the season, and we commend it without hesitation, because the moral is an excellent one."—*Albion.*

"With unparalleled candor he has here unfolded the particulars of the intrigue, taking the whole world into his confidence—'bearing his heart on his sleeve for daws to peck at'—and, in the dearth of public amusements, presenting a piquant nine days' wonder for the recreation of society."—*N. Y. Tribune.*

"The work is very amusing, and it is written in such a vein that one cannot refrain from frequent bursts of laughter, even when the Chevalier is in positions which might claim one's sympathy."—*Boston Evening Gazette.*

"A positive autobiography, by a man of acknowledged fashion, and an associate of nobles and princes, telling truly how he courted and was coquetted by an heiress in high life, is likely to be as popular a singularity in the way of literature as could well be thought of."—*Home Journal.*

"The ladies are sure to devour it. It is better and more exciting than any modern romance, as it is a detail of facts, and every page proves conclusively that the plain, unvarnished tale of truth is often stranger than fiction."—*Baltimore Dispatch.*

"The book, therefore, has all the attractions of a tilt of knight-errants—with this addition, that one of the combatants is a woman—a species of heart-endowed Amazon."—*Newark Daily Mercury.*

"If you read the first chapter of the volume, you are in for 'finis,' and can no more stop without the consent of your will than the train of cars can stop without the consent of the engine."—*Worcester Palladium.*

"Seriously, there is not so original, piquant and singular a book in American literature its author is a sort of cross between Fielding, Chesterfield, and Rochefoucault."—*Boston Chronicle.*

"With the exception of Rosseau's Confessions, we do not remember ever to have heard of any such self-anatomization of love and the lover."—*N. Y. Express.*

"The book has cost us a couple of nights' sleep; and we have no doubt it has cost its author and principal subject a good many more."—*N. Y. Evening Mirror.*

"The work possesses all the charm and fascination of a continuous romance."—*N. Y Journal of Commerce.*

A LONG LOOK AHEAD;

OR, THE FIRST STROKE AND THE LAST.

BY A. S. ROE,

AUTHOR OF "JAMES MONTJOY; OR, I'VE BEEN THINKING," "TO LOVE AND BE LOVED," ETC.

1 vol. 12mo. Price $1 25.

"The purpose of this book is so manifest to inspire juster estimates of life and character, and its purpose is so well attained, that we improve the occasion of noticing it to add our earnest approval of its lesson and moral, perforce of convictions born of our own observation and experience. We have read the book thoroughly, and like it as thoroughly. It is one of the very best books of its kind, and the author and publisher have both 'done the state service' in placing it before the public."—*N. Y. Evening Mirror.*

"The story is beautifully told, and the characters are types of moral loveliness. No one can read and ponder it, without the tears starting unbidden to the eye, and sympathising hope irradiating the countenance. Such works do much to counteract the evil tendencies of the mushroom trash that constitutes our bar-room and "sporting" literature, and the thanks of the public are eminently due to both the author and the publisher for this most acceptable counter current to the streams of demoralization which are now sweeping over the land."—*Binghampton Republican.*

"The lover of the country, who knows its scenes and duties, who can delight in the gambols of the young colt in the meadows, or enjoys the sweet perfume from the haycock the breath of the cud-chewing cow—better still, he who can swing a scythe, a cradle, or turn a smooth furrow, will undoubtedly relish this simple narrative of country life, and the pure, unadulterated native American manners and customs therein described."—*Newark Daily Advertiser.*

"It has a charming simplicity and purity, and its characters have a freshness and naturalness not often found in works of the kind. The impression of the story is admirable—adapted to inspire the young with sentiments of self-reliance, honor and integrity, and to produce charity and good feeling in all. The religious tone which it exhibits is excellent, and a genial warmth pervades the whole work."—*N. Y. Evangelist.*

"It is not only far beyond the general run of what are called, by courtesy, American novels, but it is superior to many books that have sold by tens of thousands. It has positive merits of a high order. The dialogue, incidents and characters are natural, and as a whole, it is an impressive production. We commend the novel to our readers, as a pleasant book."—*Boston Post.*

"Whoever commences reading what he has written, must give up the idea of attending to other business until the story is read through; for there is such an interest excited in the subject that one is insensibly compelled to read on to the end. There is a good spirit pervading his writings, which insensibly affects the reader."—*Boston Evening Telegraph.*

"You cannot finish five pages of this work (unless your heart be hard as adamant) without finding all the home feelings stirred within you, and you read on and on, unconscious of aught beside, unwilling to lay it by, until the last line is finished. It opens with all the sweet simplicity of Goldsmith's 'Deserted Village.'"—*Albany Spectator*

"Bell's sketches are instinct with life, they sparkle with brilliants, are gemmed with wit, and address themselves to almost every chord of the human heart."—*Louisville* (*Ky.*) *Bulletin.*

BELL SMITH ABROAD.

A Handsome 12mo. volume. Price $1 00. With Illustrations by Healy, Walcutt, and Overarche.

"The readers of the *Louisville Journal* need no introduction from us to Bell Smith. Her own brilliant pen, and her own sparkling, witching and delightful style have so often graced the columns of this paper, and have made so many friends and admirers for her, that we need say but little toward creating a demand for this charming volume. But some tribute is nevertheless due to Bell Smith for the real pleasure she has imparted in every chapter of her book, and that tribute we cheerfully pay. Her admirable powers seem so much at home in every variety and phase of life, that she touches no subject without making it sparkle with the lights of her genius."—*Louisville Journal.*

"She is ever piquant in her remarks, and keen from observation; and the result is that her 'Abroad' is one of the most interesting collections of incident and comment, fun and pathos, seriousness and gossip, which has ever fallen under our notice."—*Boston Evening Traveller.*

"It is dashing and vigorous without coarseness—animated with a genial humor—showing acute and delicate perceptions—and sustained by a bracing infusion of common sense."—*N. Y. Tribune.*

"There are many delicate strokes, and not a little of that vivacity of description which entertains. The author shows her best side when matters of home-feeling and affection engage her pen."—*N. Y. Evangelist.*

"History, art and personal narrative are alike imprinted in your memory by the associations of anecdote, merry and grave, and you feel that you are listening to the magical voice of 'Bell Smith' *at home.* Such volumes enrich and honor American literature."—*Philadelphia Merchant.*

"This is a capital book; full of life, spirit, vivacity and information—thoroughly lady-like, and telling precisely what everybody wants to hear, so far as the author knows."—*Salem Gazette.*

"Spirited and artistic! Bell Smith sparkles, and dashes on, amusing and interesting. A capital book for a leisure hour or railroad travel, or for those seasons when you want to be pleased without effort."—*Cleveland Leader.*

"We like Bell Smith and Bell Smith's book. A lively, free, dashing style, she talks on, and nothing is wanting but the merry laugh we know she is owner of to make us think we are listening to a very interesting woman."—*Chicago Journal.*

"Lively, gossiping, chatting, witty, sparkling Bell Smith, we must confess your book has quite enchanted us."—*N. Y. Day Book.*

"In freshness, piquancy, and delightful episodes, illustrative of foreign life and manners, they have rarely been equalled."—*National Era.*

www.ingramcontent.com/pod-product-compliance
Lightning Source LLC
LaVergne TN
LVHW020210110826
845151LV00003B/661
9781425534608